RENDEZVOUS
WITH DEATH

Sam Griffith

Stephen F. Austin State University Press

For more information:
Stephen F. Austin State University Press
P.O. Box 13007 SFA Station
Nacogdoches, Texas 75962
sfapress@sfasu.edu
www.sfasu.edu/sfapress

Book design: Jerri Bourrous
Cover design: Jerri Bourrous
Distributed by Texas A&M Consortium
www.tamupress.com

LIBRARY OF CONGRESS CATALOGING-IN-PUBLICATION DATA
Griffith, Sam
Rendezvous With Death / Sam Griffith

ISBN: 978-1-62288-152-9

"I have a rendezvous with Death. . .
And to my pledged word am true,
I shall not fail that rendezvous."

—Alan Seeger

"All through our growing up years,
we often walked the woods.
Usually on a Sunday afternoon.
Maybe that's why I'm a natural
for this place. In the spring
we each tried to find the first
violet bloom. I still do it here, and
when I find it, I whisper, 'This one
is for you, Wudie,' and my eyes fill
with tears, still after all these
years, missing her so much."

—Normadene Walters Jackson,
"Stories from My Childhood"

This one is for you, Mom.

CHAPTER 1

THURSDAY MORNING WAS cool, more a reminder of the recent February than a hint of the coming spring. The sky was greying, with a brisk breeze from the north. The radio said a cold snap was in store. I listened for the traffic report. I turned off Mockingbird onto a side street to avoid a stalled car blocking traffic three blocks ahead. It seemed like half of Dallas had heard the same report. The intersections were stacked up as frustrated drivers tried to force their way through traffic lights timed for school car pools and milk-and-bread runs, not rush hour. I zig-zagged my way down tree-lined residential streets, coming up behind the Carrington Building, an older, two-story, red brick office building spared from Dallas' cyclical boom-and-bust demolition and re-building spree.

Most of the Carrington housed Brooks Exploration, a small oil and gas exploration firm. Fifteen years ago it had filled three floors of one of Dallas' downtown skyscrapers. Now it occupied a quarter of its previous office space. The current term is "lean and mean" and "down-sized," an economic euphemism for a company cut to the bare-bones. But at least Brooks Exploration was still solvent, which is more than could be said about a lot of oil companies that had once flourished in Texas in the latest shale gas boom.

It was just past eight, so I knew the parking lot would be full.

Whether from the fear of continuing lay-offs or just the conservative, hard-working mindset of petroleum engineers and geologists, Brooks' employees usually were clocked in by seven forty-five. Predictable, dependable. I was sneering at their rat race existence as I eased my four-wheel drive Chevy pickup into the only parking spot left. It was next to the two large, rusting, grey metal trash bins. As I got out, I eyed my location next to the trash bins, and hoped it wasn't too symbolic of my progress in my own rat race. I decided I was parked far enough away from the bins to prevent too easy a comparison so I locked up and went inside.

My office was on the back side of the building on the second floor. I rode the slow elevator and went down the seafoam green hall to my office. Although "Noah Starr - Professional Investigations" was on the nameplate, there wasn't a line of clients clamoring for my services. Dallas seemed to have its problems under control, or, if not, I didn't seem to be high on its list of potential saviors. Oh, well. I unlocked the door and pocketed the keys. I turned on the lights and checked the telephone answering machine. The red light was blinking so I hit the "play" button. The first two calls had hung up. The third was a vacation lake lot promotion scam that offered me either a new Cadillac or a ski boat, guaranteed, if I would only take the tour of their lake development. The fourth was business.

"Noah?" An electronic facsimile of an east Texas twang. "Uh, this is Pete, uh, Pete O'Brian. Remember? Franklin High School? We graduated together. I, uh, it's been a long time, but I need to talk with you." The voice paused, the uncertainty taking the force from the words. I was used to it. Seeing a private investigator is like keeping a dentist appointment. The longer you thought about it, and the closer you actually got to going, the less the pain bothered you. A phone answering machine made it even worse, an electronic Father Confessor that made the caller feel like he was talking to himself.

The voice again: "Yeah, I got something I need you to do. Bobby Ray McClinton, he said you knew Dallas. Call me, will you?" He gave the phone number and paused for half a minute, as if unsure to tell me more. He hung up, a metallic "click." There was nothing else worthwhile on the machine, so I replayed O'Brian'a message, and jotted down the number.

I called O'Brian's number. The area code was familiar, like an old photograph you hadn't seen in years. While I waited for an answer, I rested the receiver on my shoulder and stretched to reach the small refrigerator I had in the corner of the office under the window, and got a plastic quart bottle of orange juice, shook it up, and twisted off the top and drank some. I leaned back in the chair and listened to the phone ring.

"Hello." A woman's voice, rising on the second syllable.

"Hello. This is Noah Starr. May I speak to Pete O'Brian?"

"Oh, uh, okay. Just a minute." She said. Then her voice faded. She seemed to have her hand over the mouthpiece, but I could still hear the muffled conversation. "It's him. Are you sure you want to bring him into this?" I couldn't hear the reply, but in a moment the twang from the answering machine came on the line.

"Hey, Noah?" His voice wavered with uncertainty. "Appreciate you calling me back so fast." He stopped. After a moment, I primed the pump.

"What can I do for you, Pete?"

"It's my daughter, Carolyn. She's, uh . . . she's run away. Me an' Helen are out of our minds. We, uh, we think she might have headed your way. Bobby Ray McClinton, you remember Bobby Ray? He was halfback our senior year. Anyway, he's a county deputy here now. He said you might could help. I don't know how you work, but me an' Helen can come to Dallas, or, whatever you want. Can you help me out with this?"

I remembered Pete. Even in high school, he had been one of those guys who didn't want to ask anything of anyone, and if forced to, with his back to the wall, would feel like he had lost a part of his masculinity in the bargain.

"Yeah, sure, Pete. Listen, I charge by the hour, so it might be better for you if ya'll came up here. It would save ya'll some money."

"Yeah, that'd be o.k."

"Whenever's good for ya'll. Say, when did she leave?" I asked.

"Last Saturday night."

I mentally counted the days that had passed, and shook my head. "Well, if I'm going to do any good, I need to get on it as soon as possible. The longer you wait, the harder it is to pick up the trail," I said. "Of course, you know that chances are she'll show up on her own any day now."

"No," he said, "No, I feel bad about this. We've waited for four days now and haven't heard a word. We gotta do something."

"O.k., back to my first question, when's good for you?"

"Whenever. We can be there this afternoon if you want." I glanced at my calendar.

"How about tomorrow afternoon, say about one?"

"That'll be fine."

"And Pete, I need you to bring pictures of Carolyn and any of her friends that I might need to talk to. And, if you have her cell phone, any emails, text messages you can get, maybe letters she had received lately, maybe a diary, you know, just any information you have that would help me get a feel for her and her friends. Maybe a Facebook page. Anything like that. Try to remember who she had been with during the last few days she was home. Who she may have seen, and bring their contact information, phone numbers, too. All that, o.k.?"

"O.k., buddy." He was feeling better now that he had something he could do. "We'll get that stuff together and head over and see you tomorrow at one." I gave him my address. I could hear him discussing coming to Dallas with Helen while he was hanging up.

I spent the rest of the day trying to trace a couple fathers who weren't paying child support, and trying to find the assets of a Dallas businessman that had lost a half-million dollar judgment to a lawyer I frequently worked for.

I ran some license checks to get some addresses to start with on the child support cases. Then I scanned the Dallas County land records to trace title records, looking for property the businessman owned in Dallas County. I didn't find any that he owned, but he had recently transferred five lots to another man with the same last name. Bingo. I figured the transfers were to hide the property from the court judgment. A judgement is just a piece of paper, but deep pockets and seizable assets can make even an old lawyer's eyes sparkle. And I had found some deep pockets for the lawyer to pick. I printed out and downloaded the line of title on the properties copies of the deeds.

I spent most of the afternoon on the phone following up the leads I had developed. About four fifteen, I was still on the phone and beginning to get a cauliflower ear when call waiting buzzed. I wrapped up the conversation and answered the incoming call.

It was Alice.

Alice was my girlfriend, what might be more politically correct to call my "significant other." She was a third year law student at Southern Methodist University and at the top of her class. Like most law school stars, she was on the law journal editorial board. In her spare time, she worked part time for a personal injury law firm downtown.

I had met her at a party an old friend of mine had thrown a year ago, during his second year of law school. Alice and I had talked for a couple of hours at the party, then left the party and talked most of the night and had dinner together the next night. She was brilliant, charming, and beautiful, with a smile that had immediately caught my eye and my heart. Her father and grandfather had been lawyers in Texarkana and she was carrying on the family tradition. Three months ago, we had moved in together in a smaller, older house near campus.

"What's up tonight?" she asked.

"I really hadn't thought about it. Any suggestions?"

"I'm going to be late. Frank screwed around and didn't finish proofing a comment. Stupid bastard. The law journal is supposed to go to press in a week. We'll be at the journal office until about seven. See you then for dinner?"

"Fine. You want to eat in or out?"

"I don't care. Let's just play it by ear."

"No prob'. See you then, Beautiful."

We hung up.

I wrote up a summary of my investigation of the businessman's assets, listing the properties, and then attached the copies of the deeds I had gotten from the land records office. I wrapped it up a bit after five and called it a day. I opened the cabinet at the bottom of the bookshelf and turned on the small TV Alice had given me for Christmas. I leaned back in my chair and watched the evening news while I worked on *The Dallas Morning News'* crossword puzzle. I scanned the rest of the paper while the first of the local news came on. The weatherman said that a cold front would be coming in that night. They say that anyone who predicts the weather in Texas is either a newcomer or a fool, but I guess sometimes you take any job you can get, even as a weatherman in Texas. Predicting Texas weather in general, and Dallas weather in particular, especially in the spring, is even a chancier proposition than usual. A balmy day can be run over by a blue norther that comes like an icy knife freezing the heart of the coming spring. I thought about the old joke about there being nothing between Dallas and the Arctic Circle but a barbed wire fence, and two of its wires are down. I glanced through the newspaper some more and after six, I closed up shop and went home.

Alice got home a little after I did.

"How was your day?" she asked as she put her briefcase on the kitchen table. She gave me a quick, one-arm hug and a peck on the cheek.

As I gave her a quick rundown of my uneventful day, she glanced in the refrigerator. We hadn't been to the grocery store in over a week.

"Looks like Old Mother Hubbard's cupboard, Noah, and I'm starved." She leaned an arm on the refrigerator door and winked at me conspiratorially. "Let's blow this joint, Babe."

CHAPTER
2

WE WENT TO a restaurant in the West End, a gentrified, yuppie area just west of downtown Dallas, where they had rejuvenated old buildings into upscale restaurants and nightclubs. After dinner, we went across the street to a club. It was one of those rare places where realized that some people actually liked to go out to enjoy the pleasure of their companions' conversation, as well as for entertainment, kept the volume at a reasonable level.

We shared a bottle of wine and talked about the day. Alice told me about being called on to recite in Constitutional Law and bluffing through it with the aplomb of a third year with canned briefs. She caught me up on the law school gossip, who was seeing whom, who was working for which law firm, and the latest job offers.

It was after eleven thirty when we finished the last of the wine and paid the tab. It wasn't until we got to the door that we saw it was raining. It hadn't looked like rain when we came in, so we didn't have an umbrella. We stood under the awning and talked until the rain slowed. Alice stood with her arms wrapped around my waist, under my jacket, trying to stay warm in the brisk wind, her hair brushing my face. The spring rain had come on the heels of the cold front the weatherman had predicted. I admitted to myself that he had been right, but figured even a blind pig can find an acorn occasionally. It was cold and the wind cut through us and sprinkled us with rain. In a few minutes, the rain slowed to a light mist.

The West End had been crowded when we came in, so we had had to park down a side street. We headed for the truck, walking at a quick pace. The rain had washed away the car fumes, leaving Dallas smelling, for a few minutes at least, like a walk along a country lane after a summer rain.

As we turned the corner, we saw a small crowd. It was mostly police, with a TV news crew that had just arrived and was setting up and getting out their camera, positioning the reporter in front of their van with the station's logo in the picture. A couple gawkers attempted to rubberneck around the yellow raincoated police. The rotating blue and white lights on two patrol cars illuminated the scene with uneven strobe light cadences.

I glanced over and saw the police were trying to keep the onlookers back so the plain clothes investigators could do their work. I recognized Dick Warner, a photographer for the paper. Warner primarily handled the police beat. He was trying to angle his camera down over the shoulder of a broad-faced cop for a better shot. The policeman had a disgusted expression as he watched Warner. I didn't care much for him either. He was one of those guys who rubs everyone the wrong way, and I knew if he saw me, he would talk my ear off. Besides, Alice wanted to get home, and her squeeze on my thigh while we were finishing off the wine had me in the same mood. We skirted the crowd and were heading toward the truck when Warner saw me.

"Noah, wait up." He broke towards us, a grin plastered across his hatchet face. I steeled myself for his b.s. "Ain't you gonna check it out? I thought you private eye types were like ambulance chasing lawyers, always poking into something." He horse-laughed at his joke, but straightened up when he caught my chill. "Hey, Noah, ain't you gonna introduce me?" He paused half a second, then continued, "No, I guess you ain't. Can't blame you, though." He stared at Alice with approval. "Hi, I'm Dick Warner."

"Dick, this is Alice; Alice, this is Dick."

Warner thrust out his hand, and hesitated a moment before Alice took it.

"Pleased to meet you," she said sweetly. He nodded eagerly that it was mutual.

Warner turned back to me. "Like something out of a gangster movie," he began while Alice covertly nudged me to cut him off. "Seems like the guy was strolling the streets, you see, when an SUV, 'dark, maybe black' a witness said, anyway, this car zipped by and blasted him twice with a shotgun. Bit messy. Don't think any of my pictures are going to make the paper," he said ruefully. "Blood and guts on the sidewalk don't go down good with bacon and eggs first thing in the morning, eh?" He grinned and elbowed me.

"No, Dick, and it doesn't go down too well with our evening, either. Listen, we have to be shoving off. Talk with you later, o.k.?" I slipped my arm over Alice's shoulder and gave him a passing wave.

"Yeah, sure, I get you," He said, glancing at Alice while she tried to stifle a yawn. His voice dripped with lechery.

We turned back up the street towards the truck. We walked past the TV van, the camera light flashed to life, its luminance partially blinding us in the near darkness of the poorly lit street. The reporter began his on-the-scene report in the white glare of the camera lights: "Tonight, at approximately eleven oh five, an unknown gunman shot a pedestrian just north of the West End in a drive-by shooting. The pedestrian has been identified as Keith Holland, a Dallas businessman."

I didn't hear any more. I froze, then told Alice I had to go back for a second. She wrapped her arms around herself for warmth as I turned back towards the gawkers and began to move through the crowd, easing my way past a policeman and a print reporter. A reporter was trying to take notes on a soggy pad.

The cop just looked wet and miserable. I must have crossed an invisible line because he reached out a hand to my shoulder. "Don't need to get any closer. You can see all you need from there."

I glanced over my shoulder into his dark brown, impassive eyes. "Yeah, o.k." I said under my breath as I watched the investigators study the bloody mess. It was Keith Holland, all right. His dark hair had gotten a few streaks of grey since I last saw him, but his hawkish nose, high cheek bones, and arching eyebrows were the same. His face was speckled with blood, the rain drops running down in diluted crimson streaks. The blasts had caught him in the torso, ripping apart the tan sport coat.

I heard a car pull up behind me and the creak of doors being opened. The policeman parted the crowd like Moses on a good day, and two men in emergency service blues rolled a stretcher beside the corpse. A plainclothes police investigator took a final glance at the scene and nodded to them. They grappled Keith's loose form onto the stretcher, covered it and strapped it in, and pushed it to the open doors of the ambulance.

I turned away and walked over to where Alice and Dick were standing. Concern wrinkled Alice's brow, her soft eyes had taken on a steely intensity. I nodded to her, assuring her that I was o.k.

After a strained pause, Dick asked, "What do you make of it, Noah? Alice said you knew him."

I nodded slowly, my mind still filled with Keith's bloody image. "Dick, I just don't know." Turning towards Alice and slipping an arm around her waist, I said, "What say we go home?"

She nodded.

"Dick, if you hear anything about this, let me know, will you? I'd really appreciate it."

He nodded, his eyes on the ambulance as it slowly pulled away from the crowd.

The thick mist had turned into a steady rain while I was looking at Keith, but I hadn't notice it before. I was chilled, soaked to the bone. Alice clutched my arm and snuggled against me as we walked quickly to the truck. I glanced at her. Her face was turned towards me, her cheek pressed against my shoulder like a child's when it's scared of the dark. A wet strand of blond hair stuck to her forehead. Her mascara had begun to run. She was frightened. She had seen death and it had shaken her. Deeply. Me too.

I unlocked her side first, let her climb in, and closed the door. I went around and got in. I cranked the truck while she turned on the heater. The fan whirred above the sound of the engine. Neither of us spoke on the way home. We listened to the fan, the squish of the windshield wipers, and the pounding rain. The weather matched our mood. No longer the gentle rain of a hopeful spring, but the vengeful hammering of a winter's dark night.

There wasn't much traffic, just scattered cars slicing through the mists, drivers clutching steering wheels and peering myopically through foggy windshields. We made it home in less than fifteen minutes, but it seemed like an hour. We pulled into the driveway and ran into the house.

I locked the front door and turned off the porch light behind us. Alice came from the bathroom carrying a couple thick towels. I dried my hands and face with the dark green one as I wandered into the bathroom and took off my wet clothes. I towelled off and put on the heavy terrycloth bathrobe that Alice had given me. I was beginning to warm up, but I turned the thermostat up to eighty-five anyway.

I was still cold so I went to the kitchen and filled the teapot with water. I put it on the stove and rummaged through the cabinets for tea bags, home-raised dried mint, and honey. I put them on the table along with a pair of thick mugs and two spoons. The whistling kettle called Alice into the kitchen. She had changed into a fleecy robe. I poured the steaming water, dropped in the bags, and crumbled in some mint. We stirred and dabbled until the tea was satisfactory.

Alice broke the silence. "What are you going to do about Keith?" She had dried and brushed her hair, and had washed her face. I thought again, as I often had, that she didn't need makeup; it merely complimented her beauty.

I looked into her soft brown eyes. I shrugged. "It's been a few years." I paused and sipped my tea for a minute and thought. "But I can't just let it lay. I'll call Bill Travis tomorrow. See what he's heard. Maybe stir around a bit. See if I can get any leads for him if he needs it. But the police will have it wrapped up in a week."

Alice slowly stirred her tea again absent-mindedly, then took a small sip and watched me.

"Right now there isn't anything to do. But I think I'll call back home tomorrow and see Keith's folks, maybe find out when the funeral is going to be."

She reached across the table and held my hand. Then, with a gentle squeeze, she rose, leaned over and kissed me on the cheek, her hand caressing the back of my neck. Then she went to the bedroom. I rinsed the cups and spoons, put them in the dishwasher, and put everything away. I checked the doors, turned out the kitchen and hall lights, and joined Alice.

It was after three in the morning when I got up. I had slept fitfully, that last ragged image of Keith recurring in my dreams. I slid quietly from beneath the sheets, pulled on my robe, and eased from the room. As I shut the bedroom door, I saw Alice tightly curled near the edge of the bed, her hair a tousled grey fluff on the pillow in the slight illumination of street lights that diffused through the drapes.

I put the teapot on to heat and went in the living room. I didn't turn on the lights. The pale luminance from the backyard guard light fit my mood and thoughts. I eased my way past the ottoman near the doorway and skirted the coffee table. I turned on the stereo. A country and western station was playing a Don Williams song about being a country boy. His rich voice drifted into the room, the sad song of lost opportunity matching my mood. I settled into the blue leather chair by the window. I turned it so it faced the window that looked out over the backyard and patio. Miranda Lambert was in the middle of a song about love in Texas when the teapot whistled, calling me from my dark thoughts to the kitchen.

I fixed the tea and carried it back to the living room. I propped an elbow on the chair and rested my chin on my palm. I looked into a dark corner of my memories and remembered Keith.

As I reminisced about our misadventures and our misspent youth, it dawned on me how much Keith had meant to me when we were kids, and how long it had been since I had seen him.

Keith and I had grown up together in a small farming community, where the dense forest of the Big Thicket met the pineywoods of East Texas. Back then, Columbia County was a natural Eden for teenage boys who were unwittingly following in the footsteps of Tom Sawyer and Huckleberry Finn, eager to hunt and camp out and fish along the Sabine River, a dark, murky, muddy river subject to high water flooding from sudden East Texas rains.

Keith was a year older than I. His father was a good hunter and fisherman, skills he had passed on to his only son. My father had grown up in Dallas, and had moved to Columbia County to work for the Franklin newspaper. Dad hadn't known of the joys and pleasures of country boys, and so could teach me nothing of field or brook, gun or hook. I had looked to Keith to enlighten me. And Keith had shared his knowledge with me, without the aura of superiority that often accompanies a relationship where one seems to know everything, and the other, nothing. Every summer from the age of six until I was fifteen, we would wander across fields, hunting and exploring. Property lines meant nothing; we were limited only by the distance we could walk and be back home by dusk. He had been my best friend.

I remembered us as teenage boys growing up together and getting into scrapes together. I remembered the first time I had gotten drunk. When I was fourteen, me and Keith bought a six pack of beer from a bootlegger outside of town and drank it all while camped out at a small six by eight foot, tin-roofed camp house I had built out of scrap lumber in the woods behind my family's home on the outskirts of town. We got drunk, and me and Keith acted silly and thought we were so grown up when all we really were was dead drunk.

When I was fifteen, just a few months after our first fling at drinking, Keith had turned sixteen and had gotten a driver's license, a used car, and a new crowd of friends. During the next year or so, while I grew used to not having my regular running buddy to get into mischief with, I had sometimes thought the friends seemed to have come with the car: "For Sale: 1982 Chevrolet, black two door, three wild friends." Keith's new friends had seemed an extension of the car.

Keith and I had drifted apart after that. A bobbing cork on the Sabine couldn't compete with the excitement of riding around the Dairy Queen. By the time I had gotten my license and a car, we were no longer on the same wavelength. His cars and his friends had gotten faster. No longer satisfied with the Dairy Queen, Keith had sought his fun in Bossier City, Louisiana, seventy miles and a universe from Franklin, Texas. In Bossier, if you looked sixteen and had the money, you could drink right up beside the grown-ups. I hadn't seen him much after that. He had graduated high school without much more distinction than maybe having the lowest grade possible and still get a diploma. A stint in the army had washed him from my life except for a couple of brief encounters in Dallas in the last couple of years.

I was musing and remembering, wondering what Keith could have done in the past couple decades since he had graduated from Franklin High School that had gotten him blown away, when the lights came on.

"Been up all night, Noah?" Alice asked quietly.

"Since about three, but I didn't sleep too well before that."

"I know what you mean. I kept dreaming of him. Lying in the rain like a run-over dog." Her voice broke and she pulled the collar of her pale blue robe tightly under her chin, curling her shoulders upward as if trying to keep the cold thoughts away. She forced a wane smile. "You want some breakfast?"

I nodded and rose from the chair. The radio announcer was finishing the day's weather forecast when I turned it off. "Fair and sunny," I echoed. "For whom? Not for Keith. Or me."

CHAPTER 3

I GOT TO the office a little after nine. There were no calls on the answering machine. I made a couple calls about some work I was doing for a small electronics firm that was paranoid about industrial espionage and getting knocked out of the market by one of its competitors. Then I called a north Dallas station house and asked for Bill Travis. We had shared a patrol car on the graveyard shift for six years, something neither of us did any more. Bill had gone up the ranks and was a captain, and I had left the force. But we still kept in touch, getting together at occasionally for some Mexican food and Corona beer.

"Noah, you old reprobate, what the hell are you bugging me for now," he said.

"Who's handling the Keith Holland murder?"

"Hang on a minute." The phone clanked on the desk. I tucked mine under my chin and waited. I watched a pigeon circle and land on the window ledge. It waddled along the ledge looking for breakfast, then seeing me through the glass, flew away in a flurry of feathers.

"Noah, Roger Nelson's got it. Are you on this case? It only happened last night. Awfully quick to get hired."

"Personal. Holland and I were close when we were kids. Alice and I were at the West End last night and came upon the scene while ya'll were still investigating it. She was pretty upset by it. She's not used to the blood. Bothered me some, too. What's Nelson like."

"He's pretty good, a little young, only been a detective for a year. But he's good."

"Would you keep me posted on any progress?"

He assured me he would, sent his regards to Alice and we hung up.

I called *The Columbia County Herald* to see if they knew when Holland's funeral was going to be held. The *Herald* was a small-town newspaper, still owned and run by the same family that my father had worked for. The

Lansdales had their finger on the pulse of the county. A. B. Lansdale, the patriarch of the family, answered the telephone. I hadn't talked with him for several years, so he had to get caught up on what I had been doing. I was finally able to ask about Keith's funeral. He told me that the time had not been set yet, but he was pretty sure it would be Sunday. I thanked him and hung up after promising to stop by and visit with him the next time I was in Franklin.

I called Pete O'Brian. I told him I was going to be in Franklin over the weekend and suggested I come by and visit with them on Saturday morning and save them a trip to Dallas. He asked if I was coming in for Keith's funeral. Bad news travels fast. I said yes. We agreed that I would come by around eleven in the morning. I got the address and directions and hung up.

I closed the office and went home.

I drove back home, zipping through the light, mid-morning traffic. Alice was getting ready to leave for S.M.U. Friday morning, she had class in corporate law. She was glancing over the case summaries for the day's cases.

"Back so soon? What's up?" She slid the books and papers into her dark brown leather brief case and snapped it shut. She turned her full attention to me.

"I talked with Bill Travis. Said he would keep me up on developments in the investigation. The investigator's name is Roger Nelson. He's been an investigator for only a year, but Bill said he's good." I got a glass from the cabinet and poured a glass of sweet tea from the pitcher in the refrigerator. I leaned against the kitchen cabinet. "Remember me telling you about Pete O'Brian calling me yesterday to ask me to look for their missing daughter?"

"Yes, is that tied up in this Holland thing?"

"No, but they were supposed to come up to my office this afternoon. I called them and arranged for us to meet tomorrow at their house. I thought I'd go over to Franklin this weekend. Keith's funeral will likely be this weekend, and I wanted to go by his folks' house and visit with them a bit. It's been such a long time since I've seen them. Maybe eight or ten years." I looked over at her. "You want to spend the weekend in scenic Columbia County?"

Alice grinned and shook her head. "No, thanks for the invite, but I don't think I'll tag along. You didn't come home this early so you could wait until I get out of class. Besides, I'm not really in the mood to go visit the Hollands. I don't know them and I sure don't want to spend half the weekend being introduced to strangers, and the other half explaining our relationship in Bible Belt terms. No, you go and enjoy yourself. I've got lots of work at the office, and I'll have to cut back my hours soon to study for finals, so you just go alone."

"Well, o.k. But it won't be nearly as much fun."

She glanced at her watch. "Gotta run now."

She gave me a peck on the cheek and half-turned to get her briefcase.

My arms encircled her, turning her towards me. I kissed her lightly on the lips, leaned back an inch and looked into her sparkling eyes. Then I kissed her again. Her arms wrapped around my neck, pulling me closer. We separated again. She looked at me with her eyes half closed, her lips slightly parted, the tip of her tongue wetting her upper lip. I raised her chin slightly with a finger tip and kissed her again.

She pinched my butt. "When will you be back, Big Boy?" she asked in a smoky voice.

"Sunday night, most likely. I'll call you if I get tied up."

"O.k." She glanced at the clock on the oven. "Okay, I've really gotta run now, Babe. Enjoy the homecoming." She grabbed her briefcase with one hand, scooped her navy blue corduroy jacket off the back of a kitchen chair, gave me another peck on the cheek and dashed out the door. I could hear her MiniCooper cough to life as I headed to the bedroom to pack an overnight bag. The car whined as she backed into the street and gunned away.

I packed some clothes for the weekend, I locked up the house and headed back home to east Texas.

The east-bound traffic was light on Interstate 20, mainly eighteen wheelers hauling furniture and food, their drivers riding high above us common mortals. The trucks were rolling fast. I nosed up behind an eighteen wheeler pulling a flat-bed carrying steel I-beams. A sign on the back of the truck said if I saw the truck being driven in a reckless manner to call the company offices, and gave a "1-800" telephone number. Either the driver didn't figure anyone would waste the time to call in on him, or that he was going too fast for anyone to get the phone number. He was passing all the cars on the Interstate, with me his tiny shadow.

I saw a highway sign proclaimed Tyler the "Rose Capital of the World." I made a mental note to bring Alice back in Autumn for their Tyler Rose Parade.

I drove on for a while longer, then took the Franklin exit off the Interstate, and headed north on the farm-to-market road. It had been several years since I had been back to Columbia County, but it never seemed to change. The cars were newer, and the gas stations seemed to have more orange vinyl siding each time I returned, but the land did not change. The two lane highway was shaded with pine trees, their dark green bristles in stark contrast to the lime green, uncurling new leaves on the scattered oak and sassafras trees. Tall clumps of yellow-brown winter-killed Johnson grass that clustered around culverts and road signs waved in the breeze. I was soaking up the country atmosphere when I rounded a curve and pounded through a chug hole in the pavement half the width of the road. I re-adjusted the rear view mirror that had been jarred when I hit the hole. I looked back in the mirror at the ragged hole in the highway and said, "Yeah, this is Columbia County."

CHAPTER
4

THE HOLLANDS' HOUSE was much as I remembered it. I drove slowly along the lane to the house surrounded by tall pecan trees. Polled hereford cattle stared blankly at me through taut barbed wire fences. Young calves scampered around, chasing one another on spider-thin legs, then dashing back to the security and ready nourishment their mothers offered. The winter rye grass pastures were a vivid green. About thirty yards from the highway, a large sign stood in the pasture, with a picture of a polled Hereford and the farm's name: "F. E. Holland & Son - Registered Polled Herefords" and the address and telephone number. A hay barn, of weather-grayed pine planks and rusty corrugated sheet iron roofing, stood behind the house.

I thought of Keith. If he had stayed and worked the farm, instead of going to Dallas, maybe . . . . Oh, hell, as the old song said, how are you gonna keep 'em down on the farm after they've seen Big D? But now Keith was coming home to the farm to stay.

Six cars and two pickup trucks were parked in front of the house. Word of Keith's death had spread quickly. I pulled up behind a dirty red and white Ford four wheel drive pickup. Three bales of coastal bermuda hay and a half-full paper sack of cattle range cubes were piled in the bed of the truck. There was a faded Copenhagen tobacco sticker on the battered steel bumper. There was a "Big Buck Hunter" sticker in the rear sliding glass window.

I went up the steps and knocked on the door. Through the screen door, I saw two women approaching. An elderly woman, maybe eighty years old, with wire-rimmed bifocals and tightly curled salt-and-pepper hair, sidled out the door and patted my shoulder. She held on to the screen door and tilted her head back to peer at me through the lower half of her glasses, her eyes small green circles in an uptilted, sun-wrinkled face. "You knew Keith?" she asked in a high, brittle voice. Her long throat hung loosely, the skin forming wattles.

"Not too well, ma'am," I said, "It's been a few years." I glanced at the other woman, in her sixties. Her hair was latticed grey and white. Her face, puffy from crying, was darkly tanned from years of working in the sun. Deep furrows lined the mouth and forehead. Her eyes were bloodshot, her shoulders sagged with despair. She wiped her hands on her embroidered apron. I reached for her hand.

"Mrs. Holland, I wanted to stop by and say how sorry I was about Keith," I said.

"Me too, honey," the old woman said, clutching Mrs. Holland's left arm with fingers curled and gnarled with age and arthritis, and patting her back soothingly, like she was comforting a child who had scraped a knee. "I gotta run now, Martha. Now, if there's anything I can do, anything at all, you let me know. I'll be back tomorrow with some more food." She patted the woman's shoulder again and tottered across the porch and towards the cars, swaying precariously on stiff limbs, her flowery print dress hanging as loose as a burlap sack on a scarecrow. We watched in silence until she had climbed into her car with a faded "Mike Huckabee for President" sticker on one side of her rear window and a Ted Cruz sticker on the other.

Then Mrs. Holland turned to me. "Noah Starr," she said slowly, "My, it's been such a long time. Here, let me look at you." She slid on the horn-rimmed glasses that hung from a thin silver chain around her neck, and held me at arm's length. "You've put on a little weight since I last saw you. What's it been, Noah? Eight, ten years?"

"About that, I guess, ma'am." I glanced over her shoulder into the house. Neighbors were gathered to share the family's grief and bring food.

She put her arm around my waist, and walking close to me, led me into the living room. Her manner was the same as it had been when I was ten and had come for a visit, warm and motherly. I wondered who was supposed to be comforting whom. She introduced me around to the clusters of people. Nobody mentioned Keith or why we were there. We ended up in the kitchen, alone except for a Mrs. Bartlett who was washing dishes.

"You will eat something, won't you?" She cast her eyes towards the dining table and the kitchen counter awash with cakes and pies, platters of fried chicken, and bowls of vegetables, as if wondering where it had come from and how she would get rid of it.

"No, ma'am, I'm not hungry. I just wanted to give my condolences."

Her face weakened, the bottom lip trembling, her tightly closed eyes squeezing out a tear. She covered her face with her hand and breathed deeply. Her voice faltered. "I . . . I'm sorry. It's just that it was such a shock." She glanced out the window. I followed her gaze out the window to a red and white calf nursing its mother, lunging against her udder to release more milk. She looked back at me. "Did you know Keith these last few years?"

I shook my head. "Not really."

"I did. Oh, he didn't tell me what he was up to." She paused, "But a mother knows." She glanced over at the woman washing the dishes, gently took my arm and led me down the hall to a bedroom, and quietly closed the door behind us.

I glanced around. It was Keith's old room. His high school graduation picture was on the wall, and various 4-H awards and athletic trophies still lined the shelves.

She turned to me, slowly rubbing her hands together as if she was washing them. "Come sit over here, Noah." We sat on the edge of the bed, half-way facing each other. "I got to know what happened. Why he was killed." A single tear formed, and slowly rolled down her face. She pulled a wadded up kleenex from her pocket, and wiped the tear from her face and dabbed at her eyes, and looked at me. "I knew Keith was wild." Her voice was thick and uneven with emotion. "He's been that way since high school. You know it and I know it. When he visited, he acted like an All-American boy." Her voice sank to a whisper, "But I knew." She gathered herself again. "You used to be a Dallas PO-lice man." She accented the first syllable of "policeman", with a long "o". It was a flat statement.

I nodded.

"And aren't you a private investigator now?"

I nodded again.

"Would you look into this for me. Just me. Not his daddy. Finis didn't suspect anything. He never knew Keith was into meanness. He just kept on saying, 'He's just high-spirited.' This come as such a shock to him. So he's not to know you're looking into it, o.k.? Let him just think Keith was killed in one of those random acts of violence you read about in the big city. He's dead. But at least Finis won't lose the Keith he knew."

"Mrs. Holland, exactly what do you want?"

"Mainly just that them that done it are caught. The rest I'll try to forget. Try to remember my boy like he was . . . As he was back before, like he was when ya'll were friends."

"O.k. I was going to look in to it anyway. I talked with a Dallas police department captain this morning about it, and he told me who would be in charge of the investigation. I will call him when I get back in town Monday. But if I'm going to get very involved, I will need Keith's home address, where he worked, his friends, any such information you have."

She nodded. She went to a desk, pulled open a drawer and got out a small notebook. She came and sat beside me shoulder to shoulder on Keith's old bed.

She opened the notebook. "This here is Keith's home address," she said, pointing to the top of the page. "And this is the key to the apartment." She pointed to a house key that was scotch-taped to the page next to the address. "Me and Finis went once about two years ago. It's north of I-30 off the main loop around Dallas. You know the loop I'm talking about." She paused and glanced at me and I nodded. "It's upstairs. All those apartments look alike. That was the most frustrating trip I ever took. Spent half a day going up there and wandering around on and off Interstates and loops that were jam-packed, looking for Keith's apartment. Then, we only had a short visit with Keith. He seemed like he was impatient for us to leave, so we just stayed a short while. Keith said he had a date and had to meet someone before the date. That hurt Finis. He didn't say anything about it, but he just kinda withdrew a little bit, as if he realized, deep down, that he had lost Keith, that he wasn't going to come home to raise cattle with him. We never talked much about him after that."

She pointed to the facing page that had a business card that said "Holland's Harley Davidson" and gave the address, and had a key taped to it. "And that's his business. It's a motorcycle shop. I don't know any of his friends. But maybe there's something at his apartment that can tell you about that." She handed me the notebook. It had "KEITH" written on the red cover. Two pages and two keys were all his mother had of Keith, all she really knew of her only son. She looked at the notebook and then at me as if she was thinking the same thing.

"I'll check out the apartment and let you know if I find anything."

"Could you copy those, the keys too, and send them back to me. I don't have another one, and we'll need to go get his belongings and clean out the apartment." She sounded so practical, but I knew she was just talking to keep from thinking about Keith's murder and how she had lost him long before his death.

We talked a little more and I convinced Mrs. Holland that I had already planned to investigate Keith's murder. I assured her that I would let her know what I found out. She had wanted to pay me, but I had refused, gently, saying it was a favor for an old friend. She had hesitantly accepted that. I left and headed towards Franklin.

Franklin had been a town of 5,000 when I had graduated high school in 1992, but it had more than doubled in size since then. I spent most of the afternoon driving around Franklin. I had visited occasionally, but hadn't taken time to return to my old haunts. Few things are as disconcerting as going back home after a couple decades to the small town you grew up in. It's like being in an old *Twilight Zone* episode. The town looked much the same. The old little league park was still where it used to be. The advertising panels that lined the outfield fence were different and the paint was new, but the bleachers and the refreshment stand were like they used to be. The old Piggly Wiggly grocery store had been closed for years and was now an antique store now, but from the stuff lining the sidewalk, it looked more like a bad garage sale. The old pizza parlor now sold fried chicken.

I was passing the new high school at 3:30 when it let out. I pulled into stop-and-go fast-food across the street and filled my gas tank. I leaned against the fender and watched the surge of exuberant humanity. Friday afternoon and school was out. To a teenager, it was like a reprieve from the electric chair. The big yellow buses lined up along the side of the parking lot next to the flat roofed loading pavilion. Kids yelled and shoved and laughed and threw paper wads as they waited for their buses to take them home. The line of buses stretched around the corner, but the loading went quick. The kids were as eager as the drivers to get home and start the weekend. The older kids ignored the buses and the younger students and headed towards their cars. They gathered around cars and talked and planned the weekend, then piled into the cars and pickups and roared from the parking lot.

I drove around a little longer to see the changes in Franklin. Around five o'clock, I checked into the Columbia Vista Inn. It was a fairly new two-story motel made of cement blocks painted a festive yellow. I took a room on the upper level. I parked my truck near the stairs leading up to my room. I got my clothes, locked the truck and went up the stairs to the room. It was identical to every motel room in America. Two double beds, an ugly "painting" screwed to the wall above the headboard of the bed, a low six drawer chest, and a flat screen television.

Dusk was settling over the town, the street lights flickering on, casting their eerie white glow against the encroaching darkness. The main street ran in front of the motel. It was loud with pounding rock music, accelerating cars, and whooping teenagers. From the sound of it, the town turned its streets over to its youth when it rolled up its sidewalks. I stood on the balcony for half a minute watching the cars race, maneuver, stop and swap passengers, then surge back into the flow. Unless things had changed a lot from my day, the kids were pairing up for the night's drinking and carousing, loving and fighting. Almost two decades ago, that might have been Keith out there, taking a primer course for the fast life towards which he had seemed inexorably drawn.

I called the O'Brians and told them I was in town and would be by their house at eleven like we had discussed, and reminded them to have the information and photos I had requested. I read *The Columbia County Herald*, and watched the news. I went out and got a burger for supper and brought it back to the room to eat while doing *The Dallas Morning News* crossword. I went to bed early to the cacophony of the kids' rutting season on the street outside.

CHAPTER
5

I CAUGHT THE wake-up buzz of my cell phone on the third ring. I sat on the edge of the bed and rubbed my eyes. A vertical bar of light slashed across the bed through the slightly parted curtain. After a quick shower, I put on jeans, black lizard skin boots, a starched blue oxford shirt, grabbed my leather jacket, locked up and left the hotel. I drove over to the O'Brians'.

I pulled into the driveway behind Pete's red Ford SUV with a back window sticker that said "Oil Field Trash and Proud of It". As I was getting out, the front door opened. Pete O'Brian came out to meet me. Pete was almost six foot tall and weighed over two hundred pounds of hard muscle, with a slight beer gut. We shook hands.

"How was the trip?" he asked as he led me to the house, his head down and his shoulders hunched up, his hands deep in his pants pockets. "We got the stuff you wanted."

His wife, Helen, was waiting for us at the front door. She was very attractive, a curly haired brunette with delicately boned features. They led me to the living room. It was panelled in light brown wood, with green carpet. We sat down, the O'Brians on the couch and I in a chair. The den had few books, but what it lacked in literature, it made up for in photographs of their two children and their school awards. There were clusters of photographs of a son and a daughter on the t.v. and bookshelves, and on the walls.

After Helen had served coffee, and I had declined coffee cake, we made small talk. Pete was a roughneck with Meechum Oil Company, a local drilling company I had worked for while attending Kilgore College. Helen was a tenth grade math teacher at Franklin High School.

I brought the conversation around to business. "O.k. Now tell me about Carolyn."

There was a pause. Helen leaned back on the couch, like a turtle retreating into her shell.

"As I told you yesterday, she's disappeared. She didn't come home from her date Saturday." Pete started.

"And you waited almost a week to check into it?"

"No, I went to the police Sunday morning. See, she was supposed to be home by midnight. I waited until one thirty before I called the kid. Hell, I didn't even know who she was out with. She's real popular and dates a lot. I roused Danny, that's my boy there," he gestured towards a photograph on the t.v. of a young man in an orange and black football uniform, "And he told me she was out with a new kid in town name of Chad Denton. His family just moved here from Ohio. I got the kid on the phone and he told me he had brought Carolyn home around twelve thirty. I . . . ." He dropped his head slightly, then looked me in the eye, "I guess I lost my head. I got pissed and told him she wasn't home and since she was with him I was goin' to hold him responsible if anything happened to my little girl. The bastard hung up on me." He paused, as if reliving the conversation. "Well, I'll tell you right now, I won't put up with crap like that from a punk like him. I got dressed and went down to the police station to see what they could do. They said they would look into it, but unless they could find that something had happened to Carolyn, they wouldn't really look into it. They think she's run away. Hell, she's not five years old and running away next door. She's an almost grown woman. She's gone and everybody seems to think she just run off to Dallas."

He lunged to his feet, his hands white knuckled fists. His eyes bit into me. "Dammit, Noah, the police, they ain't going to do a damn thing." He spit out the words. Helen shuddered at their impact. She pulled on his pants leg until he sat back down.

"Now, Peter, please. It doesn't do anyone any good to get so upset." She gently patted his knee, trying to calm the raging beast in him.

"Noah, please," he implored, his hands open toward me. "You've gotta help me, you gotta find her. The police, they ain't gonna do anything. They just figure she's run away from home. Her mother," he glanced over at his wife and put his hand on her tightly clasped hands, "Helen she hadn't slept since all this started. She just cries and worries. I'm, I'm . . . dammit, that Denton boy's to blame for this. He caused her to leave, dammit. It's all I can do to keep from blowing him away." His shoulders slumped. His eyes, rimmed with tears, sought mine. "Noah, try to find her for me. Say you'll look for my baby."

"O.k. I'll do what I can, but let me say this: with no knowledge of your daughter, I want you to realize the police may be right. A lot of kids run away these days." Pete hugged Helen, as if to reassure himself that she was still there.

I nodded. "I'll need some information." I said, "Who's the boy's, Chad's, father?"

"Walter Denton."

"Where do they live?"

"On the north side of the lake. Five-oh-five-five River Road." He glanced over at Helen for assurance that he gave the right address. She glanced over at him and nodded slightly. They both looked back at me.

I tried to phrase the next question delicately, then gave up. "Pete, is there any reason, any possible reason at all for Carolyn to leave home? A recent argument with you? Trouble at school?" I paused, "Pregnancy?"

Pete shook his head at the first two, but went rigid at the last one. "No, no, her mother and I didn't raise her like that. We're good Christian people. Carolyn went, uh," he stammered, "goes to church every Sunday."

"Easy, Pete. I was just asking. But kids are doing it a lot of things these days that we didn't use to do. Even what we used to call 'good girls,' too. The world's changed a lot since we were in high school, buddy."

He shook his head adamantly, quick and tight.

"O.k. How about drugs or alcohol?"

"What kind of girl do you think we raised?" He asked indignantly.

Helen patted his knee again. "Now Peter, he has to ask these questions." Then, turning to me, she said, "Let me get you our scrapbook." She was almost out of the room when she turned and explained, "She is our only daughter, our baby."

She returned in a minute with a thick pink photo album with a photograph of a little girl on the front in a plastic covered slot.

The photos in the album seemed to begin with high school. I shuddered to think how many more photo albums there were of Carolyn. I skipped over the first of the scrapbook, and glanced at the final year or so of material. Photos and newspaper clippings showed Carolyn touching all of the social bases. She was on the student council, a cheerleader, and the homecoming queen. All the things that were so important in high school. Twenty years ago, I might have thought them worthwhile, but now they seemed like a fixed beauty contest. But they weren't the things a seventeen year old girl ran away from.

My eyes kept drifting back to a picture of Carolyn posing beside a swimming pool, a teenager in a woman's body, her feminine charms scantily covered with a bright red bikini, like two thin bloody stripes. She had a great smile. It was the smile of one young enough to enjoy life to the fullest, without ever a thought of paying the piper. I saw a wallet sized studio photograph of a more demure Carolyn and asked if I could take it. Pete nodded and I slipped it out of its plastic pouch and put it in my shirt pocket.

"Do you have the list of her friends, people she had seen and been around Saturday, addresses and phone numbers and emails like I asked?"

Pete glanced over at Helen.

"Yes, I have it right here." She said, reaching over to the end table and handing me a list of names and addresses, carefully written in a small, neat script. "These are the ones she's closest to. I've already talked to most of them. They didn't know where she was."

I glanced over the list and nodded. There must have been over twenty names.

"Now Pete, this might cost quite a bit. The longer she stays away, the colder the trail. I get hundred dollars an hour, plus expenses. And I might have to call in some help. And I generally get a two thousand dollar retainer up front. Still want me to take a look?"

They glanced at each other and Helen whispered, "Just find her." She went out of the room and returned with her purse, dug out her checkbook, and began to write a check. "Who do I make it out to? Noah Starr?"

I nodded.

"Is that 'Starr' with one or two 'r's'?"

"Two."

She finished writing, then carefully folded the check along the perforation and tore it out and handed it to me.

I folded the check and the list of names and put them in my shirt pocket and stood up. "O.k. That will be all for now. I'll keep you posted on developments. If anything comes up, if you think of something Carolyn said or did that might relate to this in any way, let me know. You have the office number." I gave them my cell phone number.

Helen's face was lined with fears, unnamed pits of quicksand of what may have swallowed her child without a trace.

"Don't worry," I told her. "Kids take off all the time these days. Most are back in a week or so." I didn't mention the others. The looks on their faces told me they knew the fate of the others was far bleaker.

They walked me to the door. I left them huddled together on the porch as I drove out the driveway.

CHAPTER
6

I HEADED TOWARDS River Road, stopping along the way for a quick lunch at the Rainbow Cafe. It had a dining room in front, with a pool room behind a beaded curtain. The "blue plate" special was chicken fried steak, cream gravy and french fries. It was good to eat "home cooking", although I could almost hear my arteries clogging. I thought of the good old days when such a meal was regarded as eating high on the hog, rather than eating one's way to a coronary.

I noticed a number of teenagers in the back room, playing pool and listening to the juke box. The music was country. I motioned the waitress over. She brought a pitcher of iced tea and refilled my glass.

"Thanks, Betty," I said, reading her name tag. "Are you from around here?"

She shook her blond head. She was pretty, in her late twenties, with a good figure and a rich tan. Small crows feet fanned from her brown eyes. She had a pair of small silver hoop earrings swaying from her lobes, with small diamond studs just above the earrings. Her blue and white uniform was freshly ironed. "Naw. I grew up in Woden. Know where that's at? East of Nacogdoches. But I've lived in Franklin for the last two years." She leaned a hip against my table.

I motioned towards the kids in the poolroom. "Do ya'll get many teenagers in here?"

"Quite a few of the kickers, especially right after school. Nights, they're usually out just drivin' around and drinkin'. Not much else to do here in Franklin."

"Have you ever seen a kid named Chad Denton in here?"

"I think he came in a couple times a while back. He was in with Roger Lawson, I think. Don't think I seen him lately, though. Why do you ask?"

"I'm looking into Carolyn O'Brian's disappearance. What is he like?"

She didn't answer my question, but asked, "You a cop or something?"

"A something. I'm a private investigator."

Her eyes lit up. "Really? You from around here. Never heard of you before. Bet'cha got an office in Tyler or Longview, right?"

"Dallas. But I grew up in Franklin. Carolyn's father and I graduated together. Like I said, what's Chad Denton like."

"I didn't know him. Just saw him here some. Seemed o.k. though. Talked funny, like he was a Yankee or somethin'."

"Do you know Carolyn O'Brian?"

She shook her head, "I've never seen her in here that I know of."

"Is Roger Lawson back there now?" I said, nodded toward the back.

She glanced through the doorway into the poolroom and nodded. "That's him back there shooting pool with the John Deere cap. You want anything else?"

I shook my head. "No, thanks. Can I have the check?"

"Sure." She pulled her order tablet from the patch pocket on her apron, flipped through to find mine, tore it out and laid it, face down. She flashed a broad smile. "Do come back." She went back behind the counter.

The tab was just under seven dollars. I laid a five and a ten on the table next to the ash tray, smiled at Betty, and strolled to the back.

There were six young men passing the afternoon shooting the bull and playing pool. Several were dipping snuff, their lower lips slightly pouched out, using styrofoam drink cups as spittoons. Occasionally one of them would hold his cup to his mouth and spit, then set the cup aside.

Roger and a guy with "B U S T E R" engraved on the back of his western belt were playing when I walked in. Three sets of four quarters were lined on the edge of the table above the coin slots. Evidently a lot of them wanted to challenge the table. A folded five dollar bill had been laid beside the quarters.

Roger had the solids and was ahead. He only had one ball left to sink. He was angling the cue for a double ricochet off the rubber. He glanced at me when I came in, then turned his attention back to the table. He stroked the stick once, slowly, then with force. The cue ball hit the rubber once, rolled behind Buster's ball, bounced off the rubber, and clipped his ball It rolled into the corner pocket. The cue ball rolled slowly into line with the 8 ball.

"Side pocket," he said and sidled around the table. He picked up the blue chalk cube and rubbed it on the tip. He bent from the waist, and smoothly shot in the 8 ball. He stood up and grinned broadly.

"Crap," Buster said with a smirk, and reached for his spit cup.

Roger put the five spot in his billfold. "That almost makes us even. You won six off me last Saturday. Who's next."

The others kidded and argued over whose quarters were up next. They finally agreed on Mike, a lanky boy of about sixteen who wore a brown felt cowboy hat with the front of the brim turned down and a pair of crossed toothpicks in the snakeskin band. A small button that proclaimed "Rodeo: America's # 1 Sport" was fastened to the side of the crown of the hat just above the band on the left side. He bent over and inserted his quarters, released the balls, and racked them. There was a frayed, faded circle where his snuff can had partially worn through the back left pocket of his jeans.

Everyone else was watching me. I looked at Roger.

"You're Roger Lawson, right?"

"Yes, sir. Who are you?" He leaned casually on the pool cue like it was a walking cane, his hand resting lightly on the tip of the pool cue.

"I'm Noah Starr. I wanted to ask you a few questions about Chad Denton. Do you have a few minutes?"

His face clouded, and he glanced back at the pool table.

"Not really. I'm on a hot streak." He paused, and looked at me. I didn't move. "Okay, if it's necessary, I'll take a break."

"If you don't mind, it's important."

He glanced back at Buster, and tossed him the stick. "Keep the table for me." He went over and sat on the edge of a table, and asked, "What do you want to know?" Then he ducked his head and spit out the tight ball of snuff into his cup. He reached into his back pocket and pulled out the flat Copenhagen can, pulled off the top and took out a pinch and placed it inside his lower lip. I remembered doing the same thing when I was his age. Now I knew I was in the country, not much snuff dipping in the big city. He held out the open can, offering me a pinch. I declined with a slight wave of the hand. He put the lid back on and put the can back in his hip pocket and looked at me, as if he was now ready for questioning.

"What do you want to know about Chad?" he asked.

"Whatever you know. When did you meet him. What kind of a person he is? Anything you know about him and Carolyn O'Brian?"

"I don't know much about Chad. He moved here the first of the year. His family came from Toledo, Ohio. He's a nice enough guy. He's on the baseball team, and I think he's going out for football next year." He glanced over at the other guys, who agreed. "I met him at school. We're in English and metal shop together. He messed around with us a little when he first got to town, but he drifted into the rich kid circle. Hell, he's, I mean, heck, he more one of them, I mean, he is a rich kid, too. Got a big home on River Road. Big boat, fancy cars. We're still pals, though. He's just a nice, quiet guy."

"What about Carolyn O'Brian?"

"What about her?"

"Do you know her?"

"Sure, doesn't everybody?"

"What about her? What's she like?"

"She's real active in school stuff. She's a cheerleader and stuff like that."

"Did you ever go out with her?"

"Not on a date, but we were friends. I've known her all my life."

"Who did she run with?"

"Usually the rich kids. They have great parties. I've been to a couple of them. Lots of beer and . . . ." His voice dropped and he glanced at me, startled by his open statement to me, an adult stranger.

"And drugs?" I asked.

"I wouldn't know about that." He said suddenly, his hands raised in denial, his palms toward me.

"Had Chad and Carolyn been dating long?"

"Not that long. I figure a few weeks."

"You know that Carolyn has disappeared. What do you think happened to her?"

"I don't know. Everybody at school is shocked. Some kids think Chad did something to her. Most of the kids seem to think she just ran off to Dallas. Carolyn is always talking about being a model in Dallas, or maybe L.A. or New York. She's a real good looker, so maybe she did. Nobody really knows."

"How's Chad handling the situation?"

"Like I said, he's pretty quiet anyway. But since this, he's really kept a low profile. Poor kid. New in town and now this." He shook his head slowly, as if burdened by life's inequities.

"Anything else?"

"Not that comes to mind."

"If you think of anything, please call me. I'm staying at the Vista Inn. Here's my card. Call me if you think of anything. I would appreciate it. By the way, who's Chad's and Carolyn's best friends?"

He glanced over at the others. "Carolyn usually runs with Debbie Jenson. Chad? Since this stuff came up about Carolyn, he's been pretty much a loner." He glanced over at his friends. "But he used to be pretty close to Russell Kimberly." The guys nodded again.

"Do you know where Debbie and Russell live?" I asked.

They clustered around, took out their cell phones and scrolled their contacts lists, and gave me the kids' addresses and cell numbers, and then the directions to their homes. I jotted the information down.

"Thanks, guys. Have a good afternoon." I turned and walked out. Behind me the conversation erupted and I could hear them racking the balls for the next game as they went back to their carefree teenage lives. I envied them for having nothing more serious in their lives than losing a pool game. One of the boys had a tee shirt with the statement "Have No Fear" printed on the back.

I thought: If they had good sense, they might ought to be afraid.

CHAPTER
7

I DROVE OVER to the Franklin Police Department. It was a rustic building, made of local red iron ore rock. It had been a W.P.A. project in the thirties and looked like any number of public buildings and schools across east Texas from that era. I parked in the visitor's parking. I went in and asked to see the Chief. The balding dispatcher studied the toe of his sharkskin cowboy boot for a bit, then asked, "What do you want with him, Mr. . . .?"

"Starr, Noah Starr."

"Well, Mr. Starr, what's your business with Chief Browning?"

"I wanted to talk with him about the Carolyn O'Brian disappearance."

He looked at me steadily, then said, "Let me get him on the horn." He picked up the phone, punched in a couple numbers and waited a moment, "Yeah, Chief. Guy here named Noah Starr wants to talk to you about the O'Brian disappearance. Yeah, o.k." He looked up at me. "Last door on the right. Name's on the door."

I thanked him and went down the sea foam green hall. The bubbled, peeling paint was smudged with countless hand prints. The white acoustic ceiling tiles were yellowed. Water leak stains spotted the tiles like dark clouds. I rapped on the wooden door and paused, then entered when I was invited.

The Chief was leaning back in his high backed black leather chair, his feet on the corner of his desk. He was about six foot tall, his once-muscular frame going to fat. He was in his mid-fifties, his short black hair was white at the temples. He was wearing a rumpled tan khaki uniform with an open collar and his sleeves rolled half way up his forearms. He had a U.S. Marine Corps emblem tattoo on his right forearm. His off-white Stetson was on the hat rack by the door. The office was furnished with a grey metal desk and file cabinets. The wall behind Browning was filled with certificates and awards, with a scattering of photos of him and various dignitaries. The Chief was reading a report when I entered, and glanced at me over half-frame reading glasses.

He dropped his feet, stood up, and leaned against the desk. He took off the reading glasses and laid them on the manila covered report. He extended his right hand. "I'm Chief Browning. What can I do for you today?" After we shook hands, and I introduced myself, he said, "Sit down, Mr. Starr." He sat down, leaned forward and rested his crossed forearms on his desk.

"I'm looking into Carolyn O'Brian's disappearance and I wanted to find out what your department has found out. It would save me a lot of time repeating your footsteps."

"What's your stake in this?"

"Pete O'Brian hired me to investigate it for him."

"And you are a, . . . what?"

"Private investigator." I gave him a business card and pulled my license from the wallet and handed it to him. He looked at it, then at me.

"Have any references? Anybody I'd know?"

"Bobby Ray McClinton with the County Sheriff's Office. We went to high school here together. But it's been a while since we've seen each other. He recommended me to O'Brian. And there's Captain Bill Travis with the Dallas Police Department."

He picked up his phone. "Carl, get Bobby Ray McClinton on the phone for me. Yeah, right now." He leaned back in his chair, holding the phone under his chin. "So you grew up here? When'd you graduate?"

"Ninety-two."

"With your build, figure you played football." I nodded. "You were on the state quarter-final game team, then." I nodded again. "Hell, they still talk about that mud bath with Jacksboro. What position did you play?" I was about to tell him when he raised his hand. "Bobby Ray, Walter Browning here." The Chief smiled broadly, "Yeah, that's right, um-hum. Uh, what I called about is do you know a Noah Starr? Uh hum. He's o.k. then? You recommended him? O.k., sounds good. Thanks. By the way, when you coming to the lodge again. It's been ages. Yeah, o.k. Call me sometime next week and let's plan a fishing trip to Lake Fork. Bye."

Browning hung up the phone, put on his reading glasses and opened the folder. He put my business card in the folder and handed my license back to me. "Bobby Ray vouched for you. O.k. I've been reviewing the facts in the case. Frankly, we haven't found out much. We checked out all the angles, as much as we could." He leaned forward again, resting his forearms on the desk. He started reading the report and summarizing it for me. "O'Brian reported his daughter missing at 3:46 a.m. last Sunday morning. I've talked with him. Hell, I think he's talked with everyone from J. Edgar Hoover on down. He's been in my office three times. He thinks the Denton kid did something to her. Threw her in the river or something." He shook his head. "The man's a hot-head. Hell, I guess I'd be the same way if my daughter disappeared." He glanced at the gold framed family portrait on the corner of his desk, as if to reassure himself that his family, at least, was still together. "We looked into that angle, of course, but Denton's story seems ok for now. He is about the only thing we have, so we've covered it pretty good."

"What's his description of last Saturday night?"

Browning glanced at the file, thumbing through the pages. "Said he picked her up at her house at seven-thirty. They saw a movie in Longview. Came back here, got a pizza at Lemon's," he glanced at me. "That's just down the street, on the corner of Bois D'Arc and Louisiana. It's a teen hangout. We've checked that part out with several people who were there that night. Mainly high schoolers. Also talked with Harley Lemon, the owner. And a waitress, Stacy Muldoon. They left about ten thirty or eleven. Drove around for a while. Was seen and talked with several people. We've interviewed everyone that saw or talked with them.

"About eleven-thirty or twelve o'clock, they left. Nobody else saw her again. Denton said they went straight to her house, but he seemed a little nervous on this point. I figured they went parking somewhere. But I couldn't shake him on that story. Denton said he dropped the girl off at her house by about twelve fifteen or twelve thirty. He said he let her out, that she insisted on going to house alone. He said she had a key, and let herself in. The house was dark. He went home and was asleep when O'Brian called at one thirty. Denton said O'Brian threatened him, called him names and said he'd kill him if anything had happened to his daughter. That's about all we have. We checked all the leads, but didn't come up with anything." He took off his glasses and laid them on the edge of the desk, as if he didn't want to be associated with such a sign of advancing age.

I leaned forward, resting an elbow on the desk. "What do you think happened, based on your instincts, the report, or whatever?"

"Confidentially, I think she got in a traveling mood. Maybe had trouble at home. Maybe pregnant. A lot of the kids at Columbia High School smoke pot or use other drugs and, uh, I can't back it up, but I understand the girl was deeper into drugs than most kids around here. We nailed a dealer about six months ago. He talked his way into a reduced sentence. According to him - and I wouldn't bet a plugged nickel on anything he said - but he said Carolyn O'Brian as a big partier. Said she was a regular weekend user. As I said, I don't put much faith in what he said, but he did say it. The D.A. dangled a reduced sentence like a carrot. The bastard would have fingered his mother for the Kennedy assassination if he thought it would help."

"Do you believe she was using drugs?" I asked.

"She doesn't fit the pattern. She had good grades and all, but any more there just aren't many 'patterns' to go by. Kids are into everything. Good kids, bad kids, rich or poor, no difference except the degree they are involved in. The rich are just involved more because they can afford it. And Carolyn ran with the rich kids. Her family isn't rich, but they are comfortable. But she had the looks and charm to get in with any crowd that she wanted to be in with."

I nodded and stood up and shook hands with him. "Thanks for the information, Chief."

"No problem. Keep in touch. I take a professional interest when people start poking into my local business. You understand. Hope you can find her. The O'Brians are hurting, bad. You find her and they may be pissed at her, but that's better than the thought she may be dead, like O'Brian keeps suggesting."

CHAPTER

8

I GOT IN my car and headed north towards the lake. Franklin had grown a lot since I had been in high school, but I was still able to find my way around the main streets. I missed only one turn on the way to River Road, but I dog-legged at the next corner and got back on the right street.

River Road had been a quiet country road when I was young. It arched around the east and north side of the lake, a two lane black top that rose and fell with the hills that formed the lake. Thickets of elm and scrub oak leaned over the road, at times their arching limbs forming a tunnel through which I drove to the Dentons'. I kept glancing out my side window, trying to see the lake through the trees. Occasionally, I would see a glint of reflected sunlight on wind tousled water. When I had been young, River Road had boasted several parking places overlooking the lake. I wondered if kids still went parking there.

After almost a mile of trees, the forest broke and civilization began again. "River Road" had two meanings. One was the name of the road itself. The other was the name of where rich folks of Franklin lived. Locals used the term with the same awe, or jealousy, as Dallasites talking about Highland Parks. For River Roaders, the strip of forest was a mile wide "railroad track" that kept the commoners from mingling with the upper crust.

River Road homes were usually built on several acres with lake frontage. The Dentons' new house was no exception. It was two story, with soaring white antebellum style columns along the porch that spanned the front of the house. The tall windows were dissected into small panes by white crosshatching. Unpainted snatches of trim and scattered piles of scrap boards, empty plumbing fixture boxes and paint cans emphasized the newness of the house. Bare patches of sand glistened in the midday sun in stark contrast to the cool green of the newly laid sod, the edges of the grass blocks checkering the yard. The few forlorn pine trees that remained in the yard had high, thin branches stretching toward the sun, but the lower two-thirds of their trunks lacked limbs, testament to how dense the forest was before the contractor got there. The tree trunks bore numerous signs of recent construction including white slashes of cut bark from careless tractor drivers and overzealous pruners. Most of the raised flower beds were empty, but the rose garden in the middle of the circle white gravel driveway had been planted and mulched with pine bark. The metal tags identified the varieties of the roses dangled from the rose bushes' bare branches, glittering in the sun.

I nosed my truck around the driveway and parked beside a new, moss green Mercedes. I got out and walked around the front of the car, admiring its clean lines. I trotted up the three broad steps onto the huge, veranda-like porch. The double doors were framed with leaded glass, the beveled edges catching light from inside. I pressed the door button. A chime sounded faintly in the distance. A minute crept by unnoticed. I pressed again, twice. No response. I glanced back at the car. Someone was surely home. A new Mercedes isn't the kind of car you park until the old Volkswagen breaks down.

I thought someone might be on the lake, so I went around the house. The delicate, honeyed fragrance of scattered bright yellow King Alfred daffodils and a small purple wisteria bush wafted on the soft breeze coming across the lake. The patio was abandoned. New bone white wrought iron lawn furniture was clustered against the far side of the low brick wall that surrounded the area. The brightly colored canvas umbrella on the table was furled and tied. Only its scalloped edge wagged in the breeze.

A path snaked down to the water. I followed it, glancing at the few scrub oaks left by the landscapers. If they had left the best trees, the trees they had cut down would not have yielded enough wood to roast a hot dog. The path ended at a forty foot wharf that jutted into the lake. The new wood of the piers reeked of creosote. Against the west side of the wharf, a white and sky blue ski boat bobbed against the tires that lined the dock. I walked out on the platform and looked at the boat. It was as new as the rest of the place. Clear plastic sacks still held the life preservers and covered the seats. The big outboard engine was pristine white. There was no one along the shore so I climbed the slight rise back up to the house.

She was standing on the patio as I came up the hill, her eyes squinted into black slashes that split into crow's feet at her temples. She wore a bright blue on green paisley caftan, her blond hair wisping from under a matching scarf. Her arms were crossed tightly beneath her small breasts. In her left hand, several ice cubes swirled in a snifter of amber. Her face was a contrast of a tense mouth and sagging jowls.

"What do you want?" She asked venomously.

"I want to talk with Chad Denton."

"He isn't here now. Why do you want to see him?"

"I want to talk with him about the disappearance of Carolyn O'Brian."

She stiffened, her eyes hardening, the crow's feet deepening in her sun-aged face. "Who are you with, the Sheriff's Office or the Franklin police department."

"Neither."

"What now, the damn F.B.I.?" She snorted. "I want to see a badge," she paused, "Or a warrant. Or you out of here."

"I'm a private detective. Peter O'Brian asked me to look into his daughter's disappearance.

"Got a badge or something?" she ordered flatly.

I took out my license and showed it to her. She studied the license, reading myopically. I had a clue as to the origin of the crows feet and leather skin, vanity and fashion.

"Guess it's legitimate." she said disdainfully. "But I don't have anything to say," She spat out the last words, "Especially to you."

"I just want a few words with your son. It couldn't hurt."

"The hell it couldn't. Chad has talked with all the cops he's going to." She took a long swig from the glass, then recrossed her arms tightly. "Chad told the police everything he knew, which wasn't much. He took the girl out, yes, but he took her home and left her. He has not seen her since and doesn't have any idea what happened to her. Maybe her father did something to her. He's crazy, if you ask me. He's called here so many times we've reported him to the police and the phone company. Bet he didn't tell you we put him under a restraining order, did he? Didn't think so. He's the homicidal nut around here. You go back and talk with him. And get the hell out of here." She turned and stalked into the house, the slamming door punctuating her tirade.

I walked back toward my truck. As I passed, I glanced at the Mercedes again. A small spot of dark oil glistened on the front fender, catching the eye like the Colossus at Rhodes. I wiped it from the fender. It just didn't look right on the car. I got in my truck and wiped my finger on a cloth I kept under the seat. Sitting in the truck, I noticed a dark stain under the Mercedes. I got out and went over to the side of the car and got down on my hands and knees and looked under the car. A puddle of oil blackened the white gravel. I glanced up at the oil pan. It was crushed on the passenger's side, the deep crease ending in a tear. Oil glistened from the hole like blackening blood. I got up and brushed the dirt from my knees.

I got in my truck and put the key in the ignition. I sat a minute thinking about Mrs. Denton's assessment of Pete O'Brian. I remembered Pete from high school as easy-going. But a missing daughter can drive one to the edge of sanity. I started up, drove around the Mercedes and headed back towards Franklin.

CHAPTER
9

It was almost three-thirty when I got back to Franklin. I headed back to the motel, stopping along the way to pick up a cold six pack of Dr. Pepper and the Saturday *Columbia Herald* and *The Dallas Times*. When I got back to the motel, I got out the telephone book and looked up the Sheriff's Office's number. I punched in the number and asked for Deputy McClinton. He was off duty. The dispatcher wouldn't give me his home telephone number. I checked and, as I expected, Bobby Ray's number was not in the book. I called the O'Brians' and got his number and called him.

"Bobby Ray, this is Noah Starr. The O'Brians, Pete and . . ."

"Noah, how the hell are you?"

"Fine. About . . ."

"What's it been, ten, twelve years?"

"Yeah, about that. About the O'Brians. They said you recommended me to look into this. What do you know about their daughter, Carolyn's, disappearance?"

"Not much, Noah. The city cops are handling it. We checked into it a little. But they've got the ball, mostly. From what I've heard, they've hit a brick wall. That's why Pete asked me what to do. Me and him are in the Rotary Club together, and after our last lunch meeting, he cornered me. I told him what the police were doing, but he wasn't satisfied with that. I told him if he wanted it checked out further, he might ought to think about getting a private detective to handle it for him. He asked me who, and I thought of you. Last time I saw you, you were a Dallas cop, and I had heard that you were a private detective now. Are you going to be able to help him?"

"Don't know. Met with them this morning. Then I talked with the Police Chief and went out to the Dentons' and talked with the boy's mother."

"She's a cold bitch, ain't she?"

"Yeah. Do you know anything about Carolyn's disappearance."

"Nothing. We didn't come up with anything, and I've heard the city boys haven't found anything either. They don't broadcast it, but hell, we don't get too much excitement around here."

"Bobby Ray, what do you think happened to here?"

"The hell if I know. I figure she ran off to Dallas, it happens occasionally. You know, kids gettin' the 'Big City' lights in their eyes. Guess they've seen too much living large on t.v. and in the movies and those music videos, maybe they think they can just step into that life. But it doesn't really fit with the O'Brian girl."

"Why not?"

"Well, usually the run-aways have a bad home life. You know, the father drinks maybe, the parents fight a lot. Kid maybe doesn't fit in in school. So they up and leave for Dallas, maybe Shreveport. Maybe hoping they'll find a place to fit in there. Maybe just can't take watching the other kids enjoy a normal life while they're living in hell and figure anywhere is better than there. Some of those run-aways have told me they just want to end the lives they were living. Kinda like suicide, in a way. If you're gone away from everyone you know, you're like being dead. No one to look down on you. You're nobody to the folks in the city. You're nothing. Like I said, to some of these kids, ending it is better than staying where everybody knows you and you're on the bottom of the pecking order and they treat you like shit.

"But, O'Brian didn't fit in any of that. She was smart, pretty, popular. Hell, seems like she was in the paper every week or so doing something at school. I asked my kids about her after this come up. Betty, my daughter, is in the grade below Carolyn. Betty said Carolyn was really as popular as she seemed to be in the paper. Said she was a friendly, outgoing kid."

"Do you think something's happened to her?"

"Don't know. The Dentons are new here. I've met the kid's father, Walter. He's been real active in town since they've move here. He moved here about last September. He's plant manager out at the corrugated paper factory and moved here and got settled in before the rest of them came down. I understand the city police talked with the boy, you know because of what Pete's been sayin'. Nothing came of it. Boy's story seemed to check out."

"So you think she ran away?"

"Really, I do. That's why I told Pete about you."

"If you hear anything different, would you call me?" I gave him my mobile and office numbers. He agreed. Then we discussed Keith's funeral. He said he would be there and told me when and where it would be held. We hung up.

I finished off a can of Dr. Pepper, and picked up one for the road. I went out to the truck, and headed back to the Hollands' place.

CHAPTER
10

THE HOLLAND'S YARD was packed. At least ten cars were clumped in the Holland's yard, with a half dozen more lining the drive way to the house, pulled close to the fence with just enough room to drive by. I saw some space by the barn. I nosed around the cars and pulled behind the house. I parked beside a big four-wheel-drive weather-faded orange Kubota tractor with a ten foot bat-wing rotary brush mower hooked up behind it.

I got out and started towards the house. A tan and white collie ran up to me and sniffed a few times. I patted its head. It trotted behind the car. I was almost to the porch when I heard the dog barking. I looked over my shoulder in time to see the dog chasing a calf past the barn. In the shadow, barely a silhouette, a man was looking across the field. I went back out to the barn.

It had been quite a few years since I had seen Mr. Holland. He didn't notice me when I first walked up. He was wearing a khaki pants and a flannel shirt, with a sweat-stain old straw cowboy hat set back on his head. His arms were crossed as he stared at the western horizon. He was leaning against a massive round hay baler.

He glanced over at me. It took him a few seconds to place me.

"Noah," he said finally. He stuck out his hand. "Been a long time, boy. How've you been?" We shook hands, and he crossed his arms again.

I told him I was fine and asked how he was doing. He said he was the same. We leaned against the baler some more, watching the horizon.

"Think it's going to rain?" I asked.

"Yeah. Look at that thunderhead over those pines," he said, pointing towards the northwest. "We've been needing it. About ten inches short this year." He nodded towards the pastures. "The winter pasture is getting a little short. Cattle have almost eaten it down to the ground. Got a little hay left, though, so no major problem." He paused, and slowly looked around the farm. Then he looked at me. "You know, Noah, this farm's been in the family over a hundred years. He pointed towards a copse of large oak trees in the south. "My great-grandfather built the first house there. The old family cemetery is behind it about a hundred yards." He paused, and I listened to the wind slowly pick up and watched the cattle slowly drift together, then head down the hill towards the pond in single file.

"It's a good farm. Got my roots here. My folks lived here all their lives, their folks did, too. Been Hollands here since the early 1870's. Came here from Tennessee after the Civil War." I listened, having nothing to add.

"Did'ja see the sign as you come in? 'F. E. Holland and Son?' I put it up the year after you and Keith graduated. I even offered him half the farm. He was the only boy we had. You know that. Thought if he had a part of the farm, he would give it a try. He lived in my folks' house for a while, off and on after graduating high school. But he didn't care. The farm was just a place to stay. Did you know Keith in Dallas?"

"No, sir, not much."

"Keith was a high spirited boy. Always was. Always laughing, running around, cuttin' up. Keith is a popular guy. I've heard from lots of his Dallas friends. He enjoyed the Dallas life. The parties, the crowds, the clubs. Had a good business, making lots of money. Then, then this killin'. It just doesn't make any sense." He looked at me, and I nodded in affirmation.

"I been wonderin' that maybe if Keith had felt about the farm like we did, and stayed here, none of this would have happened." He nodded towards the trees again. "The rest of us Hollands have always been like those trees. Our roots reach deep in this land. My granddad, he told me that if he ever left this land, he would just dry up and die, like a tree with the tap root cut. Keith, he was the tumble weed. Never seemed to have any roots. But like my granddad had warned, Keith just dried up and died." He paused, then looked south towards the cemetery, "But he's comin' home for good now, back to his roots." His voice quivered. He turned his back to me, his shoulders shaking with sobs.

I stood there for several minutes until he stopped crying. But he continued to look towards the cemetery. After about five minutes, I patted him on the back, and walked slowly towards the house. As I opened the back screen door, I looked back at Mr. Holland. He stood like the trunk of an old tree, its roots reaching deeply into the soil. I went into the house.

I went down the hall, past the familiar bedrooms, and into the crowded living room. It was like a quiet family reunion. I recognized several of the faces as those of Keith's relatives.

"Noah," a brunette in tight jeans called at me over the cacophony, as she got up from the sofa and came towards me. "It's me, Anita," she said as she got close. Anita had been one of my first girl friends. We made small talk, and she told me she had married one of our classmates. He worked at the trailer manufacturing plant in Longview, and she was a grocery checker at the local Brookshires food store. They had three kids and lived just down the road. She thought that it was "just terrible" that Keith had been shot. She asked if I was going to find the one that did it. I assured her that the Dallas police would solve the murder. She was discussing her son's soccer talent when I saw Mrs. Holland come into the room with a younger woman who was holding the hand of a five year old boy. I excused myself and moved over towards her. A couple got up from the couch to let them sit down. Mrs. Holland sat at the end of the sofa, and put her arm protectively around the woman, who was attempting to hold the squirming boy in her lap. He was rhythmically kicking the sofa with the heel of his red sneakers. She looked up as I approached. I squatted down by the arm of the couch.

"Noah, you remember Debbie, don't you."

I looked at Keith's sister. Her eyes were red and puffy. "Hi, Debbie." I glanced at the boy, "And who's this?"

Mrs. Holland leaned over and ruffled his hair. He made a face and tried to avoid her hand. He tugged at his mother's hand like a kite tugging on its string in a blustery wind. "This is Tommy. You're the apple of Gran'Ma's eye, aren't you, Tommy?"

Tommy ignored her, and turned to Debbie, "Can I go outside, Mama?"

She nodded and released him. He leaped to his feet and ran through the crowd and out the front door, the screen door slamming behind him.

She looked back at me. "I haven't told Tommy about Keith. He's too young. He wouldn't understand." She paused. "How have you been, Noah?"

"O.k., Debbie, and you?"

"I'm o.k., considering what's happened and all. Mama said you were going looking into what, who did that to him."

I nodded. "I don't know what I can do, but I'll call some people I know in Dallas."

Debbie slowly nodded as she pulled a tissue from her pocket and daubed at her eyes. The people nearby looked over at her covertly, uncertain whether to console her or to let her cry. She wiped her nose. "It's just been such a terrible shock. Me and Mama knew Keith's been running with some bad people in Dallas. Have you met that guy that calls hisself 'Bob Cat.' He's got tattoos all over him. And he's mean. Him and Keith came over to my house about six months ago, and they were drinking whiskey, and cussing. They were talking about fights they'd been in at a beer joint they went to a lot."

"What was the name of the joint?" I asked.

"I think it was called "Hank's Place." I heard Keith talk about that place, but I'm not sure if that's the place they were talking about fighting at. Why?"

"I was just wondering."

"Do you think that Bob Cat guy is responsible for what's happened to Keith?"

"I don't know, but I've met a guy about Keith's age in Dallas called Bob Cat and, if it's the same guy, not much would surprise me about him or what he's in to."

"You are going to be at the funeral tomorrow, aren't you, Noah?" Mrs. Holland asked.

"Yes, ma'am."

At the mention of the funeral, Debbie broke down and began sobbing loudly. Mrs. Holland hugged her closely, gently patting her back as if consoling a small child who was scared of the dark. Debbie put her head on her mother's shoulder and cried. The room fell silent. All eyes looked at Debbie, then at me, wondering what I had said to cause her to start crying.

Mrs. Holland looked at me over Debbie's bent head. "It's going to be o.k." she said to both of us. Then to me, "She's been like this ever since we first heard about it." She looked lovingly down at her daughter. "It's going to be o.k."

I told her I would see them tomorrow and excused myself, and went out the front door. I went around the house toward my truck. The wisteria was coming into bloom, its grape-like clusters of purple flowers giving off an intoxicating fragrance. Large bumble bees climbed over the flowers. I wondered if kids still caught the white faced ones and put them on strings like we did when I was a boy. I picked a bloom and smelled it as I went behind the house.

Tommy was playing chase with the collie. He was carefree, blissfully ignorant that his uncle was dead. I wondered how Debbie was going to explain Keith's disappearance. Mr. Holland was where I left him, still looking across the pasture. The Holland males didn't face reality well. Mr. Holland never admitted what Keith had become. Keith had never been willing to grow up, and had reaped what he had sown. And Tommy, like his grandfather, was in blissful ignorance of events around him.

I got in my truck and drove back to the motel, picking up a box of fried chicken on the way.

CHAPTER
11

I WOKE UP a little after seven-thirty. As I was shaving I glanced down at the fading wisteria blossoms I had plucked at the Hollands. The flowers were crumpled and wilted on the lavatory's imitation marble top. It reminded me of Keith's lifeless body lying crumpled in the rain. I picked it up and smelled its last hint of fragrance. Then I tossed it in the trash can. From dust to dust. And so it was with Keith.

It was over six hours until Keith's funeral. Time shuffles by on dead feet when you are waiting for a funeral. After breakfast, I drove around Franklin. I passed my old high school with its clean, utilitarian lines of white brick. It had been replaced by a modernistic eyesore with wide expanses of glass and rows of windows inset at an odd angle that the architect had probably convinced the school board would have deep meaning to the young scholars. Or maybe they were just harder to hit with a rock.

I drove out to the lake, past the piers and boat ramps. The fishermen were out early. More than a dozen trucks and empty boat trailers were parked along the road. I parked a while and watched several boats bobbing in the light breeze near the dam. The two men in the nearest boat were drinking beer, their rods leaning against the sides of their boat. I went in the bait shack and bought a soda. The owner, a red-faced man with a fringe of white hair and bushy white eyebrows, asked if I was there for the fishing. I said I was not that day, but I might be back to wet a hook some other time. I asked him how the fishing was going and which lures were the best. He complained about the speed boaters, saying the only time the fishing was fairly good was at the crack of dawn or during the night. He allowed, though, that when the weather was cool, the speeders and skiers stayed off the lake. We spent half an hour of comparing the wiggling qualities of several of the lures. I bought a couple, thanked him and left.

I headed back towards town. The church parking lots were full. The sign outside the Missionary Baptist Church said, "I Will Make You Fishers Of Men". I glanced down at the small paper sack of lures, thought of what I had promised Mrs. Holland I would do to catch Keith's killer, and said "amen" to myself.

I headed towards the rural church at twelve thirty. The tan brick Church of Christ building was nestled under a half dozen ancient oaks. Cars and trucks filled the parking lot, and some were parked under the trees that circled the church grounds, and lined the farm-to-market road out front. I parked and went to join the crowd gathered outside the building.

The small sanctuary was packed. I worked my way through the crowded foyer and I signed the registry. I could see the Hollands sitting stiffly on the front row. People were drifting to them, bending over to whisper words of consolation, and then moving on.

The Hollands remained stoic, nodding bravely, accepting hugs and gentle kisses on their cheeks. They seemed to avoid looking at the large polished pecan wood coffin in front of a wall of flowers. Floral wreaths and sprays formed the background, with bright red roses and yellow carnations denying the solemnity of the occasion and the season of the year.

I edged my way outside and stood on the porch. Storm clouds had gathered while I had driven around Franklin, and were now dark and menacing. Inside, the funeral began. The singing was a capella, as it was a Church of Christ. Through the open double doors, I could hear the initial hymn, "In the Sweet Bye and Bye", followed by "Blessed Assurance". I eased back in and stood against the back wall.

Then the sermon began. The preacher started out gently, talking vaguely about Keith. He told about Keith's family and Keith's youth. Then he launched into a fire-and-brimstone tirade about the wages of sin being death. Sniffling turned to tears. Then he described the torments of Hell. The tears became wailing. After half an hour, he finally wrapped it up, with insincere assurances to the Hollands that he was sure Keith was waiting for them at the Pearly Gates. From the crying, I didn't think many were convinced of Keith's salvation, and some were now likely unsure of their own. A young man took the pulpit and read "Crossing the Bar" by Tennyson, his voice occasionally cracking with emotion.

The gathering concluded the service by singing "Amazing Grace" very slowly. The preacher approached the family and gave his personal condolences to them. Then he stood aside.

The funeral home men, dressed in similar dark blue suits, slid the coffin floral spray to the foot of the box and opened the coffin. The mourners passed by the family, pausing occasionally to pat a shoulder or whisper a word, then moved along in line to view the body. The line moved out the side door. Those who didn't want to see the body came out the double doors at the rear of the church.

I started moving towards my truck, nodding and making small talk with those few I recognized from years gone by. As I was pulling onto the highway, I saw the pallbearers carrying the coffin out the side door and loading it into the dark grey hearse. The Hollands stood at the door, watching. I drove to the Hollands' farm.

CHAPTER
12

SEVERAL CARS WERE already there. I figured they hadn't gone to the funeral. The back gate was open and a lane had been pressed in the rye grass by the vehicles already out by the trees that surrounded the family cemetery. I parked under a pecan tree in the yard and got out. I glanced at the dark clouds and pulled my raincoat from the back seat and put it on. I took the umbrella from beneath the seat and stuck it under my arm.

I walked across the pasture to the cemetery. The four strand barbed wire fence around the cemetery had been taken down on the north side, the rusty wire rolled and piled against the corner posts. The three intermediate posts stood forlornly like Calvary's posts. I glanced around and saw no cows. I presumed they had been moved to another pasture.

Keith and I had frequently wandered among the graves when we were kids and I remembered some of the graves going back to the early 1870's. They were variously marked by rocks, metal engraved tags and store-bought marble slabs. Near Keith's grave was the most interesting, a pair of gray granite markers, with the engraving on its face, each topped by a carved marble angel with its right hand pointing towards the heaven. Mr. Holland had told me that they were twin girls who had died during the 1917 influenza epidemic. They were now going to go through eternity standing over Keith, pointing him towards salvation. But from what Mrs. Holland and Debbie had told me, I wasn't sure Keith was going to be following his ancestors up to his heavenly home.

A wine colored awning was over the open grave, the piled red clay that had been dug out of the grave spilled from beneath the astro-turf rug spread out over the hump. Rows of folding chairs faced the hole. Fifty yards away, as if they had no part of the goings on, two black men from the funeral home leaned against the backhoe tractor with which they had dug the grave, waiting for the funeral to be over so they could refill the hole and load up the chairs and awning and go back to the funeral home. They too were watching the darkening rain clouds.

It began to rain. I turned up the collar of my raincoat, and opened the umbrella and headed towards the tent. Three men ducked under the awning from the trees where they had been standing. I recognized Bob Cat Ketting. He and his buddies were shaking the rain off and laughing when Ketting noticed me. We had crossed paths a few times when I was with the D.P.D. He nudged the guy to his right, and mumbled something. The other two looked at me.

Ketting hadn't changed much. His dark brown hair started with a high widow's peak and was greased back in duck tails that met below his collar. His face was aged by too much liquor, too many late nights, and too many brawls. A faint scar ran from his left ear to his chin. He was wearing a blue denim western cut suit, an open collared, dingy white shirt, and scuffed brown cowboy boots. The two men with him looked about the same, like ten miles of bad road.

As I approached them, Ketting crossed his arms. A tattooed snake head exposed its fangs on the back of his right hand. I noticed the roughly-etched prison tattooed letters on the knuckles of his right hand: H-A-T-E. A spider web spread over the left side of his neck with a black widow spider tattoo perched under his ear. "Starr," he said flatly.

"Ketting."

"What you doin' here?" he asked.

"Keith was a friend back in high school. You?"

"Just a friend. You ain't still a cop, are you?" His companions eyed me suspiciously.

"No, I left that years ago."

"Thought so." He nodded at the other two men. "This is Phil Jones," he said of the one on his left, "and this is John Marley," he said of the other. We nodded at each other. "This here is Noah Starr. Used to be a Dallas cop. Put my brother away for a bull shit drug possession case. The boy had only a little meth, and Starr and the D.A. gave him two years. What you been up to lately, Pig."

I got the idea he carried a grudge. "Private investigations. You still pimping and pushing drugs?"

He smiled tightly, exposing two missing teeth. "Naw, I keep an honest bar."

"What is the name of the place?"

"Hank's Place, a couple miles north off I-20. Stop by some time and I'll front you a beer. For old time's sake." He glanced over at the open grave. "Or for Keith's sake." He paused a moment, then said, "I'm really gonna miss him. I wonder who the hell did it?"

"Me, too. Got any ideas?"

He shook his head.

"I might stop by and discuss it? I want to find who did it, too."

He glanced towards the house. The hearse and the family cars were slowly coming across the pasture, the vehicles lurching over the uneven field. The rest of the cars in the funeral procession were snaking into the yard and dispersing into the field, their headlights glittering off the heavily falling rain. Umbrellas were popping open like mushrooms after a spring rain. The mourners were streaming towards us.

He looked back at me. "Like I said, come by some time, and we'll talk it over." he said. "Where we have some privacy."

I agreed and moved towards the edge of the awning. They withdrew from the tent, aware of the curious stares of the family's friends and their inability to fit in the rural society gathered there.

The crowd moved under the shelter, clustering towards the back, gently suggesting who should take the seats, nudging the older people towards the limited number of chairs. The family settled in the front row as the pall bearers struggled to unload the coffin from the hearse and put it over the dark chasm. The funeral home workers set up the flowers behind the coffin.

The preacher began speaking but his words were drowned out by the rumbling thunder and the crack of lightning. The crowd seemed to shrink together like frightened sheep. Rain pounded on the tent like it was a loosely stretched drum head. I strained to hear, but couldn't hear a word over the din of the rain. When the preacher and the people near the front bowed their heads, I knew it was almost over. The preacher then went to each family member, shaking hands and speaking to them. The pall bearers took off their red boutonnieres and placed them on the top off the coffin and moved away to join their families.

The crowd drifted back to their cars. The wind was gusting the rain across the field and across the awning, soaking everyone. Debbie and Mrs. Holland looked back at me as they were being ushered towards the funeral home's car. The car carried them to the front porch of the house. I saw them get out and move into the house under umbrellas.

I headed back across the field towards the house, the wet grass soaking my pants legs to the mid-calf. At least a third of the mourners had stopped at the house. I went in to say goodbye. Mrs. Holland, her eyes red and puffy from crying, saw me and came over to talk. She insisted I eat something. I finally agreed to eat a piece of pecan pie. We went in the kitchen. She got a small plate and a salad fork from the dish drainer. She placed a piece of the dark brown, syrupy pie on the plate and handed it to me. I picked off several of the pecans from the top of the pie and ate them. Mrs. Holland asked me if I wanted something to drink. I nodded yes. She asked if I still drank tea. Again I nodded yes. She poured me a glass from one of the gallon jugs on the table. She stood and watched me eat and drink for a few minutes. When I finished, I thanked her and got up to go.

She patted me on the shoulder gently. "You'll let me know if you find out something, won't you?"

I assured her I would, thanked her for the pie, said goodbye to her and left.

I went back to town, checked out of the motel, and headed back to Dallas.

CHAPTER
13

I got back home by seven-thirty. Alice was home, her MiniCooper in the garage. I pulled in the driveway, killed the engine and unloaded the truck. Alice was in the kitchen, typed papers strewn across the table. She looked up and offered her cheek when I came in. I bent over and kissed her and gave her a hug. Then I pulled up a chair.

"How was Franklin?" she asked, laying the red pen she had been editing a law journal article with on the pile of pages and focused on me.

"About the same as always. More people, fewer trees. Like most nice rural areas, city slickers want to savor the country life, move there and then reconstruct the suburbs they moved there to get away from, and screw it up for everyone. Hell, it's the same old story."

She smirked. "Yeah, Noah Starr, keeper of the pristine Texas wilderness, circa 1950. Did you find out anything about Keith?"

"Not a lot. Did meet some of his friends, though. A guy named Bob Ketting invited me to drop by his beer joint and discuss Keith's demise. If I could stick him with it, the Dallas P.D. would probably give me an medal. I pinched his brother on a drug bust back when I was on the force. Wanted to get him, too. He was involved in all kinds of criminal activity, but I could never make anything stick on him. But he was still involved. If Keith was running with him, that would explain a lot."

"Do you think Ketting killed Keith?"

"Based on his past history, he would be likely candidate. But I don't have anything to suggest he personally did it. I'm just saying that Ketting runs with a rough crowd. I mean, Ketting looks like a hundred miles of bad road. The folks he runs with would steal the nickels off a dead man's eyes. They would kill anyone that crossed them. So I've got lots of suspects."

"You will be careful, won't you? I don't want to go to Franklin for your funeral."

"I'll be careful, Babe. Now that I've found you, I'm not going anywhere."
I glanced at the papers. "Accomplished much?"

"Put in about four hours Friday, and seven yesterday at the office. We sent out the discovery request in the Jernigan case, so now we're just waiting for their answers." She glanced down at the papers. "And we have a couple good comment papers for the law journal, too. This one," She held up the top article, "is really good. It's on 'Terry' searches. Discusses the common law basis for the Fourth Amendment. You might enjoy it."

I picked it up and glanced through it. "Is it going to be published?"
"Likely."
I handed it back to her. "I'll read it then."

She gestured towards another stapled sheaf of papers. "This one may not be published, but you might like to read it. You like history. Traces Texas community property law from the Visigoths crossing the Pyrenees into Spain in 407 A.D."

"Sounds good." I leaned over the table and kissed her gently. "Speaking of sounding good, how about you and me calling it a night. Franklin was nice, but it was lonely."

She wrapped her arms around my neck and kissed me deeply. We stood up and, arms around each other's waist, went to bed, turning off the lights as we went.

CHAPTER
14

I WENT DOWN to the office early the next morning. In Dallas, like most big cities that rely on automobiles for transportation, you either leave an hour early, or spend that same time caught in traffic. The good thing about my business is that I did not have to be at the office to work, so if I was running a few minutes late in the morning, I could just start making phone calls from the house or just skip the office until I was heading by that way later in the day when the traffic was better. But I had a specific purpose that required my office files, so at 7:15 I headed out to the office, shaved, showered, and in a crisp clean shirt and ready to take on the world, or at least my little corner of it. Heck, I could have been going to a real job.

I even beat most of the office help at the Carrington Building and got a parking place right next to the main back entrance. It crossed my mind that the last time I had parked this close to the door, I had come at 6:30 on a Sunday morning.

I went down the quiet corridors. An office building before the business day starts is like a mausoleum, silent as a tomb. I didn't see anyone in the halls or the elevator. I went to my office and glanced over the mail and checked the answering machine. I wrote down the names and numbers and put them to one side to call later. The only thing that seemed half-way pressing was a call from a bankruptcy lawyer I was running some trails for. I learned early in my police work that it's no good to call businessmen or professions before nine. They usually aren't in the office until then, and if they are, they are usually putting out their own fires that were more important that mine. I would call him later.

On the way back from Franklin the night before, I had decided that my next step would be to check up on the Dentons. Chad seemed to be the logical focus of my investigation, since he was the last person known to have seen Carolyn alive. I knew that there wasn't a lot that I could find out about a juvenile. Even if he has been in trouble with the law, the records were usually sealed. And since Chad had recently come down from Ohio, there shouldn't be anything to find out about him in Texas. Especially since Police Chief Browning didn't seem to be focusing on him as a prime suspect, and had emphasized that he felt Pete O'Brian's accusations were unfounded. My experience was that when someone has a record, and are anywhere near the scene of a possible crime, the police figure that guy is good for the crime, and focus on that person as the perpetrator until proven wrong. Since the police didn't feel that Chad had anything to do with Carolyn's disappearance, but seemed to have a pretty good grasp of what was going on in their town, I wondered if Chad was as uninvolved in her disappearance as the young men at the café had said he was.

I figured the next avenue of investigation would be in Toledo, Ohio, where the Dentons had come from. I didn't know much about Ohio, and nothing about Ohio law. A larger problem was that Mrs. Holland couldn't afford any kind of expensive investigation, so a trip to Toledo was out. So I thought of the only person I knew in Ohio, Linney Lowery. I rolled through my phone's contacts list and found his number. One advantage of being on a big city police force is that you meet so many people. If you stayed in touch with them over the years, the old contacts sometime come in handy down the road. Over the years since I had left the force, I had occasionally gotten calls for help from ex-cops in private investigation or in security who needed a hand in finding someone or checking out someone. They would give me a ring and ask me to do them a favor for old times. Sometimes I would do it for free if they were in something where they couldn't pay, sometimes for a nominal fee. Several times the old police contacts would just refer a whole investigation to me, paying client and all. So I kept up the old contacts. And sometimes I used them myself.

Linney Lowery was an administrator on the police department of a Toledo suburb. We had become acquainted when Linney had been on my shift in Dallas when he first got his badge as a police officer, and we had remained friends even after he had moved back to Ohio where his wife had come from. They came to Dallas visiting every few years and we still got together and had dinner and reminisced and catch up with each other's lives.

I punched in the numbers and listened to the phone ring. He picked up on the second ring.

"Hello."

"Linney, it's me. Noah."

"Noah, how're you doing, old buddy?"

"Fine, how are you and Diane?"

"Happy as clams. You planning to come this way for a visit?"

"No, but I need your help on something."

"Anything, what you got?"

I outlined the disappearance of Carolyn, then said, "I need to check out the Dentons. The kid was the last one to see her, and, although from what I've heard, he doesn't sound like he was involved, it's the only thing I got. Plus maybe it'll calm her daddy down a little."

"What do you think happened to her?"

"She didn't just vanish. The police chief thinks she ran away from home. He suggested Dallas and said she could have been in the local kids' drug scene some. I'll look around here in Dallas, see if I can find any leads. We both know that if she ran away from home, she's likely to surface in a couple days, and come home. But it really doesn't feel like a run-away. I've known Pete since high school, and, besides, talking with him and his wife, I didn't feel the false notes you hear when you're investigating one of these situations and the family is hiding the facts. There was a lot of tension and anxiety, but they didn't hold back on anything I asked them. No, I don't believe it's a run-away."

"What do you think happened then?"

"Linney, I just don't know. That's why I'm calling you. The Dentons came from Toledo. They are the only thread I have, so I'm following it."

"What do you want me to do?"

"Just find out whatever you can about them. I don't really expect anything worthwhile to come of it, but you never know. Like I said, she didn't just vanish in thin air. Something happened to her. And for her age, she's been gone too long without a telephone call to assure the folks. I am beginning to feel like Pete, that something did happen to her. But what? And who? And like I said, the Dentons are the only possible lead I have now."

"I see. Your instincts are usually on the mark, Noah. And from what you've told me, it doesn't sound like a run-away. I'll get on line at the office and run some checks. If I get even a hint of anything, you'll get it. Who do you want checked?"

"I guess the whole family." I gave him the names and general descriptions of the Dentons and any other information I could think of.

"How quickly do you need this?"

"Soon as possible."

"Sure, no prob'. Still got the same phone numbers?"

"Yeah, If I'm not in, just leave a message and I'll get right back to you. You got my email address?"

"Yeah."

"If you would, could you email copies of anything you find?"

"O.k. You and Alice still together?"

"Yeah."

"When are you two going to tie the knot and make an honorable woman of her?"

I laughed. "She is an honorable woman, but the question is, can she make an honorable man out of me?"

"Noah, Noah," he said with fake sorrow, "She's a good woman, but that might be too big a job even for her."

"Really, though, we've talked about it later this year, after she graduates and gets started in her practice."

"She is graduating this year?"

"Weeks away, buddy. And let me tell you, getting out of law school will be as much a relief for me as for her. We are both ready for real life."

"Well, I'll get on this for you, Noah, and get it to you as soon as I find something. And you remember us for the wedding invitations."

"You and Diane are always on my 'A' list, Linney."

We hung up, and I leaned back and thought about the day and where I needed to go.

I called Bill Travis again at the station. He was the kind to be early every day of his life.

"Got anything new on Keith Holland?"

"Nope."

"That was short. You want an early lunch?"

"Hell, it isn't eight o'clock yet. Must be nice to be your own boss, work when you want. Some of us have real jobs, you know. "

"Say about eleven at Bodacious Barbecue on Beckham?"

"Make it about eleven-thirty and I'll be there. You buying this time?"

"You got it." And hung up.

Eleven-thirty on the dot, Travis walked in. He was forty-seven years old, tall and lanky, with brown hair greying at the temples and a full mustache, and wearing a dark grey, western cut suit and dark grey lizard skin cowboy boots. He hung his pearl-grey Stetson on the hat rack and came over to my table.

"If you're really paying, let's get moving and get in line, Boy."

I saluted left-handed. "Aye-Aye, Cap'n."

After we were seated, both of us with a plate of barbecued pork ribs and all the trimmings, I asked him what the police had uncovered on Keith's murder so far.

"Do you know much about Holland?" he asked.

"Not much these days. Like I told you, we were high school buddies, but hadn't seen him these last few years. Why?"

"Just he was into a lot of bad stuff. If you and him were too close these days, I'd have to wonder about you." he said with a smirk.

"As if you don't already."

He laughed and excused himself to go get a couple more jalepeno peppers. When he got back, he explained. "We've been watching Holland. He and his friends were selling methamphetamine, ice, crank, bad coke, even some angel dust and who knows what out of a bar on the east side."

"'Bad' coke? Is there any 'good' coke'?"

"No, but some is worse than others. They sell coke that's cut with everything in the chemist's book. Coke's bad enough and it can screw up both mind and body. But some of the chemicals they cut their stuff with is more dangerous than the coke itself. And the meth they're selling is cooked up by some brain dead dip-shit who's so dumb he couldn't spell cat if you spotted him the 'c' and the 'a'. They stir together a bunch of chemicals and cook it down and dish it out. What ever happened to health foods. Damn."

He shook his head in a quick jerk and snorted. "No wonder kids are so screwed up today." He bit half of a jalepeno, then took a strong swig of tea.

"What is the name of the beer joint? Hank's Place?"

"Yeah," he said glancing up from a well-gnawed rib. "How'd you guess?"

"I met a couple of Holland's friends at the funeral. Bob Ketting, Phil Jones and a John Marley."

Travis nodded as I named each man. "Those are the ones. Ketting is the ring leader. He owns Hank's. You ever been there?"

I shook my head, "No, but Ketting's invited me in for a drink and a chat. Thought I would take him up on it."

He nodded. "Couldn't hurt. But, hell, Noah, be careful. That Ketting's mean. We picked him up for a murder last year, but the witness refused to testify. The D.A. wouldn't go to the grand jury with it because he didn't have a witness. Can't really blame them, because we couldn't provide them with any hard evidence. But it was Ketting. I'd bet my badge on it."

"Yeah, I know what you mean. When I was on the force, I was on Ketting's tail, too. I couldn't make anything stick back then either. Has he gone down for anything yet? He hadn't even been convicted for so much as jay walking back then."

Travis nodded. "Oh, yeah. You mess with enough shit, some of it sticks. He's got a long rap sheet. Think he's been down to the station house more often than I have. But he's only done one two year jolt for possession of stolen goods. He was in the prison at Eastham."

"Eastham? He must have been a bad egg to get sent to the 'Ham on his first sentence."

"He was. He's in the Aryan Brotherhood. He was implicated in a couple of prison stabbings of blacks. They couldn't make the charges stick, but it didn't take them long to transfer him from the Belo I farm to 'Ham where they can handle the worst of the gang members."

"Still with the Brotherhood?"

"Some. You know, you only get out of the Brotherhood feet first. He knew quite a few members before he went in. Those folks kinda go with the territory, go with what he's involved in."

"What else is he involved in?"

"I've heard him and his gang are in drugs, pimping, fencing stolen goods, a little burglary. Maybe even a contract killing, though that's just underground rumors."

"What a charmer. And ya'll have only sent him down once?"

"Well, he's not as stupid as he looks, but he is that mean. And he generally has at least one level between him and the real action. He just got a little careless on the stolen goods charge. Frankly, he's been getting a little careless with the drugs. Too many paths lead back to Hank's. Even got a couple whores working out of the hot sheet motel just down the block. Just getting too much going on around him. You know, he's messin' in his own nest. Just the way I like it." He grinned, and wiped barbecue sauce off his fingers with a paper napkin. "Next time we get the bastard, he's gonna grow old, real old, in the joint. Couldn't happen to a better guy."

"Was Holland really involved with Ketting, or just run with him?"

"He was involved." he said flatly, looking me straight in the eyes for emphasis.

I nodded. "What about Keith's cycle shop? Was it dirty? He owned it, didn't he?"

"Best I can tell, it was not involved. But his other business compadres hung out there a lot. Plus a cycle shop is a necessity for them, with all the bikes they run."

"Have ya'll checked his apartment or the shop? His mother gave me the key to his apartment and I'm going to go through it. Want to come along."

"No, unless it'll tell us who capped him, we don't really want to go through his dirty dishes. You watch too much t.v., Noah." He began eating another rib. "You know, Holland's not a real priority for us. We just figure a business competitor, or maybe even partner, capped him. Simple. Works for us." He put down the rib, and started on the potato salad. "You knew Holland was a felon, didn't?"

I shook my head.

"Yeah, he was on six year's probation for burglary of a habitation. And he was also pulled in twice for selling drugs, once for selling to kids."

"Selling drugs to kids?"

"Cases were weak, though, so the D.A. let them slide when he got the burglary conviction. The drugs lead back to Ketting. And the drugs, that's where his whores come from. They pick up run-aways, on street corners or the bus station. Give them a place to flop for a couple days. Get them strung out on some drugs. Then put them on the street to earn their keep. I've seen some of the kids. Really cute kids. Ought to be home being a cheer leader at the home-coming game, not turning tricks in the back seat of a john's car." He pointed at me with a pork ribs for emphasis. "You want to know what I think, I'll tell you. I think you old buddy Keith Holland was involved in Ketting's prostitution and drug dealing. If he hadn't been capped, he would have gotten pulled in soon. I've checked around. The Feds were maybe getting ready to move on Ketting. Maybe Ketting got nervous of a loose end. Who knows how it'll shake out."

"How about the shop?" I asked

"We haven't had too much trouble from the shop. Heard they smoke a little pot down there while they work on their cycles. Nothing to make us dig deeper. Holland seemed to be keeping the shop legit. Of course, I kinda wonder where he got the money to open it."

"I'll let you know if I find anything," I said.

He nodded. He pushed the plate to one side. "Appreciate it. Just keep me posted if anything surfaces that I'd be interested in, o.k.?"

I nodded. "You ready to go?" We shook hands and I paid up and we went left.

CHAPTER

15

I WENT BACK to the office. The light was blinking on the answering machine. Two calls were from lawyers wanting me to serve some papers, one was a lawsuit, the other was divorce papers. I called them back and told them I would pick the papers up at the district clerk's office and would get them served. The third call was from Alice asking me to pick up some groceries on the way home.

I checked my watch. Two thirty. The afternoon clientele at Hank's Place clientele should be well into their cups by now. I decided to take Ketting up on his offer. I closed the office and headed south.

The early afternoon traffic was very light. I took Loop 635 south, and then turned off on a side street. Two blocks down, on the corner, was Hank's.

Forty years ago, this area was a nice residential area with family-owned neighborhood shops. Twenty years ago, it was a transitional neighborhood, occupied by earnest blue collar workers pursuing the American Dream to improve themselves. They had evidently been successful enough to move to better neighborhoods, leaving the area to pawn shops, cheap liquor stores and a couple dilapidated motels falling into unkept rubbish heaps, inhabited by alcohol-laced denizens, blown, like cast off paper, along the gutters of society, there but unseen and unnoticed until a crime of violence focused a policeman's attention on them. The motels' broken neon signs reflected the shattered dreams of their daily or maybe hourly residents.

I parked in the broken asphalt parking lot next to an old faded blue Dodge pick-up with a green dented fender and no back glass. One of its front tires was almost flat, and a back tire was so bald it was showing cord. A Budweiser logo and a "America for Americans" sticker shared the bumper. There were two cars, an early '90's Ford and a rusted-out orange Dodge so trail-worn that its rusted and dented body sagged low on its worn springs. It was ready for the auto crusher in a wrecking yard. There were four motorcycles near the door, two chopped Harley Davidsons, a 450 Honda, and a light-weight Suzuki that looked embarrassed to be in such macho environment.

Hank's wasn't a tavern or a club. It was a bare-bones, basic beer joint. It was run-down, with a peeling paint job. The big front plate glass window had been painted over with a scene of a buxom siren enticing men into her room for the ultimate odyssey. I went up the two cracked cement steps and pushed the red door open.

The bar was very dark. I went in and stepped to the right so I wouldn't be silhouetted against the glaring light of the outside. I took off my sunglasses and let my eyes adjust to the darkness. I was wearing boots, khaki slacks and a starched blue oxford shirt and was still way overdressed for the joint. When my eyes had adjusted to the light, I glanced around the room. Everybody was watching me. The bar was to my right and ran the length of the room. A fat man with a goatee and curly, shoulder length hair tied in a thick, greasy pony tail, was behind the bar, leaning back against the refrigerated boxes that lined the wall behind the bar. He was wearing a sleeveless Harley Davidson tee shirt. His thick, hairy, tattooed arms were crossed above his gut. A chromed chain hung from a studded belt with a skull and cross bones buckle to a fat, pouch-like wallet that stuck out of his back pocket.

Four men were gathered at the back pool table, lit by a red and white Budweiser that hung close over the table, casting its focused circle of light in the middle of the green felt. The lamp was plastic, colored to imitate stained glass. The men stood frozen with their pool cues poised, ready for either stroking a pool ball or a skull. They evidently had experienced unwelcomed interruptions of their pool games in the past, and were waiting for me to make my move before they reacted. I recognized two of them as Ketting's companions at Keith's funeral, Jones and Marley.

I went over to the bar, keeping the pool players in the corner of my eye, and leaned my right side against the bar.

"Old Mil," I said to the bar tender. He raised the lid of a refrigerator box and pulled out a cold bottle. He hooked the cap in the church key nailed to the side of the box and snapped the cap off. It fell into the heaping full box of bottle caps underneath the opener and slid to the floor. He set the beer in front of me.

"Three bucks," he said flatly.

I laid a five spot on the bar. I took a drag on beer. It was ice cold. Condensation formed on the bottle immediately. The bar tender took a couple of dingy white napkins and laid them in from of me. I set the beer on a napkin, and looked back at him. "Just the way I like my beer, ice cold."

"Only way to drink it." He said flatly. He stared at me impassively, evidently unwilling to be drawn into my scintillating conversation.

"Bob Ketting in?"

"No."

"Expect him back soon?"

"No." He glanced towards the crowd. They stiffened. He leaned towards the bar, his hands resting on the surface. I slowly eased from the bar, while appearing as nonchalant as possible. I picked the bottle up, my fingers wrapping around the neck. That's what I like about beer in bottles, always a handy weapon in a pinch. One of the pool shooters was easing towards the door, the pool stick resting on his shoulder. I glanced back at the bar tender. He was leaning forward. His left hand had disappeared under the bar.

I flipped the bottle, catching it by the neck, the mass of the bottle extending forward, and swung it in a glancing blow on the bar tender's temple. He staggered, and like a punch drunk boxer clutching at the ropes, groped the bar for support. His left hand held a sawed-off shotgun by the short stock. I grabbed the barrel with my left hand, pointing it away from me. The tender's eyes were losing their glazed look, focusing on me. I swung the bottle again and jerked the shotgun from his loosened grip. I dropped the bottle and thumbed the gun's safety off. I shifted it towards the man on my left who was stepping towards me like Casey at the bat. He froze in mid-swing.

I heard the bottle clank onto the bar, roll to the edge and bounce on the floor behind me. I glanced down and toed it across the floor away from me so I wouldn't step on it if things escalated into a two fisted tango. The three men still at the pool table were in motion. One man had his pool stick at ready. Jones was reaching into his back pocket. Marley was disappearing through a back door.

"You better be pulling out a comb, buddy." I told Jones. "Just ease it out." I pointed the shotgun towards him. He pulled out a fat black automatic pistol and pointed it loosely towards the floor. "You know it's a felony to carry a gun in a bar, don't you?" He didn't look very concerned about a blotch on his record. "Put it on the table," I said, pointing with the shotgun.

He laid it on the table beside him. I urged him back with a small wave of the scattergun. I stepped forward and stuck the pistol in my belt. We were in a stand off, but I held the bigger cards. They weren't going to rush me, but I wasn't making much headway myself.

Ketting stepped from the doorway through which Marley had disappeared. He held a 12 gauge pump riot shotgun at chest height. Marley stepped from the doorway and away from him to Ketting's right, holding a cocked nickel-plated army .45 caliber automatic. Both hands gripping the pistol, his arms stiff out in front of him, he stepped a couple yards to Ketting's right. A spare clip stuck from his belt. They had certainly raised my ante, topping my cards.

When he saw it was me, Ketting lowered the shot gun slightly. "Starr, you stupid bastard, you almost got your ass blown away. What the hell are you doing here?" The others relaxed. Marley gingerly lowered the hammer on the .45 and stuck it in his belt in the small of his back, and pulled his shirt tail over it. I lowered my gun.

"I thought I would take you up on your offer of a beer."

He leaned over the bar and glanced at the bar tender. "Why the hell did you hit Stan? Shit." He glanced at me. "All this for a beer?"

I laid the shotgun on the bar and smiled. "Stan got antsy when I asked about you. Must 'ave been a misunderstanding." I smiled broadly. "What about that beer?"

Stan groaned and staggered to his feet, rubbing his head. He glanced at Ketting, then at me, then at the shotgun I had laid in front of him.

"Another Old Mil, please." I said pleasantly.

He glanced back at Ketting, who nodded and said, "Gimme one too." He looked back at me. "You dumb shit. All this trouble for a beer. You're worse'n a bull in a china closet."

He laid the riot gun on the bar and came over to me and we shook hands. Stan put the beers on the counter, an Old Milwaukee for me, a Budweiser for Ketting. Stan reached for the sawed off shotgun, but stopped, his hand froze in mid-reach when I glanced at him. His glare faltered and he glanced at my bottle to see if it was moving into a weapon mode. I was holding the bottle loosely. He glanced back at me.

I nodded and said, "You ought to put that away. Might get rusty on this wet bar." I gestured to the bar, half covered with the beer I had spilled moments before. "Mind cleaning this up?"

He put the gun under the counter and wiped the bar with a dirty cloth.

I leaned against the bar, and rested my elbow on the surface. It was still wet.

"Don't you got a dry rag back there somewhere, Stan?" I said as I glanced at my sleeve, the pale blue oxford cloth almost navy blue with moisture. I took a long drag on the beer while Stan looked for another cloth. He wiped the bar again.

Ketting took a package of Marlboros from his shirt pocket, shook out one and lit it with a disposable lighter. He crumpled the empty pack and tossed it behind the bar into a large, plastic lined trash barrel almost filled with empty bottles.

Marley walked up behind Ketting and motioned to Stan for a beer. Stan opened the box and uncapped a Budweiser and set it in front of Marley.

"Get me another pack of coffin nails, John," Ketting said. Marley disappeared into the back room. Ketting inhaled deeply, blew out the smoke and drank some of his beer. He leaned against the bar, resting his elbows on the counter. He looked over at me, and said, "You got your beer. What da'ya really want?" He took another drag on his cigarette, holding it between his thumb and forefinger, in his cupped hand.

"Like I said at the funeral, I'm looking into Keith's murder. Thought you could help me out."

"Bothers me, too." He glanced over at Marley who handed him the cigarettes. "Thanks." He put the pack on the counter in front of him and looked back at me. "What can I do to help?" He took another swig of his beer, then looked at the bottle. He swirled the beer in the bottom and drained the bottle. He tossed it in the trash can, burped, and asked for another. Stan set another before him.

"Do you have any idea who could have hit Keith? Or why?" I asked.

He looked at me closely, his left eye squinting from the smoke that wafted into his eyes from the butt that hung in the corner of his mouth. He plucked the cigarette from his mouth, dropping an inch of ashes on his shirt. He brushed the ashes away and crushed out the cigarette. He took off the cellophane wrapper and opened the cigarette package, shook out a cigarette, and lit it. He pointed the pack, with a couple white cigarettes sticking out, in my direction, offering me one. I shook my head slightly. He laid the pack on the bar, and leaned back against the bar again and asked, "What do you know about my," he paused, "Business interests?"

"I've heard about the pimping and drugs. Heard that Keith was involved."

"No, I'm not involved in anything illegal. Just trying to make a buck out of this bar." He waved his hand expansively. "But, even so, there's some folks who grudge a man trying to make a honest livin'. Know what I mean?"

I nodded. "And Keith?"

"He had a cycle shop over on Galatin."

"You see him much?"

"Oh, he'd come in for a couple beers after work. Just friendly drinkin', ya' know."

"So you're not involved in any drug selling or prostitution?"

He shook his head.

"How about fencing?"

"Hey, I made a mistake a few years ago, o.k. I done my time. That wadn't my fault. A regular customer told me he was moving to Odessa for a job in the oil fields. Offered me a big screen t.v. for a hundred dollars. Said he didn't have any room in his car to haul it out to Odessa. How's I to know he stole it? Cops been on my ass for years, tryin' to find some'in' to git me on." He pointed to a twenty-five inch t.v. on an overhead rack over the backbar. "That one, I still got the receipt for it. They ain't gonna nail me again. I'm legit."

I motioned towards the riot gun with my beer. "Isn't it illegal for a felon to have a gun?"

"Belongs to Mel over there. Ain't that right, Mel?" One of the pool players nodded.

"Look, Bob. I don't really care if you're pimping for the Queen of England. I just want to find out about Keith. Did he have any enemies?"

"Don't we all, man? About two, three weeks ago, he was in a knock down, drag out fight right here. Had to finally cut the bastard to take the fight out of him."

"Who was he fighting?"

"Guy named Murphy, Jerry Murphy. Used to be a regular here."

"What were they fighting about?"

"What else? A woman."

"Who was she?"

"Some young thang he come up on."

"What was her name?"

He looked over at Marley who had been watching us steadily while nursing his beer. "What's that gal's name?"

Marley set his beer down. "Kerry, Carrie, somethin' like that." He finished the beer and tossed the bottle, and motioned for another. I shot him a quick glance, then looked back at Ketting.

"Yeah, that's her name, Carrie. Keith said he'd seen her on one of his trips back to Franklin, then he met her up here in one of those north Dallas bars he went to."

"How old was she?" I asked.

"Keith said she was twenty-one, but I figured she was a little younger, eighteen or nineteen or so. Hell, I don't care as long as she ain't 'San Quentin quail', know what I mean." He nudged me with an elbow and leered.

I nodded. "Yeah, sure, Bob. A date's hard to find sometimes, huh?"

"Yeah, any port in a storm, eh?" He laughed and elbowed me again.

Marley slapped him on the back and started laughing. "Any port in the storm. Ain't that the truth?" The guys in the back began to laugh with Marley.

"Would you recognize her if you saw her again?" I asked.

"Sure. Doubt she'll be back, though. I only saw her with Keith."

I pulled out a photograph of Carolyn O'Brian and showed it to him.

He took it and nodded. "That's her. Boy was she a hot little number. Always climbing all over Keith." Marley nodded in agreement, smirking.

I took the photo back. "Was Keith involved in drugs?"

"If you mean usin', ain't everybody? A little toot now and then is just livin', ain't that right, John?"

He nodded.

"Was Carrie?"

"Hell, why do you think she was with him. Of course she was. Old codger like him couldn't get something like that without a little bait."

"When did you last see her?"

"Hadn't seen her since before that fight I was tellin' you about couple weeks ago. Only saw her on weekends back then. Usually Saturday night."

"When did you first see her?"

"About three months ago. Why are you interested in that girl? Thought you were interested in gettin' Keith's killer. You think she was involved?"

"No. I'm just trying to get a feel for Keith's life. When did you last see Keith?"

"The night he was killed. Came in about early afternoon. Left here about nine."

"Where was he going?"

"He was talking about hittin' one of those north Dallas pick-up bars he went to a lot."

"You ever go with him?"

"Hell, no. Nothin' but a bunch of stuck-up rich bitches up there. I stick with my kind, ain't that right, Johnny?"

Marley nodded.

"Did he meet many people at those bars?" I asked.

"He went a lot. And you see what it got him."

"You think someone from one of those bars shot him with a shotgun?"

"Could be. He picked up a lot of those rich girls. Bring 'em down here. Hell, their noses up in the air. They thought they was slummin' when they came here, like they were afraid to take a drink because they might catch somethin'. Maybe one of their rich boy friends got jealous and blew him away.

"You know, them rich folks is just as violent as everybody else. They can just afford to hire one of those hot shot lawyers and get off. Look at that oil man over in Fort Worth. Hired "Race Horse" Haynes and got off. If I'd shot somebody, they'd have my ass in Old Sparky or whatever they call that poison needle stuff they use to kill people with in prison these days."

"Did Keith ever sell coke to those rich folks?"

"I don't know anything about Keith sellin' drugs." he said emphatically. "An' I don't like what you're suggestin' about him, either. He was the one killed. Get off his case, man."

"I didn't mean anything by it. I was just asking." I said, trying to placate him.

"The hell you didn't. Keith's dead and you're trying to cover up for the guy who done it. What'd he do, pay you to dig up the dirt on Keith so he can get off. The 'needed killin' defense. Get him off by showing that

Keith needed killin' and the bastard did society a favor by shootin' him." He squared off at me, his hands clenched. "Look at you in your starched shirt. You act like you're his friend and you're nothin' but a paid pimp tryin' to get the killer off." He was screaming. "Get outta my bar. I see you around here again and I'll kick your ass to hell and back."

I glanced around the bar. Everyone was primed for round two. I didn't figure it would end as well as the first one. I drained the last of my beer. "You got me wrong. I'm trying to find Keith's killer, not protect him. I may be back for more information." I put the bottle on the bar. "Thanks for the beer, Bob."

I turned and walked out, putting my sunglasses on as I left.

I got in my truck and drove the six blocks to Keith's motorcycle shop.

CHAPTER

16

THE SHOP WAS open. The Harley-Davidson eagle emblem was painted on the front glass in black paint. Circling the emblem was "KEITH HOLLAND - HARLEY-DAVIDSON SHOP." A lighted sign with similar wording hung from a rusted round steel bar that stuck out from the corner of the grey brick building. The sign was broken. The three foot square pane facing me was half gone, the jagged hole exposing the sky through the hole in the back pane. A sparrow was flitting along the bottom shard of plastic, turning its head and eyeing downward into the space between the signs panels, as if wondering if it wanted to raise its children in such a run-down neighborhood. I knew how the bird felt. I didn't want to even visit the area.

Several cycles were parked along the street. Most of them were chopped and lean, with high handle bars, and back-slung seats. I caught a mental image of Peter Fonda in *Easy Rider*. I went in. A cow bell attached to the wheezing pneumatic door closing mechanism clanked as I entered.

Customers and employees alike turned toward me, cold and restrained. Keith's business seemed to attract about the same warm clientele as Ketting's, though not as friendly. I went to the service counter. After eying me for half a minute, everyone returned to their business. I looked at a display of tee shirts with Harley-Davidson logos, and heart warming sentiments like "Kill 'em all and let God sort 'em out." Not much of a "forgive and forget, let bygones be bygones" type of folks.

A stocky man with black shoulder length hair tied in a pony tail and a black mustache and goatee came over after several minutes. His bare arms were covered in intricate tattoos of dragons and snakes. He wore round wire rimmed glasses, tinted almost black. He rested his thick hands on the counter, the knuckles perpetually black with ground-in grease, his fingernails had half an inch of oily grime underneath.

"What'cha need?" he asked flatly.

"I need to talk with the manager."

"He ain't in. You a salesman?"

"No, I am here about Keith Holland."

"He ain't in."

"I know. He's dead."

"So what you want with Rick?"

"I wanted to find out if there had been any threats against Keith recently. Find out who he ran with and what he had done that could have gotten him killed."

"You a cop?" He leaned back from the counter, his voice getting loud. All eyes turned on me. Several of the customers and at least one of the employees seemed to be fading into the background, their business completed.

"No, I'm a private investigator. I am trying to find some answers for the family."

"I.d.?"

I laid my license on the counter. He looked at it and handed it back.

"So?"

"So I would appreciate some help. Is this Rick guy in?"

He looked over his shoulder at a skinny, pimple-faced kid at the back of the parts racks. "Dinks, tell Rick there's somebody here to see him. And tell him why."

We all stood silently until Dinks returned with a man in grey coveralls, wearing a black leather baseball cap with the Harley logo printed in red. He was wiping his hands on a greasy shop towel.

"Yeah?"

"I'm Noah Starr. I'm looking into the death of Keith Holland for his family."

"Uhm."

"I needed to ask those who worked with Keith if there were any unusual occurrences just before he was killed? Any fights? Mad girlfriends? That sort of a thing?"

"Naw. Nothing like that. Nothin' unusual. Just regular stuff for Keith."

"I was over talking with Bob Ketting at Hank's, and he said something about a fight a couple weeks ago with a guy named Jerry Murphy over a young woman named Carrie. Did you hear anything about it?"

"Yeah, sure. Looked like it was a hell of a brawl. Keith was stove up for several days. Had a couple big bruises on his face, and a split lip. Said he had to cut the guy."

"Just regular stuff?"

"Oh yeah. Keith was always whuppin' up on somebody. Shit, me and him have laid into it more 'n once. That Keith, what a kidder. Reminds me of one time, me and him was drinkin' over at a beer joint, one of them cold days where you just don't feel like doing anything but drinkin' all day just to keep warm. Seems like it was last February." He turned to a guy behind the counter. "When was that ice storm last year. You know, the one that the sleet stayed out for days?"

"January, last January."

He looked back at me. "Anyway, me and Keith was drinkin', an' . . . What say you come around the counter and step back to my office, what did you say your name was?"

"Noah Starr."

"Yeah, Noah." He stuck out his hand as I came behind the counter. "I'm Rick Martin." He turned and led me down the hall, and into a small side office next to the shop. It had a grey metal desk, a brown plastic covered office chair with grey duct tape over the seat and back with tufts of fiber and cotton poking out new holes, two orange plastic and metal straight chairs, and a couple bookshelves of grease and grime covered parts books and shop manuals. An inverted hub cap was on the corner of the desk, half-filled with cigarette butts. An old car distributor served as a pencil holder.

Rick waved a hand towards the orange chairs as he went to a coffee maker. "Coffee?" he asked over his shoulder.

I said yes, black, and he poured me a styrofoam cup and handed it to me. He sat in his chair and leaned back. He blew at his hot coffee, then tested it. I sipped mine and set the cup on the edge of the desk.

"What were you telling me about Keith, and a bar fight back last January?"

"Oh, yeah. Anyway, me and Keith had been drinkin' Jack Daniels Black Label whiskey all day. Must've started about mid-morning. By late afternoon we wuz pretty lit. Know what I mean?"

I nodded.

"Anyway, we was sipping and talking and this guy, hell, neither of us knew him, he set down on the bar next to Keith and got a beer. Seemed like a pretty nice guy. Didn't cause no trouble. Just nursing his beer and watching the t.v. up over the bar, thinkin' his own thoughts.

"Well, after a while of me and Keith just sittin' there drinkin' some more, I heard Keith say 'tap him' real quiet like. Then he said it again, real quiet, like he was talking to hisself. I asked him what he was talkin' about, and he said to me that, as he put it, old Jack Black was tellin' him to tap, you know, punch, that guy. Hell, he hadn't done nothing to nobody, but that's the way Keith's mind run sometimes, especially when things was slow and he had been drinking too much whiskey. I tried to talk him out of it. Hell, I didn't want no trouble. I just wanted to sit and drink. Keith just ignored me and kept on saying 'tap him.'"

"All of a sudden he just spun that bar stool, and caught the guy right in the eye with a hay maker. Knocked the guy off his stool and into the floor. But the guy still had his beer bottle in his hand somehow. It was one of them long neck Budweisers. And he grabbed it by the neck and laid it across the side of Keith's head before Keith was hardly off his stool. Knocked him cold as a wedge. He looked at me, but what the hell was I supposed to do. I just apologized and said that's how Keith was when he drank whiskey. You know what the guy said?"

I shook my head.

"The guy said he was the same way with tequila, and said that's why he quit the shit, got him in too much trouble. Seemed like a nice guy like I said. Even helped me load Keith into my car. But that was old Keith." He paused a second. "I'm gonna missed the old fart, you know?"

"Yes, I do. Keith and I grew up together, and even though we hadn't really seen each other in recent years, it still bothers me that he was murdered. His family asked me to check into it since I live up here in Dallas."

"Was Keith a hell-raiser back when you two ran together."

I nodded, and thought of Bossier City.

"Figured he was. Always seemed to have a wild hair. Always into something."

"How well did you know him?"

"We were as close as you can get. We drank together, fought together, bar hopped together. I was even best man at his wedding."

I looked up suddenly.

CHAPTER 17

"YOU DIDN'T KNOW he was married?"

"No, like I said, I hadn't really known him since high school."

"Well, he got married to some old bitch back fifteen years ago or so. Thought he was too old to fall for that old bait and switch trick. Know what a gold digger is?"

I nodded my head.

He continued without acknowledging my response. "A girl with no heart looking for a man with no head. And she found it with Keith."

"What was her name?"

"Betsy, Betsy Johnson was what she was going by then. He called her 'Bet,' as in 'You bet, Bet.' He said that a lot. Don't know what her maiden name was, though. Hell, bet she didn't remember, she had been through so many men."

"You know where she is now?"

"No, I don't. But I can sure tell you she had been around the track quite a few times before she hooked ol' Keith. Keith was doing pretty good back then. Had this shop. It was doing better back then. Had a used car dealership, even a nice house in north Dallas. I mean, she was a knockout. You know the type, the kind that would make Dolly Parton look skinny, if you know what I mean?"

I nodded.

"Real pretty face, though beginnin' to show too many years in too many bars. That's where he met her, in a bar. You know the type, the great lookin' barflies that will be dried up and wore out by the time they're thirty-five. Anyway, she give him what he wanted, and once she had him hooked, she reeled him in. He decided he couldn't live without her and was going to marry her. I tried to talk him out of it. But no soap. He married her, and within the year he had something to really drink about."

He leaned forward, resting his crossed forearms on the desk. "Did'ja hear the one about the young single man and the old man?"

I shook my head.

"See, there's this young man, and he had this old man for his best friend, you see? And every time the young man saw the old man, the old man would say, 'Son, when you marry, you'll be at the end of your troubles.' Well, that went on for quite a while. Old man always telling the young one that every time he saw him. So one day the young man up and marries and the old man didn't see him for several months. Then the young man comes to see the old man, and the young man looks like hell. You know, tired, worn, sad and run down. And this stub of a young man asked the old man, saying, 'Hey, you told me when I got married, I'd be at the end of my troubles. It's been hell these last few months. What happened?' And the old man smiled, and said 'I didn't say which end of your troubles you'd be at.'" He burst out laughing and rocked back in the squeaky chair.

I laughed, and then asked, "What about Betsy?"

"Oh, hell. She ran through his money, just like I told him she'd do. Got him so deep in debt that he had to sell the car lot just to keep the creditors at bay. Wasn't long after that he lost the house. Then she cleaned out all the bank accounts and just split. He finally got divorced about three years ago. But after that, he wasn't the same. Broodier. More violent. That's when he got in that shit with the cops. Things just never was the same after that. Guess some guys just can't take having their guts ripped out. Guess he was just one of them. He seemed so happy-go-lucky that nothing seemed to bother him. Then she got to him and just ripped him apart.

"Most of us just figure its part of the price you pay for the company, eh? You know, they come, they go. Kinda like cars, and the money spent is like car payments. Only sometimes those high priced sports cars drive off on their own." He smirked at his joke. "Or run over your heart."

He sipped his coffee. "Damn, this stuff's cold," he said, looking into the cup. He pulled a drawer open. "Want something good to drink?" He pulled out a half-empty quart of Old Crow. "Want a nip?" He poured the rest of the coffee into the trash can and filled the cup. He leaned forward with a loud squeak of rusty springs and set the bottle on my side of the desk.

I declined with a small wave of the hand.

"So, after Betsy took his money and left, what happened then?"

"Keith changed."

"Changed? How so?"

"Well, he was always kinda wild. You know that."

I nodded.

"But it was a fun-lovin', Devil-may-care type of wild. Not real meanness, you know?"

"Yeah, I know what you mean."

"But after Betsy, he started getting involved with Ketting." He paused. "Not that I'm saying anything against Ketting." He said quickly, his hands raised, palms towards me as if meaning no offense.

"I understand. Is that when he got involved in selling drugs?"

He glanced up at me quick and hard. "I don't know what you mean."

"I've talked to the police. They told me that Keith was selling drugs with Ketting, out of Hank"'s."

Rick slowly leaned back in his chair and slowly sipped his whiskey.

"They also told me that this place seemed clean. Did you ever know of Keith selling drugs out of the shop?"

"Never heard of it." he said coldly.

"Listen, I don't care about the drug dealing. That's the cops' job. I'm just trying to get a lead on Keith's murder. How involved was Keith in the dealing?"

"I wasn't involved in any of Keith's side-lines, shall we say. I run the shop. Listen, I had a couple scrapes with the law. Back a few years ago. I've been straight ever since I got out of the joint. I told Keith that I was legit. I wasn't goin' to screw up again. I have two felonies. The next one, they'll put the "bitch" on me. I just can't risk it. I've got a wife and family. It just wasn't worth the risk."

"So you knew that Keith was selling drugs?"

"Oh, he told me. Tried to get me in on it. Kept telling me how much money he was making. But I couldn't see it was doing him any good. Every night he would go bar hopping up in north Dallas, at them fancy bars up there. Blow his money on high-priced bitches. End of the month, he was as flat broke as I was. And I'd have spent the month with my family and that's what's important. Besides, looks like the fast life didn't help Keith too much, anyway."

"Ya'll still went out drinking. And you went to Hank's."

"So. I'm off parole. It's no big deal going to there."

"I've been to Hank's." I said.

"Just a bunch of good old boys, drinkin' and havin' fun."

"Is Ketting a big dealer?"

"I wouldn't know. Hell, I don't want to know. I keep my nose out of their business. And they let me keep my nose. And let me keep the rest of me."

"Listen, I'm not making much progress in finding Keith's killer. Seems like the drug angle is the most likely angle. Tell me what you can. I'm not going to tell Ketting. Let's just say he and I aren't on the best of terms. Just level with me."

He looked at me for a bit, then said, "O.k., if it'll help find Keith's killer. What do you want to know?"

"When did Keith get into the drug dealing."

"About the time Betsy started getting her hooks in him. He started getting in a hole, financially, to keep her happy. But she never was satisfied. Always wanted more money. Go, go, go. Always had her butt in the car, out spending money. He couldn't tell her no."

"Was Ketting already selling then?"

"Yeah. He was already selling coke out of Hank's."

"Pimping?"

He nodded.

"Fencing?"

"Yeah, those go with the drugs. Gotta make the money to take the ride, you know."

"So when Keith needed money, Ketting offered him the way to make enough to keep Betsy happy."

"Yeah, but it didn't help. She still left." He drank some more of the whiskey and pondered life's riddles.

Seemed like Rick was right about one thing: Keith's fast lane life style was a dead-end road.

I thanked Rick and left him flying with his Old Crow. As I went out the door, I glanced back at him. He was drinking straight from the bottle. I thought about a couple rough years on the police force when I drank too much, and said, "Never more."

CHAPTER

18

A COUPLE DAYS had passed since I had gone to Hank's. I had just returned to the office from a two hour conference with a defense attorney I had been hired by to do an investigation for an upcoming murder trial. From the facts I had uncovered, the defendant didn't seem to be guilty of this murder, but his past four felony convictions, and his stormy relations with the deceased, including an argument with the deceased the night before the murder made his innocence a weak defense to raise to a Dallas County jury. Plus the fact that the only alibi the defendant had was two other felons. The defendant was pragmatic and felt a five-year sentence for voluntary manslaughter with no enhancement was better than to risk a murder conviction, "bitched" up to life as a habitual criminal. If the D.A. got the conviction, he'd get a finding of use of a deadly weapon which would require the man to do half of the sentence flat time with no reductions for good time. Couldn't blame him: five years, which with good time, maybe make parole in two or three years, which sure beat thirty years served flat. He was going to take the plea.

I sat down and started back at the monthly billings. I hated dunning clients, but Alice reminded me, sometimes less than subtly, that income is an important consideration in operating a private business. The next file was the O'Brians. The trip to Franklin and my investigation had eaten the retainer and then some, and I was no closer to finding the answer.

I hated missing child cases. They were expensive, with a constant fear that the child had met a terrible fate, balanced with a realization that it was likely that the she had merely gone to stay with a friend's house after a spat with her parents. Though these cases usually resolved themselves, with the kid coming home to screaming but relieved parents, occasionally I would end up spending countless hours following leads that led nowhere, eventually forcing me to meet with the parents and giving them the sad news that their story had no end. At least, no end I could discern. After a few tears, and usually a few recriminations about paying me what seemed to be an exorbitant bill for no results, either I would suggest, or sometimes they would, that I end my search. Such an occurrence always reminded me, usually too late, that I should keep closer tabs on my billings, and not let the clients get to me for too much, because disappointed clients invariably never paid the final bill. Guess I couldn't really blame them, though it didn't make my checkbook balance very well. If my creditors knew how many bad debts I had, they wouldn't lend me enough money for a cup of coffee.

I reviewed the O'Brians' bill. I had over twenty-five hours already, plus milage and expenses. Almost twenty-five hundred dollars. Less their retainer, they still owed me almost a five hundred dollars. For what? Not much, that I could tell. I didn't know how much they made a year, but I bet that a couple grand and counting for something like this would put a crimp in their checkbook.

The telephone rang.

"Noah Starr Investigations," I answered.

"Mr. Starr? This is Helen O'Brian. Have you found anything yet?"

I admitted I hadn't.

"You got to settle this soon. Pete is getting tenser and tenser. I'm scared he's going to explode. He's raving about killing the Denton kid. I'm scared he's going to shoot the boy. Or maybe himself. I mean, he's that unbalanced. Last night he was stalking around the house cussing Denton and loading and unloading his pump shotgun. Noah, I'm worried. I've never seen him like this. I'm worried about him. What can you do?" Her voice grew shrill with fear.

I tried to calm her. "I've followed a few leads here in Dallas. I admit I haven't come up with anything yet. But I have a few more things to check in to, though I don't think I'm making any headway finding her." I didn't know if it would serve any purpose to tell her that her daughter had been running around with Keith Holland.

"What else can you do, Noah?"

"I will call the Dallas police again and see if they have had any contacts with her. I'll check a few loose ends in Franklin and follow them."

My report didn't seem to console her. "O.K. I know you're doing the best you can." She paused, then said, with her voice breaking, "I've lost Carolyn. I've come to accept the fact that she might not be coming back. Now I'm scared I'm going to lose Pete, too. Noah, I need you. Pete needs you. He'll listen to you. Please come back and talk with him. Try to make him understand. You can save him. I can't. Will you come, Noah?" She paused. "Please?"

I glanced down at the bill, and knew it wouldn't be paid, much less money for any additional time. But I had lost more money on other cases. At least this was helping, and I used the term 'help' loosely, someone I knew. "Yeah, I'll come.," I glanced at my crowded calendar, "I'll come, Helen." We hung up.

CHAPTER
19

I FIGURED IF I was going to be going back to Franklin, I might as well go by and talk with Mrs. Holland a few minutes and see how they were coping.

I called Bill Travis to see if he had any new information in the Holland case. He didn't, but said he wasn't in the "loop". He gave me the direct telephone number for Roger Nelson, the detective in charge of Keith's investigation.

I thanked him and called Nelson. I introduced myself.

"Yeah, Bill Travis said you might call and asked me to give you a hand if I could. What do ya need?"

"I wanted to see if the police had any leads."

"Nothing."

"By nothing, do you mean you're not ready to slap cuffs on the killer, or just nothing."

"Just nothing." Nelson said.

"Not even a lead?"

"No. The crowd Holland ran with includes a lot of people for whom clipping someone is no big deal. Several of his close friends have either gone down for murder or have been suspected of it. Are you aware of the drug dealing angle?"

"Yeah, do you think that's involved?"

"I'm not sure yet, but that is hazardous duty business. People get tapped all the time in that business. The drug dealers are murdering bastards. They'll kill anybody, even little kids, with no second thought. Maybe your friend crossed one of his partners. Or the business competition. Who knows."

"I take it this isn't getting the highest priority."

"Don't misunderstand me, Mr. Starr. We have so many new murders that a week-old case is old news, way old news. And, frankly, because he was involved in drug dealing, Holland just is not on our "A" list for manpower allocations. Most of these type cases are solved by an arrest of a dealer who wants to cut a deal and get a nice plea. They'll spill their guts for a deal. I figure we'll solve it, if we ever do, through the back door with a plea bargain statement down the road."

"I understand. I used to be a cop, too."

"That's what Bill said. That's why I'm being so up front with you."

"I appreciate it. I just hoped I could report back to his family some sort of conclusion. This is tearing them up."

"Yeah, I bet it is. Wish I could help. Say, give me your phone number, and if anything comes up, I'll let you know, o.k.?"

I gave it to him and thanked him and we hung up.

I called Mrs. Holland. She answered on the second ring. When I said hello, she recognized my voice immediately.

"How are you doing, Noah?"

"Fine."

"Have you made any headway on that business we discussed." I heard her muffled voice. It sounded like she had her hand over the mouthpiece of the telephone. "Bye, Finis. I don't need anything at the store. See you after a while." Her voice came back on the line strongly. "That was Finis leaving. I can talk now."

"No, ma'am. I'm still looking into it. I've talked with the police and they are still investigating," I lied. "I'm sure they'll track down the answer. Usually, in these kind of cases, it's somebody they know, maybe someone he had a business deal with." I thought of what Nelson had said about it being a possible drug deal gone bad. "Maybe someone he had a fight with over a girl. I'm following up on one of those leads now."

"Yes. Keith always was one with girls."

"But don't get your hopes up. You can never tell about murder. Oddest things can set people off."

"I guess you're right, Noah." She paused. "Finis hadn't been the same since this happened. Outside, he tense, almost rigid, like he's compensating for what he's really feeling inside. And inside, Noah, there's nothing left. He's empty. He's like an old tree with the heartwood all dead and gone, just a shell waiting for the littlest wind to knock it down. Guess he'll never be the same. Guess I won't either. But I got Debbie and Tommy. Finis, he just really lived through Keith. I'm hoping he'll someday, I don't know what the word is, just get back to living. Get back to working the farm. It always meant so much to him. But he hasn't even plowed a spot for a garden this year. But I wish you could wrap it up for me, though. Just so I'd know."

"Mrs. Holland, I wanted to ask you a question, though."

"Yes, Noah."

"Do you know Carolyn O'Brian?"

"No, can't say I do. Who is she?"

"She's from Franklin. A junior now."

"Where at, U.T.-Tyler?"

"No, at Franklin High School."

"I don't follow high school much these days, Noah. How's this involved in this with Keith?"

"I don't really think it is, but her name came up. She's a cheerleader at the high school."

"Wasn't she the one I heard about that ran away from home?"

"Yes, that's her."

"I saw something about her in the paper, I think."

"Did Keith ever mention her?"

"Keith? Why would he be talking about a girl half his age?"

"Nothing, just curious."

"You don't think they're connected, do you?"

"No, not really."

"Well, no, I've never heard Keith talk about her. I mean, my goodness, he's old enough, you're old enough to be that girl's father." Her voice had that emphatic tone of a mother chastising a child. She paused, and quietly said, "He was, he was old enough."

"Well, Mrs. Holland, I'm thinking about being in Franklin in the next day or so, and I'll stop by and catch you up on what's I've found out. It's not much but I want to keep you posted."

"I would appreciate it, Noah, and look forward to seeing you." We hung up.

I leaned back in my chair and put my boots on the edge of the desk. There was always a lot of pressure in a missing child case. But it's twice the pressure when it's somebody you know. A lot of pressure to do the job quick and cheap. And in my business, neither of the two occur with any frequency, much less in the same case.

I thought about Keith Holland, and it occurred to me that I hadn't searched his apartment yet. I still had the ring of keys his mother had given me. I opened my desk drawer. I picked up the keys and looked at them. Several of them were obviously door keys. I checked Keith's address. It was in north Dallas. I locked the office and left.

CHAPTER
20

IT WAS AN easy drive up the Dallas tollway. The apartment complex was called Forest Pines, an interesting name in light of the fact that pines don't grow in Dallas, and there hadn't been a forest there in decades. It looked like every other apartment complex in Dallas: identical two-story buildings set "casually" along curving streets. The apartment numbers were hard to find, and seemed randomly assigned. It took me fifteen minutes to find apartment 2324. It was an end apartment on the second floor.

I parked out front between a B.M.W. and a blue minivan. The stairs jutted out from the building. Brown steel frames and flat, exposed pebble steps. The stairs, purely functional, had no aesthetic appeal, but were definitely in keeping with the architectural blandness of the apartment complex. I went up the stairs two at a time while I dug the keys out of my pocket.

I tried a key, but it didn't work. Then I tried another key. Bingo. I unlocked the door and went in and locked the door behind me.

Keith had a nice apartment. The floor plan was standard, with two bedrooms, a large bathroom, a kitchen with adjoining dining room area, and a large living room/den area with a small fireplace. There were some ashes and the charred ends of several small oak logs in the fireplace.

The rooms were larger than most apartments. The furnishings were very nice, and the rich beige carpeting was thick beneath my feet.

I took a quick walk through the apartment for an overview. I didn't know exactly what I was looking for, but like the U.S. Supreme Court once said about pornography, I would know it when I saw it. I decided to start the search at the back of the apartment and work my way to the front. I went into the back bedroom and turned on the light switch. Keith had a home office in the room. In addition to the bedroom furniture near the door, there was office furniture along the back of the room, including a desk, file cabinet, book shelves, and office chair. A cork board hung over the desk. Assorted scraps of paper were thumbtacked to the board. The book shelves were generally filled with motorcycle shop manuals, most of which were grease stained with blackened fingerprints from use, together with a scattering of investment books and a couple of western paperback novels.

I turned my attention to the grey metal file cabinet. It was locked. I pulled out Mrs. Holland's ring of keys again, and found one that looked like it would fit and tried it. The key turned and the lock popped out. I put the key ring back in my pocket and pulled out the top drawer. There were rows of manila folders, all neatly labeled. I glanced at the names. Most were related to the motorcycle shop.

In the bottom drawer, I found a manila envelope under some mechanic pamphlets. I glanced in and found a list of addresses and another ring of keys. Attached to each key was a string holding a metal ringed tag, with an address. I put the ring of keys in my pants pocket. I glanced over the addresses, folded the list and put it in my shirt pocket. I finished looking through the file cabinets, but didn't find anything else of interest. I went out of the room, turning off the light, and went into the bathroom.

I looked in the medicine cabinet. It contained a disposable razor, a well-used toothbrush, some aftershave, an assortment of prescription and over-the-counter medicines, and a tube of toothpaste squeezed in the middle with the cap missing. I opened the caps of the medicine bottles, and looked in each one. They seemed to be what the label said. I closed the medicine cabinet and looked in the linen closet.

The linen closet had four shelves, so I started at the floor level, working my way to the top. I got on my knees, looked around. The bathroom scales seemed standard, but I turned it upside down and with my pocket knife, unscrewed the cover on the bottom and removed it. The springs were normal, so I put it back on the floor. A paper sack against the back of the closet contained some cleaning aids and odds and ends. I stood up and brushed the dust off my pants, then squatted down and prowled through the lower shelves, among the worn out towels and wash cloths on the bottom shelf, and even opened the clear plastic sack and looked inside the hollow tubes of toilet paper. I looked through the better towels on the next shelf, taking them out and feeling each one for any hidden contraband. And looked through the various toiletries, blow drier and assorted stuff on the next to top shelf.

I put the lid down on the commode and stood with one foot on it and the other foot on the low shelf, and looked on the top shelf. In the very back of the shelf was a folded dark green towel. I touched it. It contained something. I slid it to the edge of the shelf and got off the commode and, cradling it in my hands, sat down on the commode and began to carefully open the folds. Inside was a thick wad of one hundred dollar bills and two one-gallon sized plastic freezer bags.

I carried the bath towel into the dining room and laid the towel on the table. I pulled up a chair and sat down and counted the money. It was in three bundles, held together with rubber bands. Two bundles each contained ten thousand dollars in one hundred dollar bills. The third contained seventy-three one hundred dollar bills. I laid the money to one side.

I turned my attention to the freezer bags. One contained a white powder. I opened it and looked closer. I hefted it in my hand. Almost half a pound, maybe, of cocaine. An elephant couldn't put that much cocaine up its nose. Keith would have had to use a funnel to use that much cocaine. So much for the idea of "personal use".

The other bag contained a large off-white colored, grainy textured disk about three-quarters of an inch thick. Part of the disk had been broken off, and bits and crumbs of the disk were in the bottom of the sack. It was crack cocaine, a cooked up compound of cocaine and baking soda that gave an immediate high when it was smoked, and an addiction about as fast.

When I had been on the force, the only drugs had been pot for the kids, dime bags of heroin for the junkies, and diet pills for the truckers. Coke, crack, methamphetamine, "ice" and the numerous "designer drugs" like Ecstasy were still rare, an ignorance that was unappreciated as we were sent to chase down eighteen year old kids with a couple marijuana cigarettes by a hard-nosed district attorney.

I leaned forward and rested my crossed forearms on the table, looked at the cash and drugs, and thought about what I had found. The drugs were consistent with what I had been told by Travis and the mechanic. Now I knew that Keith was involved in drug dealing. Big time. The cocaine fit his life style, running the north Dallas clubs, meeting Carolyn O'Brian and other girls who were attracted to the glitz he offered.

The part that didn't fit was the crack. Crack was generally a black man's drug. Connected to gangs and territory. Evidently Keith was an equal opportunity dealer, but I couldn't see the crowd he ran with at Hank's being crack heads. The main white drug was cocaine for the affluent and meth for the blue collar crowd. I hadn't found any meth yet. But if he was involved in selling crack and cocaine, there was a good chance there was some meth around somewhere. Meth, Ketting and the Hank's crowd - that all fit together into a nice dirty ball. Now I had a goal. I left the drugs and money on the table and went back to my search.

The front bedroom was where Keith slept. I looked under the bed and found house shoes and dust balls. I flipped the mattress off the bed, and fluffed through the pillows. I found a chromed Smith and Wesson .38 caliber revolver and a spare quick-load cylinder in the drawer of the bedside table, along with a small vial of cocaine. I set them on the table and searched on.

I found an assault rifle with a long banana bullet clip wrapped in a sheet standing in the corner of the closet. On the top shelf of the closet I found a Adidas shoe box. I set it on the bed, sat down beside it and popped the lid. It contained seven bundles of one hundred dollar bills wrapped with rubber bands. I quickly counted a couple of them: one hundred bills in each. Another seventy thousand dollars total. I put it on the table with the rest of the loot. I also found twelve DVDs in a small grey soft leather suitcase, and tossed the bag on the bed.

I went through the chest of drawers. I poured the contents of each drawer in a pile in the center of the floor. Nothing but socks, underwear, and shirts until I got to the bottom drawer. I found photo albums and some photo processing envelopes. I laid them on the bed.

I didn't find anything else in the bedroom so I emptied a pillowcase, put my loot in it and I carried the stuff back to the kitchen table. I sat down and opened the first photo album. It was full of photos of naked women posing for his camera. The background looked like the pictures were taken in the living room and front bedroom of Keith's apartment. I glanced quickly through the book for Carolyn. She wasn't in it. I looked through the next album. There was more of the same. I kept flipping pages. She was on the last couple pages. She had a great body for a teenager, but her teenage image of seductive poses weren't up to *Playboy* standards. She was still a kid posing as a siren, calling Keith to his own personal odyssey towards his destruction.

I unzipped the leather bag and looked at the backs of the DVDs. Each had a single woman's name, except one that had "Donna" and Bridgette" printed on the spine. I took out the one labeled "Carolyn" and took it to DVD player. I turned on the t.v. and the DVD player, and inserted the disc and pushed "PLAY" on the remote. From the angle and the layout of the room, the camera had been in the bedroom closet. I stood back and picked up the remote control and pushed "FAST FORWARD" for about two minutes until a person appeared.

It was Keith and Carolyn. Keith and Carolyn entered the bedroom arm in arm. His shirt was open and her blouse and bra was missing. I hit "STOP" and then the eject button. Ketting was right about Keith knowing Carolyn. I put the tape back on the table and turned my attention to the kitchen.

I went through all the kitchen cabinets, looking in all the cans and packages. I went through the drawers. In the back of the silverware drawer I found another pistol, a snub-nosed .38 caliber, and put it in my belt. I poured out the flour and sugar into the trash can. Besides weevils in flour, there was nothing unusual. Same for the sugar. Maybe I just had seen too many old detective movies where the Star of India diamond is found in a butter dish. But I thought of the cash, guns and drugs, and kept on looking.

I shoved the trash can next to the refrigerator door and began to take all the food out one item at a time. I would open a package, glance in, then dump it in the trash can or pour it down the sink. I left the brown lettuce in the vegetable bin. I poured out the clabbered milk in a thick lump. The mustard jar held mustard and the mayonnaise jar was full of mayonnaise.

Then I opened the freezer. Evidently, Keith was big on microwave food. I turned on the hot water and began to toss the frozen food packages into the sink to thaw under the water. As the packages thawed, I tore open the containers and poured the contents into the other side of the sink to thaw. I tossed the packaging in the trash. I went through half a dozen frozen dinners and three frozen vegetable containers. I had to run the hot water over the frozen hamburger for three minutes before I got it all thawed out. It was hamburger all the way through. I melted the ice cubes out of the trays. There was even a home-packed freezer bag of peaches. I figured Mrs. Holland had put them up for Keith.

Against the side of the freezer, next to where the ice trays had been I found a thick package. The contents of the freezer bag was wrapped in aluminum foil. I opened the bag, took the contents and unwrapped the aluminum. The one hundred dollar bills had a rubber band around them, and little yellow post-it note that said "$50,000". I fanned the money. They were all one hundred dollar bills. Fifty thousand dollars in very cold, cold hard cash. I didn't think he earned that kind of cash from tune-ups at the cycle shop. I put the money on the kitchen table and continued the search of the kitchen. I didn't find anything else in the kitchen, so I moved on to the living room.

I started with the end tables. They were hexagon shaped and made of dark stained pine. They were enclosed on all sides with a door on one of the sides. Inside were various odds and ends that had accumulated and been tossed in there.

Then I turned to the blue plaid couch. I took out the sofa cushions, unzipped them and pulled out the rubber foam cushions. I tossed it all in the middle of the living room floor. I felt along the back of the couch and along the sides next to the arms. I pulled the couch away from the wall and looked behind the couch, then tipped it over and looked under the couch. Then I looked at his recliner. It had a pouch on the right side to hold t.v. programs and remote controls. Keith's also held a 9 millimeter Beretta. I slid the barrel halfway back. It had a bullet in the chamber. Keith seemed to feel he was running in an untrustworthy crowd, but considering what happened to him, I guess he knew them well. He should have been more careful. Just because you are paranoid doesn't mean someone isn't trying to kill you. I took out the chair cushion and tore it open, and tossed the scraps into the pile. I searched around the seat but couldn't find anything else but bread crumbs. I turned the chair over. The edge of the fabric on the bottom of the chair was thumbtacked. I think I mumbled "Eureka". I squatted down and pulled off the bottom thin gauzy cloth. Keith had nailed some tacks and hung a net. A paper sack was in the net, out of sight. I hefted it. It weighed several pounds. I opened the sack and pulled out a gallon freezer bag. It looked like "Ice", top flight methamphetamine crystal. Good old Keith, your full service drug dealer. Name your preference and bring your bucks.

I put it on the kitchen table and sat down to think. I looked at the addresses and telephone numbers I had found. Many of them were from east Texas. I recognized several prefixes that were in the general area of Columbia County. I figured I needed to check out some of those addresses. Lots of home-made drugs. Lots of down home rural locations. I wondered if the answer to Keith's murder was back in Columbia County, in some back barn on an isolated farm under the pines. I would have to check it out. But I needed some back up.

CHAPTER

21

WHEN I GOT back to the house, I called Jake Holliday. I had met Jake when I was on the force, but I hadn't appreciated his unique abilities until I had become a private investigator.

Jake was a big man, competent and sure of himself. He had a tour in Iraq and one in Afghanistan as an Army Ranger. Sometimes when he was drunk, he would tell me stories of search and destroy missions he had been on. Jake was very self-contained, which I attributed to too many late night helicopter raids. I guess old habits are hard to break.

I met Jake when I was investigating a murder of a self-styled "ladies' man" who was suspected of cuckolding a man named Belter. Belter had a dubious past and was once rumored to have had connections with the old Dixie Mafia. My snitches told me they had heard word on the street that Jake had killed the Romeo, but I could never get any proof. Jake was known to be available for such things.

After I had left the force, I had come across Jake several times. We had been wary of each other at first, but over time, we had grown used to each other and recognized the other's strengths. We understood each other, and had a common view of life as we knew it, a view of the underbelly of society, among the flotsam and scum of society. We weren't so cynical as to feel that everybody was like those we spent too much time with, but we knew that was the way things were on the streets on which we made our livings. Such common ground had led to a wary friendship.

It was reassuring to have someone to call when you needed a hand, knowing that when you called, he would be there and back you up one hundred percent. I needed some help now, Jake's kind of no-questions-asked, where-do-you-need-me help.

Last I heard, Jake had taken to hanging out at the Blue Room, a low rent beer joint in southeastern Dallas. It was a place where you could sit around and have a couple beers, and talk football, politics, women, or whatever topic was flying that day, and shoot some pool. And know that if there was a fight, it wouldn't be too serious. Just enough to get the blood flowing good.

I picked up the telephone and hooked it under my chin. I didn't figure the Blue Room was the kind of place to invest in a web site, so I pulled out the phone book from the bottom drawer of the desk, leaned back in my chair, and looked up the Blue Room's number. I found the number, punched them in, and waited for the ring.

"Blue Room," A man answered. "What can I do for you?"

I asked to speak to Jake.

"Who the hell is this?" A voice growled. A warm telephone persona is so essential to developing a good business.

"Noah Starr," I said. "Just put Jake on the horn." I heard him call for Jake across the joint, over the bar noise of mingled juke box country music and conversation. I heard someone ask who it was. When the bar tender told him, I heard a muffled voice. The bar tender relayed the message that Jake told him to tell me to go to hell, he was busy. I told him to tell Jake that if I had to come down there, I was going to kick Jake's butt all over the bar. The bar tender laughed and yelled that across the bar. I heard the buzz of catcalls and profanity from the high-class clientele.

In about thirty seconds, Jake came on the phone. "Yeah, what's the problem? Talk quick. My beer's gettin' warm."

I need you to give me a hand. I need some back-up. Are you free for a couple days?"

"I can make time. What's up?"

"I don't want to get into it one the phone. When can we get together?"

"Where you at?"

"At home."

"Is it something big?"

"Yeah. Wouldn't call you for peanuts. I got some big potential back problems."

There was a short pause. "Want to meet me here?"

"Yeah. About thirty or forty minutes o.k. with you?" He agreed and we hung up.

I left the house and drove to the Blue Room. It was a big square box of a building with a flat roof. The brick exterior had been painted blue years ago, but it had faded to a faint pastel, peeling paint, and streaked with rust around the rain spouts. I pulled into the asphalt parking lot before three, and there were already a half dozen cars and a couple of pickups out front. Most the vehicles had some rough miles and looked like they had gone to hell and back more than once. Maybe if the patrons didn't drop by the bar so early, they might could afford a little better transportation.

The Blue Room wasn't like that Boston bar on t.v. but it was a good place for a cold beer on a hot day. I enjoyed an occasional beer, and the Blue Room was as good a place as any to drink, and better than most. If I still drank as much as I did when I was younger, I would have moved to the Blue Room and hung up my toothbrush in the men's room and lived there.

As soon as I got inside, I stepped to the right of the door, so I wouldn't be silhouetted against the light of the door. I let my eyes adjust to the darkness. I heard Jake yell to me, so I started to ease my way in the direction of his call, like trying to grope your way to a seat in a crowded theater after the movie had began. He was sitting at the back in a corner with a can of Budweiser in his hand, and two empty cans and an ashtray half full of Camel cigarettes. He motioned me to the table with his beer can. We both sat with our backs to the wall, with our chairs about a foot apart, so we could talk and not be overheard. Jake waved the bartender over.

"What you want, Noah? Old Mil, right?"

I nodded.

"Hey, Walt," he yelled to the bar tender over a George Strait tune on the jukebox. "Bring me another Bud and an Old Mil for my buddy."

Walt nodded and brought the beers, the Budweiser in a can, the Old Milwaukee in a bottle. He tossed a couple napkins on the table and set the beers down and pick up the two empty cans. Jake drained the beer he was holding and hand him the can. Jake reached into his shirt pocket and pulled out a wad of bills and a pack of Camels and laid them on the table. He peeled off a few ones and handed them to Walt. The cold beers were already wet with condensation. I took a long draw from the bottle, nodded my satisfaction. I usually drank Corona, but the Blue Room wasn't the kind of place that had Coronas or other foreign beer. Their idea of a "foreign" beer was one that had been brewed in New York.

I leaned back, letting the back of the chair rest against the wall and hooked my boot heel on the edge of the table and sipped my beer and looked around the room.

A thirty-year-old construction worker with huge, tattooed forearms and curly black hair was challenging a middle aged welder at the pool table. The welder had on a tall baseball cap and a khaki shirt with "MIKE" stitched in block letters over the pocket and lots of little burn holes on the sleeves. Neither was good enough to run the table, but they were well matched. The construction worker sighted down his stick, gently stroking it through his arched fingers, trying to ease the six ball into the corner pocket. I heard a dull metallic thud and glanced down at his feet and saw a chrome plated automatic pistol laying on the worn linoleum next to the instep of his left boot. He was so intent on his pool shot he didn't even hear the gun fall.

Jake and I glanced at each other and grinned. Jake had a pool cue leaned against the wall beside him. He got it and leaned forward and tapped the guy on the shoulder.

He scowled at Jake for breaking his concentration. "What the hell do you want?"

Jake smiled broadly and tapped the floor by the gun with the stick. "Nothing, buddy, but I thought you might want to get your bar gun."

The man glanced down quickly, then looked sheepishly at Jake, and glanced around. Several other patrons had seen or heard the gun fall and were watching. He looked embarrassed, and picked up the gun and slid it into the front of his jeans, and pulled his faded green tee-shirt down over it. "That's the second time this week that thing's fallen out. Teach me to loose a couple pounds. It used to fit pretty good."

Walt had been watching the exchange and laughed out loud and called across the bar, "Hey, Tom, can't you read?" He nodded towards a printed official-looking sign taped to the bar-back mirror that said that possession of a firearm in an establishment that sold alcohol was a felony.

Tom picked up a green cube of pool chalk and threw it side-arm at Walt, who ducked just in time. "Hell, no, I can't read."

The other people in the bar began to laugh and hoot.

He glanced over at us and said, "Ain't that the way it is? One little silly assed screw-up and they won't let you forget it for the next ten years." He pointed towards the sign. "Ain't that a kicker? Bar's where you really need a gun. Right?"

He turned back to the pool table and stroked twice and shot. The cue ball clipped the edge of the six ball that ricocheted off the rubber and rolled toward the middle of the table. "Damn," he said and went to the bar and took a swig of his beer and lit another cigarette. He sat on a bar stool and watched the welder sight his next shot, his cigarette dangling from his mouth, the smoke eddying towards the ceiling.

Jake leaned back in his chair and glanced over at me and asked, "O.k., bud, what's the deal?"

I told him about finding the money, the drugs, and about the keys, addresses and directions.

"I need to check it out. It's the only lead I have right now as to who might have killed Keith. I figure one of the country locations is a speed lab. If I'm right, I'll damn sure need someone to back me up."

Jake nodded. "Those speed bastards are crazy. They are so deep into their own shit they think chickens can tap dance." He stubbed out his cigarette. "They fry their brains on stuff they cook up in the back barn, based on a recipe drawn up by a dumb cook who couldn't pass a high school chemistry class, hell, somebody they met in the joint most likely. Sum'bitches are as paranoid as a just-kicked cat. And they are all armed to the teeth these days. Whatever happened to 'peace and love' pot smokers?" He swigged his beer again, then he paused and looked at me steadily. "We're gonna need some firepower, if we're going in there and you're right about a drug lab."

He stood up and pulled a flat round tin of Copenhagen snuff from his back pocket, and sat down and leaned back again. He pulled the lid off and held it to his mouth and licked some. His lower left lip pouched out as he packed it between his lip and gums. He tossed the can on the table and took another swig of beer and waited for me to speak.

I nodded. "Yeah, it could get sticky. You mind?" Since I was pulling him into a possible fire fight, it seemed polite to ask him if he wanted the heat.

He shook his head. "When do you want to go?"

"It'll be about eighty, maybe a hundred miles one way." I glanced at my watch. "If we leave pretty soon, we would be there by six or six-thirty. Then we could scope it out before it gets too late. What do you think?"

He nodded. "Want to go in my truck? It's got four wheel drive. We might need it when we get out there in the Boondocks. Yours wouldn't pull a sick whore out of the mud." He grinned. "But you buy the gas."

"No. Mine'll be o.k. for this run. May take yours if we decide we have to go back, if it looks rough."

He looked at me squarely. "Are you getting paid on this deal?"

I shook my head.

"Damn," he said. "So I get a split of what? Nothing." He smirked. "How do you pay your bills, you silly bastard? You need to let me introduce you to some of my friends. They actually PAY for services rendered." We stood up and he drained the last of his beer. I took another swig at mine and set it down.

"You gonna waste the rest of that?"

I nodded.

"Don't you know that there are millions of thirsty drunks in countless Third World countries who would love to have that beer. Haven't you ever heard the expression 'waste not, want not?'"

"Well, I didn't want it, so I'm wasting it." I stood up.

He laughed and said, "You ready to go?"

I nodded. "I'm going to go to the house and get some fire power and meet you at your house in about an hour, o.k.?"

He nodded and we left the bar.

CHAPTER
22

I GOT BACK to my house and laid out my athletic bag on the bed and started packing. I got out my nine millimeter Beretta from the bedside table and tossed it on the bed. I got the shoulder holster and the three spare clips from the closet shelf, then reached back in for a box of bullets.

I went to the study and got the twelve gauge automatic shotgun from the gun case and emptied the shells out of the chamber and magazine onto the chair, then picked up a thick, blunt shell and read the faint printing on side of the plastic shell tube. The shells had number eight shot. Big enough for quail, but I needed larger shot for self-defense. I looked in the ammunition drawer, and got out three boxes of double-aught buckshot and laid the thin boxes each containing five cartridges on the table. I opened a package and took out four fat bricks of red cartridges and lined them standing up on the coffee table. I rolled shotgun sideways, holding the wooden stock with my left hand, and slid the first one into the slot on the bottom of the front stock. I pulled back the ejection lever on the side of the barrel slowly, letting the shell slide into the firing chamber, then released the lever. It shot forward with a metallic clank, chambering the first shell. The sound was ominous in the silence of the house. I finished filling the magazine with the other three shells. I made sure the safety was on, and picked up the extra boxes of buckshot shells, grabbed a box of number four shot shells and carried it all to the bedroom and laid it on the bed.

I reached into the side of the closet and got out my hunting vest, and put it on, feeling how everything was fitting. I put the extra pistol clips in the left side pocket. With my gun in my right hand, I would reload it with my left hand, so I needed them easily available. Then I started filling the elastic loops across the chest of the jacket with shotgun shells. I put the extra buckshot shells on my left side because I would reload the shotgun with my right hand, while I held it in my left hand. When I ran out of buckshot shells, I finished filling the cartridge loops with the number four shot cartridges. I put in a couple days worth of clothes in the bag together with my shaving kit. I laid a set of camouflage hunting jacket and pants on the bed, together with a heavy leather bomber jacket. I got out some gloves, and put a pair of lace-up hunting boots beside the bed. Knowing how Texas weather can change in the blink of an eye, especially in the spring, I tried to carry something to wear on a possible stake out, no matter how hot or cold it got.

I went to the kitchen and filled a thermos, and brought it to the bedroom. I checked to make sure I had Keith's list of locations and the ring of keys.

I was almost finished when I heard Alice drive up. She came in the bedroom, but stopped short when she saw the firepower on the bed.

"Noah, what are you doing?" She said somewhat breathless, as if the thought that I might need all the guns had knocked the breath out of her.

I told her about finding the drugs and money, and the list of names. "Got to check out the addresses I found at Keith's"

"And the guns?"

"Don't know what I might find. These are just for security."

"Noah, a police whistle is for security. A guard dog is for security. Even a little twenty-two caliber pistol in a purse is for security." She glanced at the shotgun and pistol, and the hunting vest filled with shells. "This is preparing for an invasion. What do you expect to find?" The fear in her voice matched the concern that clouded her eyes.

"I don't know. I've heard about drug delivery and maybe manufacturing. I expect that somewhere on the list may be a drug lab. I'm going to find out whatever is there, and hopefully find someone who can give me a clue as to why Keith was killed. Was it because of his drug involvement? What? I just don't know. But I don't have any other leads to follow right now."

"I'm afraid for you, Baby." She hugged me, then quickly stepped back. "Can you take that thing off." she said, referring to the vest. I took it off and tossed it on the bed. She hugged me again, long and tightly. "I've never limited you, Noah, you know that, but I have a bad feeling about this. Is there any other way?"

"Not that I can see. The police aren't doing very much. They've checked the obvious, but to them, the obvious answer is that one of Keith's drug friends capped him. It makes sense, and most likely is what happened, but I told Mrs. Holland I would try to get to the bottom of his murder."

She hugged me again, even tighter, her head nestled under my chin, her hair tickling my nose.

I pulled away enough to kiss her forehead, then her lips, my left arm around her, my right hand lifting her face to me. "I'll be careful." I nodded towards the guns. "This is just precaution. Besides, Jake's going with me."

Her moist eyes widened. "Jake?" she said quietly.

I nodded.

A tear rolled down her cheek. I wiped it away, then kissed her wet cheek. It was salty from the tear. I kissed her lips again. There was no response.

She leaned her head back slightly, and looked me in the eyes. "If you are taking Jake, it must be bad."

I shook my head. "Not necessarily. I just don't know what I may find, and I figure Jake's the best security I can have. Besides, I may be gone a couple days and figure I need someone to talk to."

She forced a smile. "You're going to be careful?" She asked.

I nodded.

"Bullshit." She whispered. She hugged me again tightly. Then she cupped my face with her hands, bringing my face down to hers and kissed me deeply, her eyes almost closed. She leaned her head back slightly and looked at me again. "A couple days, huh?"

I nodded.

"You're going to call me and keep me posted, aren't you?"

"Yes, 'Mother.' I'll even wear my galoshes and use an umbrella if it rains."

"Please don't get flippant with me, Noah. I just feel bad about this. Hug me again." We hugged, Alice burrowing close like a little puppy trying to get warm, then she asked, "When are you leaving?"

"As soon as I am packed."

She froze. "Tonight?"

I nodded. "Sooner I start the sooner I get through. Look, I don't expect any real trouble. The main reason I am taking Jake is that if I need to talk with someone, the two of us can intimidate them better than just little ol' me. A little intimidation can lead to a lot of talking." I kissed her again. "I'll be careful. And I will check in every chance I get. I really expect to just drive around, and if anyone is still at any of the locations, talk with them about Keith if I can." I paused, and glanced at the pile on the bed. Alice's eyes followed mine, then looked back at me. "Well," I said hesitantly, reluctant to upset her more, "Babes, I'm packed."

She nodded and we kissed lightly again, and I picked up the guns and hunting vest, and Alice picked up the athletic bag and thermos and followed me out to the truck. I stowed everything behind the seat. I turned to see her wiping a tear from her eyes with the heel of hand. She turned her face from me, wiped her face again, then wiped her hand on her clothes, and turned back to me with a stoic smile.

"I'll be careful." We kissed again, and I got in my truck and backed onto the street. Alice had her arms wrapped tightly around her shoulders, as if cold from an inner chill. I blew her a kiss and she waved. I accelerated slowly, and as I turned the corner, I waved at her and she was out of sight.

CHAPTER
23

I PULLED INTO Jake's dirt driveway, and up behind his black Chevrolet pickup which was parked under the add-on carport he had built himself. Jake lived in a small two bedroom wood frame house in east Dallas near Mesquite. His porch light was on. I got out and went up to the door. As I stepped on the first of the wood steps to the side door, he opened the screen door and beckoned me in. "Hell, boy, we gotta stop meeting like this." He laughed and beckoned me in with a broad wave. "Come on in, I'm almost ready." He turned and went back into the house, with me behind. The kitchen was forties style, with dingy white painted wooden cabinets, a gray masonnite counter top and a single deep sink half filled with dirty dishes. He gestured to the electric coffee maker. "Get'cha a cup," he said, and went down the hall, his sock feet slipping slightly as he went down the worn linoleum floor.

I opened a cupboard and got down a cup and poured some coffee. I made myself at home and looked in the refrigerator and got a splash of milk, then some sugar, and I went down the short hall towards his bedroom stirring my coffee.

He glanced up from a small green duffle bag when I came in. "How long do you think we'll be?"

I shrugged. "Maybe a day, likely two or three. Don't know what we'll find 'till we get to stirring around."

He nodded. He pulled a couple pair of heavily starched Wrangler blue jeans from a chest of drawers, and tossed them into the partially filled bag. He continued to rummage through the bedroom, getting items and casually tossing them into the bag.

I glanced around the room. There was an aging dog-eared photo thumb-tacked on the wall. Three young shirtless G.I.s, with ammo belts across their shoulders, their rifles propped casually against their hips. They were leaning back against a low wall of tan sand bags, each young soldier's pose an imitation of a John Wayne movie poster. I looked closer at the photograph. It had been bent several times, the creases wrinkling some details. In the background were several heavily up-armored Humvees lined up by sand bag emplacements and barbed wire.

Jake looked over my shoulder. "That's in the Anbar Province. I was there on my last tour in '06." His voice was flat.

I glanced at him and back at the photo. He was looking deeply at the picture and pointed at the soldiers from left to right. "That's me there. Thought I was tough as a boot back then. Didn't know what tough was then. That's Bob Lemmert. From Alabama. Got it in a firefight in Mosul. Other guy's Jim Hellen. Called him 'Hell on Wheels.'" He snorted. "We thought that was funny, but what the hell did we know? Hell, we thought it was fun to rappel out of a helicopter into a Taliban-held village in the middle of the night. Hell, it'd be darker than Egypt. Couldn't see your hand in front of your face. Slide down the ropes. Assassinate or nab our target, then catch a copter back to base." He paused, remembering. He pointed to Hellen. "He got shot up bad in the mountains of Afghanistan on a mission about a hundred miles out of Kabul. Carried him out on my back under fire and he medivaced out. He was shipped home and I lost track of him. We thought we were so tough back then. Goin' where we were sent and killin' who they said. Seemed pretty simple, but while we were doin' our 'duty,' the other ninety-nine percent of the American boys our age were going to college, smoking pot and getting some from cute college girls. We were tough but, looking back on it, we would have been smarter to chase American girls on campus than chasing the Taliban through the mountains." He paused, patted me on the back and said "Hell, live and learn. But if I hadn't been there doing that, you wouldn't be here, and I wouldn't be gettin' ready to do . . . hell, what was it again we're doin'?" He turned back to his packing, then glanced back at me. "I said 'What is it we're doin', Noah?'"

"Hell, I don't know, just checking out some loose ends. See if we can find what got Keith killed. At least enough so I can tell Mrs. Holland something to put her mind at ease."

"What are you packing?"

"Beretta nine millimeter and automatic twelve gauge."

"Really think we'll need much?"

I shrugged. "Doubt it. Rather be ready for whatever than be in the woods with nothing but my winning smile."

He handed me a blued pistol. "My new baby." I held in my right hand and carefully appraised it, pushed the eject button and caught the bullet clip in my left hand and looked at the bullets.

"Ten millimeter?" I asked.

"Yeah. Glock. Hit that other button on the side."

I jacked the receiver back and the chambered bullet popped out, hit the floor and rolled under the bed. I glanced at him.

"Forget about it. I always leave it loaded. Empty gun's about as useless as tits on a boar hog."

I pushed the button and a red laser light appeared on the wall. The point of light wavered across Lemmert's chest. Jake looked at the photo and laughed. "That poor bastard was always in somebody's sights. But ain't that the sweetest little thang. What did the Beatles say, 'happiness is a warm gun?'" He put two boxes of bullets in the side pouch of the duffle bag. He went to the closet and pulled a half dozen banana-shaped ammunition clips in separate olive green canvas pouches off a side shelf with his left hand and cupped them against his ribs, and reached towards the back of the closet under shirts and a blue suit hanging on the clothes bar and pulled out a black rifle with large magazine and short plastic stock. He dropped the banana clips on the bed and ejected the clip from the rifle, and jacked out the spare shell onto the bed. He leaned the rifle against the bed and put the shell back into the clip and reloaded the clip. He slid the rifle's clips into pouches on a green cloth web belt. He got a sheathed short knife out of the night stand drawer and put it on the belt, and clasped the belt into a circle. He slung the belt over his shoulder, clipped the duffle bag closed and swung it over his shoulder, and picked up the rifle and went back to the kitchen and laid the stuff on the table. I picked up the shoulder holster for the Glock and followed him out of the room, turning off the light switch as I went. I slid the clip back into the pistol and turned off the sights, and slipped the gun into the holster and put it on the table. I sat in a chair and drank my coffee.

Jake put on a pair of brown sharkskin boots that had been beside the door, went to the living room and returned with a blanket-lined blue jean jacket with brown leather gloves sticking out of the side pockets, and a dark brown cowboy hat.

He re-filled his cup with coffee and gestured towards me with the pot. "Want some more?" and filled my cup when I nodded. He poured out the rest, rinsed the pot, and put it in the blue plastic dish drainer, and sat down. He reached into his shirt pocket and got out a pack of cigarettes and shook out one, opened a match box, struck the match with a thumb nail and lit the cigarette. "Tell me more, buddy."

I cupped the mug in both hands. "Not much more to tell." I sat the cup down, reached in my pocket and took out the page from Keith's address book with the addresses. "Going to go look at these properties. See if any of them could possibly click either with Keith's death or the drug angle. Quien sabe?"

He glanced over the list. "Several of them seem to be in or near Flood County. That's over by your neck of the woods, isn't. Near Columbia County?"

I nodded.

"Haven't the feds busted a few speed labs there in the last year or so?"

I nodded. "Yeah, that's why I figured I might need you. In one case, I even heard that several county deputies were caught up and involved with the labs, so we might not get all the legal back-up we might want."

"For you that might be a strange position, but believe me, I've been there more'n once."

"Still want to go?"

"Sure, why not? Already packed. Let's hook'em." He went through the house turning out the lights, and we carried his stuff to my truck. "Sure you don't want to go in my truck, might need the extra clearance and the four wheel drive." I shook my head. "No, mine'll do. Thanks anyway."

We tossed his stuff behind the seat. He turned off the porch light, locked up and we left.

CHAPTER
24

WE SETTLED INTO the truck, put our cups on the dash and a Patsy Cline tape on the CD player and bee-lined to the Interstate. I put the truck on cruise control at sixty if I needed to drop back legal for the Dallas police, and accelerated to seventy-five and headed down the inside lane, past the tired office workers heading home.

I handed Jake the page containing Keith's list of addresses. He clicked on the dome light.

"Any of them you recognize?"

He shook his head slightly. "Not right off. You got any better directions to 'em than these notes?"

"Only what's there."

He shook his head again. "Let's see, east of, is that word 'Yantis,' on highway...?" He leaned over, holding the note near my face so I could watch the road and glance at where he had his finger pointing to an address. "Can you make the road out?"

I glanced at it, at the road, back at it, then back at the eighteen wheeler that suddenly decided to veer into my lane. I tapped the brake and slowed a bit, pulling in behind the truck. When it looked copacetic, I glanced back at the paper, then took it in my hand to hold it closer. It was in pencil and hard to see. "Yeah, that's Yantis. Road could be a '575', either a county road, or Farm-to-Market road." I handed it back to him. "I can't make it out here. Let's go to Yantis, find a café for supper and try to figure it out." I leaned over and opened the glove box and handed him a map of Texas. "While you're not doing anything, check and see where we get off the Interstate, and see if that '575' rings a bell."

"You want me to check out these other addresses?" He asked.

"If you want to. I've glanced over them, and the first one on the list seems to be the nearest one. We'll get some supper and good lighting and figure out in what order we'll do the rest."

He nodded and folded the note and put it in his shirt pocket and pulled out a pack of Camels, shook one out and lit it. He rolled the window down a little and blew most of the smoke out of the truck. He unfolded the map and started getting a feel for the roads around Yantis and the surrounding area.

"Before we leave Dallas County, we'd better get something to keep us warm the next couple nights, unless you have Alice and one of her girl friends for me in your duffle bag. Lots of east Texas is dry. Too many of them Baptists."

"Baptists?"

"Yeah, you know, they're pretty rabid about not drinkin'. At least in public."

I smiled. "What do you have in mind?" as I started looking for a liquor store sign.

"Oh, well, if the duffle bag suggestion is a no-go, how about something, you know, about nine years old with a nice golden tint."

I spotted a sign, signaled and darted through a break in the right lane of traffic and off the interstate. I pulled up in front of an old stop-and-rob glass fronted store that had been remodeled into a liquor store. We got out and went inside. When we opened the door, a loud beep sounded and the Pakistani attendant jerked his head around, looking up from his small i-Pad screen. He leaned back, his hip against the counter, his left hand out of sight.

Jake caught his movement and glanced over at me, then smiled broadly at the hard faced clerk. "It's o.k., buddy, we're not here to knock you over. We're just here for a little antifreeze." He thumbed over his shoulder. "It's getting nippy out there." He saw the whiskey and headed down the back aisle.

I nodded at the clerk and followed.

"You gettin' anything?"

I shook my head.

He got a pint and what used to be a quart-sized bottle of the same.

"Two? You expecting a drought? How long do you think we'll be gone?" I asked.

"Well, it could be longer than you think, but the pint's a good carrying size for sittin' in the woods. And the liter's for refills. A pint won't last long in this weather. And, damn, that's a dry area of the state."

I nodded. "Yeah, better get whatever survival supplies you need now. Course, you don't know, we may be to hell and back before we're finished this little road trip." I glanced at his bottles. "Ready?"

"Let's rodeo, Hoss."

We went to the counter, the clerk still trying to appear nonchalant with his hand still under the edge of the counter. Jake got a cup and filled it with ice out of the an ice chest next to the Lotto machine.

"We must look pretty rowdy; you haven't hardly moved your hand since we came in here."

He stared at us for a second and realized that he couldn't ring up our purchases while holding the gun under the counter. He brought the cheap snub-nosed .32 caliber revolver out and laid it right beside the cash register.

Jake reached under his jacket for his wallet. The clerk's hand moved toward the gun again. Jake slowed and said "Careful. Just gettin' my cash, friend," he said to the clerk, his hand still resting on the gun handle.

I waved Jake's money away. "Keep your money. Consider this a down payment for your help."

"Let me get a couple more bottles then. This could be all I get."

"Too late. We're out of here." I paid the clerk. "What's the deal with the gun," I asked.

He handed me my change and closed the cash register. "Robbery last night," he said in barely understandable English, with a heavy Pakistani accent. "My cousin shot. Three times. Dead."

"Sorry," I said, and we picked up our bottles and left, the glass clanking together in their slender paper sacks.

As we slammed the truck doors and cranked the truck, Jake said, "Shit. I'd be a little touchy myself." He poured four fingers of Jack Black into the ice cup from the liter bottle, and put the bottle on the seat. As we hit the interstate again, he lit another Camel, took a long swig of the whiskey and turned up Patsy singing Bob Wills' "Faded Love" and softly sang along. He couldn't sing very well, but considering what he was doing for me for free, I decided not to call him on it.

He got the map and the notes out again and began to trace addresses on the map. He continued reading the map and the notes, occasionally taking a swig of the whiskey. He held the cup and swirled the ice absentmindedly. He lit another cigarette, then got out a pen and made notes on Keith's papers, all the while humming along with the music.

After about twenty minutes, we had passed through Mesquite and were in to the blackland farm land. A full moon lit up the landscape. The land, dark as charcoal had been plowed for cotton and small grains, the furrows of the plows like corduroy over the rolling plains. Cattle grazed around five foot tall round hay rolls scattered in the pastures.

Jake folded the map and put it on the truck seat under the whiskey bottle. "Got anything else?" Jake asked.

I reached into the driver's door pocket, and pulled out several cds and handed them to Jake. He glanced at the labels and inserted a Chris LaDoux cd.

"What's the best way to get to Yantis?"

"State Highway 19 north out of Canton," he said. "Then you dog leg east from Emory."

I nodded. "Nineteen is right there off Interstate 20 at Canton, isn't it?"

"Yeah." He drank from his cup and stared at the passing fields. The music was only a background mosaic for our musings. I thought of Keith, and our pilgrimage to his past, and wondered if we would need our guns. Keith's death, and Keith's tattered life, weighed on me.

Even when I was on the force and frequently had to deal with random murder, I was unable to separate my emotions from the job. I felt the pain of the victim's family, their shock and loss, but it was their loss. The void that suddenly existed in their lives, a black hole that had, without warning, inexplicably obliterated part of their lives. Someone had once said that we are each actors who are called to perform an improvisational play on the stage of life. The survivors of those deaths were unwilling actors for whom a central character in their individual life play was suddenly gone, leaving them to attempt to carry on the play, improvising around a void that is never filled, an amputee with phantom pains that never fully heal.

But Keith's death was more troubling to me. I personally knew the survivors. Regardless what I found out, I would have to edit what I told them. They had done nothing to warrant having to suffer the full story of Keith's life. Mrs. Holland did not deserve to know the painful facts she sought to save her husband from any more than he did. They deserved the sanitized version, with only enough information to give them what is now fashionably called "closure." I would try to give Keith's killer the legal justice he had denied Keith. Although Keith's drug dealing may have contributed to the destruction of countless people, his murder was not some poetic justice, a rough street approximation of *quid pro quo*. Murder as vengeance for the murdered man's misdeeds are more Dante than Dallas, more *Tempest* than Texas.

No, Keith's death was meaningful only to the killer on an individual vengeance level. Repayment for a real or intended slight, maybe a drug deal gone awry. Who knew. Only the bereaved family tries to find a cosmic justification or explanation for the mindless, meaningless death.

For me, though, this death was personal, a destruction of that cocoon of youthful memories of my adventures with Keith, memories now inextricably bound to a vision of Keith's blood splattered, rain-soaked body. My life, based on my security in my past now contained that same void I had seen in the eyes of other survivors, and I felt diminished by that realization. I drove along in my dark thoughts, until I turned off on Highway 19, and headed towards Yantis.

CHAPTER
25

WE DROVE NORTH on highway 19 to Yantis, and pulled into a combination gas station-diner. I filled the dual gas tanks, then pulled up beside the building near the front door and went in. There was a slightly sagging screen door with the screen pushed out and torn just above waist high, where countless hands had missed the door frame and shoved the door open with the screen wire. A cow bell attached to the top of the screen door clanked when I opened it, and clanked louder when I let it slam behind me on its spring. The wooden door to the diner was covered with local business cards and scraps of paper advertising various services like garden plowing, pasture mowing, hay baling, fire wood and hay for sale.

I paid the teenage clerk with buck teeth and a bad complexion for the gas and joined Jake at a corner table.

He had slid into the back booth against the wall, and was turned sideways, with his right arm resting on the back of the booth, and his crossed legs stretched out on the seat. He was the picture of country comfort. He was looking over a menu, holding it casually in his left hand. I picked up a home-typed, laminated menu up from behind the napkin holder and glanced over it. Jake's cigarette was smoking in the plastic ashtray. A waitress, weighing at least two hundred and fifty pounds of bouncing, rolling fat barely covered by a over-stretched concert tee-shirt with a black and white picture of Clint Black, came to the table, her huge stomach and hips quivering with each step.

She smiled with a sincere over-eagerness to be friendly. "What'chall want to drink?"

Jake ordered coffee, and I asked for iced tea, and she moved slowly away. I glanced around the diner. It had eight mismatched plastic laminated tarnished white tables, four lining the back wall, and four more in a row lined up next to them. The kitchen was in the next room, with an open doorway between the two rooms. The interior designer had overlooked the doorjamb half of the hinges which had been left on the door frame. Near the check-out counter were several home-made plywood shelves that held small quantities of various groceries: two cans of Spam, four boxes of dry Skinner spaghetti, a few small boxes of crackers next to a stack of sardine tins, that sort of thing.

Next to the front door was the check-out counter with the cash register. A Texas Lotto machine, and a dozen clear canisters containing rolls of various scratch-off Texas lottery games were clustered next to the register. Behind the bored clerk reading a "National Enquirer" newspaper were various small containers of non-prescription drugs and racks of cigarettes, packages of chewing tobacco and rolls of snuff.

The waitress was back with our drinks in less than a minute, and took our orders. After she left, Jake reached in his pocket and laid out Keith's list of addresses. He leaned sideways and reached into his back pocket and pulled out the road map. He moved everything over to the edge of the table against the wall, and opened the map. He re-folded the map so only northeast Texas was visible. He tapped the ash off the tip of the cigarette and put it in his mouth. He tilted his head slightly sideways and squinted his left eye as he tried to evade the hot smoke that circled and drifted into his face. Jake got out his cell phone and tapped in the addresses on his map app. He got out a fountain pen with an insurance agent's ad on the side and pointed to Yantis on the map.

"We're here, pod'ner," He said, pointing to the map. He glanced at the directions on Keith's list again, then inked a road east. "This map doesn't seem to have the county roads and pig trails on it, but, best I can figure," he said as he glanced at his cell phone's map, and then he began to retrace the line he had just drawn, "We go east from here, then hang a left about here, and then look for this here road number. I guess it's a county road. We'll see what we see." He glanced at me as I stirred a couple packs of sugar into my tea, watching his actions with half my attention.

I nodded. "In a rural area like this, though, I'm not sure we should ask many directions."

"Yeah, I agree. If we are just scoping out the lay of these places, no reason to have too many Jethros follering behind."

"'Jethros'? " I said with mock incredulousness. "These are my country brethren, these are truly the Jeffersonian ideal of the 'educated yeoman.'"

"Noah," he sneered. "You take another gander at the checkout gal one more time," he said, pointing to the front of the store and laughing, "And then you tell me if she isn't closer to a Jethro hayseed than the Jeffersonian ideal."

"Well maybe she's not the best example," I laughed. "But let's try to keep beneath the rural 'radar'. We don't want some Aunt Sally somewhere sending the county mounties after us. Can't get much done if we have to explain ourselves, plus I don't want anyone, including the police, to figure out what we're doing, at least until we figure it out ourselves."

"Are we getting any closer to figuring that out?" He asked with an emphasis on the "we."

"Give me a break. You do the map work and leave the heavy thinking to me." I said with a smile.

He laughed. "Yes, sir, Kemo Sabe. For what you're paying me, I'll follow you blindly, which I am, of course." He sucked slowly on his cigarette, and exhaled. "I feel like I'm with Captain Ahab, searching the vacant emptiness for a Great White Whale. When you get a chance, yell out 'thar she blows' so we can head home, o.k., bud?"

"First time I see a clue, you'll be the first to know."

We continued to look at the map and Keith's notes and Jake's phone screen. After a while, our food came, and we moved the map to one side until she left, then arranged the map in the center of the table, and ate while we organized our search.

"Has it occurred to you that you have no idea how old these addresses are?" I nodded.

"Sometimes these drug labs don't stay longer than a single cooking."

"What else do we have but these addresses. Keith wasn't just a casual user. He was up to his ass in this shit. His biker buddies aren't the type to hang around him for his clever wit. And his apartment had too much firepower and drugs to be a casual conduit. No," I said, emphasizing my point by pointing to the map with my fork full of chicken fried steak, "The answer is here, and if not the answer, the missing link is here. He was killed because of the drugs. Somehow, someway, the drugs killed him. As the ad said, 'Drugs Kill.' Usually directly, sometimes like Keith, because of his involvement. We keep rooting around and we'll find the string that will lead back to the killer."

"Just keep 'rooting around.'" He snorted derisively, "Hell, I love your country colloquiums."

"Hell, boy, even a blind pig finds an acorn sometimes."

Most of the directions and addresses on Keith's list seemed to be within thirty miles of where we were. We decided, since it was dark, to drive around and see how many of the roads to the locations we could find. We would wait until dawn to investigate.

We finished our meal, stretching our drinks until we had finished our review of the map.

"About ready, Navigator?"

"Aye, aye, Captain."

I put money down on the table for the meal and tip and got up.

On the way out, Keith got a couple more packs of unfiltered Camels.

As we walked to the truck I said, "Aren't you concerned with giving me cancer with all your second hand smoke?"

"Hell, no. Aren't you concerned with giving me lead poisoning by getting my ass shot off by some hopped up hillbilly?"

"Hillbilly. Don't you need some Appalachian mountains to have a 'hillbilly?'" I shook my head, "You can take the city slicker out of the city, but you can't take the city out of slicker. Just navigate, sucker," and laughed.

He laughed and flipped his cigarette butt across the parking lot.

We got in and headed north on 19, until we came to our first turn. Jake drank some, and smoked a lot, but we found four of the seven locations in our thirty mile circle. The other three were dead ends, at least in the dark. We finally ended up in Winnsboro and got rooms at a small motel. I went to bed tired but feeling like I was finally making some headway towards Mrs. Holland's request.

CHAPTER

26

I GOT UP early the next morning, and beat on Jake's door before five thirty. He opened it in about ten seconds. He was fully dressed, and ready to roll, his small overnight bag under his arm, puffing a cigarette that he held cupped in his hand, holding it with his thumb and forefinger.

"What took you so long? Thought you were going to sleep the day away." He said.

"Let's roll then." I went next door to my room and got my athletic bag that I had left on the end of the bed. I slammed the door shut behind me and we went down to the truck and drove to the office and checked us out. I came back to the truck and slipped the receipt behind the visor.

"You know, Noah, you're in a strange business. Here we are driving all over hell and Texas looking for speed labs so we can try to track down a pusher's murderer, and you're keeping receipts for your accountant."

I didn't say anything. He seemed to have summed up my existence succinctly. I cranked the truck and we drove to a nearby cafe. The eastern sky was turning red with the first hint of the coming sunrise when we finished breakfast and got in the truck and headed east. My grandmother used to tell me the old weather adage, "Red sky in morning, sailors take warning; red sky at night, sailor's delight." I wondered if we should take warning, too, as we headed towards the blood-red sky.

We had already mapped out our circuitous trip over a couple hundred square miles of heavily wooded east Texas rolling hills, trying to avoid overlapping paths more than necessary. We didn't know what we were looking for, or what we would find, so we would have to visit all the locations. The order of our search was irrelevant. Just lots of long, boring hours of driving. What I had told Alice was true: Jake's presence might be my salvation, keeping me from being bored to death over the next couple days.

We drove towards the nearest location on Keith's map. After about eight miles, we turned onto a small black topped county road, and followed its wandering course under a thick shelter of oak trees. You know you are in the boondocks when the address isn't even on a phone's map search. Scattered along the road side were occasional mail boxes, usually painted dull aluminum, perched on leaning posts. We tried to figure out our location by checking the numbers on the boxes, but they didn't seem to have a clear order, so we gave up and just watched the scenery and looked for the indications on the list.

We rounded a corner and drove past a dairy farm. The area around Winnsboro and further west towards Sulphur Springs was heavy dairy country. The golden Jersey cows, with huge swollen udders, stood stoically waiting for their turn at the door of the long cinder block milking barn. On the other side of the barn, freshly milked cows were wandering down the hill towards the green pasture, stopping to nibble a blade of grass here and there on their way into the day's cycle.

I slowed down a little and enjoyed the scene. The farm house, a light brown brick ranch house set off from the road a good hundred and fifty yards amid old oak trees. Two young boys ran from the house towards the road, their school backpacks swinging in their hands. They kept looking down the road in the direction we were heading. When they saw me looking, they both waved. I waved back. You just don't get that kind of friendliness in the big city. The boys' openness reflected the country-side's positive attitude towards people. I remembered it from my childhood, and every time I would go back home to Columbia, I could feel, under the gloss of big-city urbanization, it still had the same country goodness. Then I thought of why Jake and I were trolling these rural roads: Looking for a drug lab in these folks' back yard so we could track down a murderer. The city's deadly tentacles reaching into the rural backwaters. We were truly lost sailors on a blood-red troubled sea.

As I capped the hill I saw the red flashing lights and yellow top of a school bus that had pulled onto the shoulder of the road to pick up a little girl at her mailbox. Her mother, still in her pale teal robe, helped the girl up the first step, then stepped back and, wrapping her arms tightly around herself to keep warm from the morning chill, watched her daughter drift towards the back of the bus and away from her. The mother slowly eased along the side of the bus, as if hesitant to be separated from her daughter.

I pulled up almost even with the front of the bus and stopped, waiting for the bus to move. The bus's flashing red lights were like warning strobes. I watched the bus driver, who was craning his neck to look in a large mirror aimed at his passengers, watching the girl select her seat on the almost empty bus. He glanced back at the highway, pulled the folding side door closed with the lever, and released the clutch. As the bus pulled back on the highway, he turned off the blinking lights. The mother stood still, her hand raised in a goodbye wave, her eyes following the disappearing bus. I accelerated and watched the bus disappear over the hill top to get the two boys.

About three-quarters of a mile later, Jake said, "Slow up, there should be a right turn off onto a little road somewhere along here."

I cut my speed to about thirty miles an hour and watched closely. A dirt road went over a rusted metal culvert, and past a rusted, sagged barbed wire fence that was choked with sassafras trees, vines, and weeds, a thick mass that blocked the view from the road. I glanced over at Jake, and said, "Think this is it?"

He shrugged. "Your guess is good as mine."

"Might as well try it. I got a feeling we're going to see a lot of dead-ends and missed turns, so we might as well get used to it."

I glanced in the mirror and didn't see any cars. I stopped next to the mailbox, and glanced at Jake. "I think we ought to park up the road and walk up."

"Don't look like there's been lots of traffic lately, but what say we pull around the corner up there," he said, pointing ahead of us. I nodded and pulled down the road a bit and parked against the fence.

We got out, and pulled the back of the seat forward, exposing the club cab compartment behind the seat. We got our pistols out of our bags and put them in our waistbands, pulling our shirts down over them. We walked back to the driveway, and turned in and headed toward the house.

The house was a dilapidated wood frame house, with a badly patched roof, partially old weather-stained white shingles covered in places with green rolled roofing, and partially rusted sheet iron. Some of the foundation piers had shifted, causing the house to sag like an old swaybacked horse. There were no cars in the yard, just scattered trash everywhere. A rusted out fifty-five gallon barrel stood near the open side door. It had been used as a burn barrel to get rid of household trash, as was common in rural areas without trash pickup. Behind the house was several sheds about to fall down, the winter-killed weeds and vines almost covering them.

We went up to the house, looking all around for any sign of life. We went up on the rotten porch to the front door, carefully testing each step. I glanced in a dirty window but between the dim daylight and the dirt on the window, couldn't see anything. I knocked on the door a couple of times, but no one answered. I tried the doorknob. The house was unlocked, so I went in, with Jake right behind he, his right hand casually under his shirt tail resting on his pistol. It was obvious why the house wasn't locked tight, as there was nothing usable in the house, just a couple broken chairs and an old rat-eaten yellow and green plaid couch with a brick under one corner. Trash was piled in corners and scattered around on the floor. I glanced at some of the trash to see if there was any addresses or names, but didn't find any. We looked around about ten minutes, which was about nine and a half minutes more than it needed, and left the house and walked back to the truck.

"What do you think?" Jake asked.

"Doesn't look like anyone's been here for weeks if not months. One dry hole."

He nodded. We got in the truck and u-turned on the shoulders of the road and headed back towards the main road and the next location on Keith's map.

We went back by the dairy farm. The unmilked cows were still patiently waiting their turn. I sped up and turned on the radio, hitting the "scan" button to find a strong signal. Neal McCoys' "I Know What Love Is, What's It To You" came on, so I hit the scan button again, and left it on that station.

When we got back to the main road, we turned north and drove a little over thirty miles, went under Interstate Thirty, and through Mount Vernon. We drove on for several more miles, then turned back east again on a small county road. We drove for several miles, then turned again, onto a blacktopped road. It hadn't received much maintenance and I had to swerved frequently to avoid chug holes.

Jake kept glancing at the map and Keith's notes, watching the scattered houses pass as I drove slowly down the road. He finally said, "Your guess is good as mine. What he wrote down was not meant as a guide, just a reminder. You just take a stab, or if necessary, we could ask around."

"Yeah, if we don't see anything that looks out of place, we might have to just stop and ask the neighbors. If there was a lab here, there would have been lots of traffic and lots of strangers. They wouldn't have mixed too well, if they tried to blend at all. The neighbors would have noticed. These people might be 'Jethros' to you and to the drug cookers, but they notice everything." Jake nodded, "Yeah, the country is where you aren't a stranger after the first week, but you're still a new-comer after a decade."

I kept looking for about a half mile, then stopped and turned around. "This road seems to be running out. If this is the right road, I think all the traffic would go out the other way, towards the county road and State 37. Let's go back that way and look again. If nothing springs out at us, we'll just stop and ask around and see if there was a place that's had lots of traffic in recent months."

"About the only way I can see we can hope to make any progress. Like I said before, 'even a blind pig will occasionally find an acorn,' but the there might be a lot of looking between the acorns if we don't get just a little lucky."

We got back to the county road again without seeing anything suspicious. I u-turned again and went back down the black-top road, driving slowly. Jake sat silently, looking at each house carefully, studying each detail for something out of place for the country.

We were easing by a white clapboard house with green shutters set under a big pecan tree when I noticed an old woman leaning against a hoe in a small flower garden beside the house. She was watching us studiously. She was wearing a sun bonnet that concealed her face.

"You know, Jake," I said, "I bet she watches everything that moves along this road and she knows everything and everybody in this are. I bet she's been here since Adam and Eve were dating. Let's chat with her."

"Sounds good to me, I need to stretch a little anyway." He took a final long drag on his cigarette and slowly blew the smoke out and flicked the butt out the window.

I pulled into the next driveway I came to, two dirt ruts leading to a padlocked steel gate. I backed out and headed back to the old woman's house. She hadn't moved, but continued to watch us.

We pulled into her driveway, got out, and walked to the edge of her flower garden. The last of the daffodil blooms were fading. Thin lines of lettuce and turnip greens were already up and growing.

"Good morning," I said.

"Morning," she replied to me and glanced at Jake who nodded.

"Nice place you got here."

"Thank you."

"Been here long?" I asked.

"Since 1959. My husband, Cyril, God rest his soul, and I bought the land from his mama. We built this house ourselves, and just added on as we needed rooms." She turned and pointed with her left hand, the fingers knotted with arthritis. Her right hand clutched the hoe for support. She was wearing a faded blue dress with a floral pattern. She must have been about five foot eight or so when she was young, but her back was bent over with age. She wore loose plastic framed bi-focals that she kept pushing back in place with a knuckle of her left hand. Her dull grey and white hair was cut short and barely wisped from under the sun bonnet. Her skin was wrinkled and sagging and brown from decades of work in the sun. I nodded when she looked back at me.

"Who ya'll looking for?" She asked.

"An old acquaintance left some addresses and locations of where he had been out in this area. We've been trying to find him or at least where he was. But we don't even know when he was last here."

"What kind of directions do you have?"

"Not much. We got off 37, and made the right turns. Then it got us to this road, but no directions where on this road the house is."

"Well, I've lived here almost sixty years and I know everybody on this road, and their kin folks, too," She said, her voice cracking as she spoke. She emphasized the "kin folks" part, her voice rising, as if that statement proved her grasp of the community's comings and goings.

"Any of the houses along here been rented out to strangers that you know of in the last year or so? Maybe with lots of traffic?"

She shook her head."No. The old Carter place was vacant for a couple months, but the Nicholas' girl, what's her name," she paused as she thought, "Oh, yeah, Betty, Betty something, she and her husband rented it. But they wasn't strangers. Lord, no, I've known Betty since she was in diapers."

"Is her husband from around here?"

She shook her head. "No, from up around Paris."

"What does he do for a living?"

"Who?"

"Her husband, Betty's husband."

"He's a welder over at Mount Pleasant at that place where they build them metal gates and cattle fencing."

"We were looking for a place that most likely had lots of traffic in and out. You know any place like that around in the last year?"

She thought for a second, glancing down, then slowly easing her hoe out to scrape a small weed from between two daffodil bulbs. She straightened up and looked back at me, her hand resting again on the hoe handle. "Seems like I heard about a place like that. Give me just a minute to think." She pulled out a kleenex from her breast pocket with her left hand and, leaning the hoe against her shoulder, slowly took off her glasses and cleaned the lenses. She daubed around her eyes, then unfolded the kleenex and wiped her face. The morning had begun to heat up, and like is frequently the case in east Texas in the Spring, the extremely high humidity made the temperature feel hotter than it was. She carefully folded the kleenex and put it back in the pocket.

She looked at me, then at Jake and said, "Well, there was this one place, but it's not on this road."

"Where was it?" I asked.

"You go back up to the main road up there," She pointed in the general direction with a casual wave, "and go south towards Mount Pleasant, and it's the first road south of this'n. You can't miss it."

"Where is it on that road?" Jake asked.

She looked suddenly at him, as if surprised at him speaking. The she looked back at me, and slid her glasses back up on her nose with her knuckle. She thought for a second. "The first one's Myrtle's," she said quietly, almost to herself. "Two, three," she said quietly, as she mentally went down the road. "It's the fourth house, kind of set off from the road. It's brick."

"What makes you think its the one we're talking about?"

"You said strangers around here and lots of cars, in and out, in and out. Myrtle, she lives on the corner of the road, me and Myrtle been friends since before I married my Cyril, we even went to school together at White Chappell school. It was only to the eighth grade, but that's all a lot of us got."

I glanced over at Jake who was rolling his eyes. She paused and I tried to steer her back to the house.

"Lots of people went to the brick house, huh?"

"Heavens, yes. Myrtle said people would be going there at all hours. Said she was woke up more than once at two, three in the morning by someone tearing by the house."

"Did she ever meet the people that lived there?"

"Just onct she said. Said she was at Jackson's store, it's a little gas station and feed store over there at Midway. Said she was in getting a little gas for her car and these two guys come in in this red truck. Said it was real loud. Said she had heard and seen that truck go back and forth to that house several times a day, and onct when she was driving by, it was there. That's how she know'd they lived there."

Jake and I nodded. We were finally getting somewhere and we wanted to keep the spigot open.

"Did she talk with them."

"They pulled in, and had to wait until she got through with the pump. They were talkin' and cussin' pretty bad, she said. Myrtle said she looked at them real hard when they would cuss, but they just kept on cussin'. But she said they looked so mean, she was scared of them living down the road just a piece, until they moved. They had tattoos, and long scraggly hair. Said there was a woman there with them. Even she had a tattoo. Myrtle said she looked older, like she had had done a lot of hard living in her life. Said her skin was tough, and she was so skinny."

Jake and I glanced at each other.

"When did they move?" I asked.

"It's only been a week or so. Said all of a sudden, in mid-month, that's kinda odd cause most people move on the first of the month when the rents up, you know?" She pushed her glasses back into place and glanced at both of us for agreement.

We both nodded.

"Myrtle said a bunch of pick up trucks and one van, like them U-Haul vans, but without any name on it, you know. They all showed up and started loading everything up real sudden like. Myrtle can see the house from her living room window, and she said she just watched 'em work like ants, loading stuff in boxes."

"Did she see what they were loading?"

"There was lots of regular household stuff, you know beds and mattresses and chairs and stuff like that. But she said must have been some professional movers 'cause most of it was packed up in big old cardboard boxes. She said she was never so glad to see anyone up and move in all her born days, and she's had some bad neighbors before. Somethin' odd, though. Myrtle said she never seen any animals over there, but she said the place stunk to high Heaven."

I glanced at Jake who had a trace of a smile, like a dog catching the first scent of a trail.

"Smell?" I prompted.

"Yeah, smelled like ammonia or rotten eggs or something. Myrtle said she had never smelt anything like that. Said you can still smell it all the way over to her house when the wind is right."

"Does Myrtle know where they moved to?"

"No, she was just glad they left."

"Who owns that place?"

"I don't know. You could ask Myrtle, she might know."

"Would you call Myrtle and tell her we'll be over there in a little bit to talk with her?"

"Well, sure. I was going to call her anyhow."

I nodded to her. "Thank you, ma'am. I do appreciate it. We won't keep you from your gardening any longer."

"Oh, I enjoy the company. Don't get much company, and don't visit much except at church, so I always enjoy someone to drop by. Stop by again when you come back by, o.k."

I assured her we would, and Jake and I walked to the truck.

"Sounds like that old blind pig's done pretty good, wouldn't you say?"

Jake nodded. "And they moved the lab in the last few days. Maybe because of Holland's murder."

"I was thinking the same thing. I just hope that that Myrtle woman knows who owns the house so maybe we can stay on the trail."

We got in and drove to Myrtle's house.

CHAPTER
27

WE PULLED INTO Myrtle's driveway in less than five minutes. It was a white frame house. An older tan Chevrolet, so clean it looked like it just came off the showroom floor, was parked in the attached white and blue metal carport. I saw a hand pull the curtain from a window and peek out.

"Looks like we're expected."

We walked to the door and rang the doorbell. It opened immediately. Myrtle, an elderly woman, held the door open about three inches and looked around the edge of the door.

"You the ones that Emma said were asking about the house down the road?"

"Yes, ma'am. If we could have a few minutes of your time."

She paused for a second, thinking about it. "What's your name?" She said hesitantly.

"Noah Starr. I'm a private investigator." I pulled out my card holder and showed her my license.

She took it from my hand and tilted her head back to read the license with her bifocals.

"O.k. But who's he?" she said pointing at Jake.

"This is Jake Brooks. He's helping me with the investigation."

She nodded and stepped to the side of the door, and let us walk in past her.

She pointed towards the living room and slowly led us down the short hall. She walked stiffly, her hands slightly flailing to maintain her balance. When she got to the couch, she backed up and placed her hands on the arm and slowly lowered herself towards the seat, finally dropping the last couple inches as if she had lost her balance. She stuffed a couple pillows behind her. I shuddered to think about her driving anywhere.

"It's a burden getting so old." She said as she continued to arrange the pillows for her comfort. She looked up at Jake and me. "I'm a poor hostess. Do be seated." As I stepped towards a chair, she said, "No, Mr. Starr, come sit by me." She patted the couch seat beside her. "If we're going to visit, it's just so much easier on me if you sit close. I will be able to hear you better."

"Yes, ma'am." I stepped to the couch, and sat just a few inches from her, where she had indicated with her patting hand.

"What do you know about the house down the road with all the traffic?"

"It's like I told Emma, there was always someone coming and going, loud noises."

"What about the stink?"

"It was something terrible. Smelled like a chemical plant. Sometimes stronger, sometimes less, but always there. I don't know how you could make so much stench."

"Do you know who owns the house?"

"Why do you want to know?"

"Well, from what you have told us, we think these people are the ones we're trying to find. And that smell you talked about was from their methamphetamine lab. They were 'cooking,' well it's called 'cooking' but its making methamphetamine, what's called 'speed.'"

She looked at me blankly. It occurred to me that the raciest illegal thing that went on when she was young was maybe making illegal whisky.

"Do you know what methamphetamine or speed is?"

She shook her head slowly.

"O.k. Methamphetamines is a drug similar to what's in some diet pills. It's called speed, among other names. People like your ex-neighbors will go to rural areas and make the speed by mixing a lot of chemicals together and then heating it to have a chemical reaction, basically cooking the mixture. It's like baking a cake. Then they sell the drugs for lots of money. They have to go to rural areas because it smells so bad that the police could easily find them in the city. In the country, they try to get a real isolated place, or move around a lot, to keep from getting caught."

She nodded slowly. "So those mean men I saw were into drugs?"

"Yes, ma'am."

"They could have hurt me."

"I figure they weren't a very big risk to you. They were trying to keep what they thought was a low profile, so I don't think they would have attacked you or anything. They just moved on when they feel any pressure come up." I paused, and decided not to mention Keith. Then I said, "So you can see why we want to track them down?"

"Oh, honey, I sure do." She patted my hand.

"Do you know who owns the house?"

"Sure, it's my nephew, Luke Patterson."

"And where does he live? I would like to talk to him. Maybe he knows where they moved to. Anything."

"Sure, he lives in Winnsboro." She pointed to an end table next to Jake's chair. "Would you hand me the phone book beside you there next to the telephone?"

Jake brought it to her. It was a thin book, not even a half inch thick. I thought of the huge phone books in Dallas. She began to flip through the pages, holding it close to her face.

"Here it is." She kept her finger on it and handed the booklet to me. I jotted down the telephone number and address.

"Thanks. Would you call him and tell him we'd like to stop by and talk with him about his renters?"

"Certainly, honey."

"We'll go over there at the house and look around a little bit if it's o.k. with you, then we'll be going on over to your nephew's."

"I'll call him as soon as you leave and tell him you're on your way."

Jake and I got up, then I helped her to her feet. She escorted us to the door. I turned and shook her hand. "We do appreciate your help, ma'am."

"Oh, you're welcome, honey. Now you be careful. Those men are mean. I'll pray for you." she said, patting my shoulder as we walked out.

I turned toward her and said, "Thanks, we can certainly use all the prayers we can get."

We went to the truck and drove down the road to the empty house.

I parked in front of the house and we went to the door. The door was locked, so we walked around the house, looking in the windows. They had moved in a hurry, leaving papers and trash scattered around the rooms. Out back we found a trash pile that was partially burned. We squatted down and rustled through the unburned papers on the edge of a blackened pile of ashes.

"Here's something," Jake said, handing me a handful of loose tablet pages, the edges singed, and the tops of the pages unevenly torn.

I shuffled through them. There were code or nicknames, and beside them were quantities and large dollar amounts. There were no addresses or dates.

I folded them and put them in my pocket. We kept looking. I found what seemed to be a portion of a broken chemical beaker tube. We didn't find anything else so we gave up and went back to the house. I tried the back door. It was a cheap, plywood interior door. Exposure to the elements had caused the layers of plywood to peel, exposing the door's framing and the interior plywood of the door. I could have easily kicked it in, but didn't figure Mr. Patterson would want to replace it, and I knew I didn't.

"Let's see if there's an unlocked window," I told Jake.

We spread out and began to look at the window locks. I found one and called Jake over. I got out my pocket knife and pried the screen off the window and set it against the house. I pushed up the bottom window sash and pulled myself up on the window ledge and went in. Jake followed me. We were in a bedroom.

In the diffused sunlight from the window, I could see the room was in poor condition. Someone had put a fist through the wall in the hall. A broken piece of sheetrock the size of a coffee table was sagging against the interior of the wall. A large stain circled the light switch, like the tracks of so many animals around a watering hole where countless dirty hands had reached for the switch. The off white paint was discolored from years of heavy abuse. Dents and scuffs lined the walls. A string of stains strung across the far wall where someone had thrown a drink. The once-tan carpet was crushed and trampled down, stained and dirty. The tenants obviously hadn't had a regular cleaning service. If cleanliness is next to Godliness, they were at least consistent.

I went into the hall. "I'll go this way," I said, pointing towards the kitchen. "You check out the bedrooms." He nodded, glanced around the empty bedroom, peeked in the closet, and said, "Clean as a hound's tooth. Next room. How's your search going, Noah." I was almost out of the room, and turned and said, "Kiss my . . ." and walked out of the room, the last word unspoken. Jake laughed behind me as he went to the next room.

I went down the hall to the kitchen, glancing at the trash and empty beer cans along the wall. The kitchen was as run-down as the bedroom. The cabinet doors were ajar. Several of the drawers were partially open where they had been hurriedly emptied. The sink was filled with several chipped jelly glasses and eight or ten beer cans. Several loose plastic baggies were scattered to the right of the sink. The empty box they came in was on the floor together with other trash.

I opened the refrigerator door and stepped back from the stench of warm, rotting food. Several days in a closed hot refrigerator with the electricity off had not improved tenants' food supply, but they obviously didn't eat too high on the hog. Half a package of generic lunch meat was coated with green mold, and an open loaf of bread had a black fuzzy fungus growing on one side. A bottle of catchup and half a jar of mustard were in the refrigerator door. I glanced in the freezer compartment but found nothing but some standing water and an empty plastic ice sack. There was a broken glass in the corner of the floor, where it had been kicked, a silvery trail of glass shards leading from where it had been dropped. A three-legged chair tilted against one wall, a matching leg was by the outside door.

I knew that the cooker would need water and drainage, so I figured the drugs were made either in the kitchen or in bathroom. I squatted down and looked at the kitchen cabinet horizontally trying to see if there was any trace of chemicals. I saw a scattering of powder to one side of the sink. I stood up and looked at the powder and the stains around it. There was a clean spot in the middle of the dusty halo were the cooker had stood. The filter for the end of the kitchen faucet was against the back wall of the counter. I knew that the water supply hose had been attached there, with a drain hose into the sink. I got out a ragged piece of paper off the floor and used it as a scoop to pick up some of the powder, then folded it into a small, tight envelope. I opened one of the baggies and slipped the folded paper into it and put it in my pocket. I put the rest of the baggies in my back pocket.

I didn't see anything else in the kitchen, so I went to the living room. It was as dirty and run-down as the rest of the house. There were three windows in the room, two facing the road. A single window shade remained intact over one of the windows facing the road. The wooden rollers for the other two windows were there, but were the shades had been torn off. Above each window were two nails where I figured sheets or tarps had been hung to keep outsiders passing along the highway from seeing in. The carpet was in the same condition as in the bedroom, except even dirtier, with more stains and several cigarette burns. Patterson lost his shirt renting to these guys. It would take him two years rent just to get the place livable again.

Jake came into the living room. He had a ten millimeter bullet in his hand.

"This is all I found, Noah. There is lots of absolute trash, but I didn't find anything else."

"Where did you find it?"

"In the floor of the other bedroom. Talk about a pigsty. Jeez."

"Come in the kitchen," I said.

He followed me in there, and I showed him where the cooker had been.

"Yep, you were right. They were cooking something here, meth, ice, who knows, but this place was jumping. Seems like they had a lot of traffic through here, too. Figure they were doing any selling out of here? Wouldn't be too smart, though to bring in the heat, or have a casual buyer know where the cooker was."

"That's how I figure it. No, I doubt they were selling here. I figure Myrtle's idea of lots of traffic and ours is two different things. I think they thought they were keeping a low profile, but this rowdiness is just their nature. They cooked it here, then distributed it at their regular places."

Jake nodded. "Anything else here, or do you want to truck over to Patterson's and see if he can shed some light on what's going on, hopefully tell us where they moved to."

"Keith's list is at least current. This was where he got his supplies. And if he knew where it was made, then he was likely involved in making it too.

He was part of this whole drug organization. But that still doesn't tell us who shot him or why."

"Let's keep looking. At least we are on the right track."

I agreed and went to the bedroom and shut the window. The house didn't need any more damage. We went to the front door. It had a spring loaded door knob lock. I unlocked it and after Jake and I went out, re-locked it and slammed the door behind us.

CHAPTER
28

WE DROVE BACK to Winnsboro, and after asking direction at a gas station while I filled up again, we found Patterson's house. It was a brick home in a nice area of town. The yard was neatly kept, with flower beds and trimmed shrubs. It was nothing like his rent house. We went up to the door, and I rang the buzzer. Jake took another long drag on his cigarette, and when the door opened, flipped the butt into the shrubbery.

"Are you Luke Patterson?" I asked the man who opened the door. He was in his sixties, with a grey circle of short cut hair around a large bald spot. He had a large stomach, and very pale skin. He opened the door wide and asked, "Are you the gentlemen Aunt Myrtle called me about?"

"Yes, sir, we are."

He motioned us to come in and we went into the den. The television was on, with several people yelling at each other while the host kept telling them to listen to each other. The audience was hooting and hollering and egging the people on. Patterson looked embarrassed for us having caught him watching such a show and said, "There really isn't much on this time of the day." He turned the t.v. off and sat down and motioned for us to sit down.

"What can I do for ya'll?"

"We just came from your rent house down the road from your aunt's."

He nodded. I figured Myrtle had told him every detail of our conversation.

"We went through the house. Have you seen it since they moved out?"

He shook his head. "No, I was going to get my son and go this weekend and clean it up and re-rent it."

"It's going to take longer than a weekend to get it ready to rent. It's been trashed."

He looked hurt. "They put down a hundred dollar clean up deposit, but they never even came by for it."

"It'll take a lot more than a hundred dollars to fix the damage. Did they tell you they were going to move?"

"No, first thing I knew about it, Myrtle called and said a lot of trucks showed up one day last week. She said they were gone in a couple hours."

"Who rented the place?"

"A man named Robert Ketting."

"Medium height, with greasy hair combed back."

"Yeah, that's him. Don't see many people with hair like that anymore. Do you know him?"

"I've dealt with him before over the years. I met him when I was in the Dallas Police Department. I also found traces of chemicals on the kitchen counter. They had been making drugs at your house out there."

A look of anguish flashed on his face. "This is terrible. I never knew. Really. They just rented the place and paid the rent. I never went there and checked on it. They would just drop the money by here."

"How did they pay, cash or check?"

"Cash. Always cash."

"Did you get references or a previous address?"

"I didn't get references. It's hard to rent out in the country, unless it's somebody that already lives there. But I did get his address." He went to a small table and got a writing tablet with the label RENT HOUSE printed in large, shaky handwriting on the front. He brought it to me. I glanced in. It had a list of the rent payments since 1983. I flipped to the end of the list. Ketting had rented the place in January. He had paid every month's rent, but was late. He had given a Dallas address. I jotted it down.

"Where did you get the address?"

"Off his driver's license."

"Did you meet any of his friends?"

He shook his head. "No, he was with somebody just about every time he came by, but they would stay in the car usually."

"How did you meet him. How did he find out about the place for rent?"

"I put an ad in the local paper, and he called. He seemed pretty nice, but he spoke a little harsh."

"Cussed a lot, huh?"

"Yes, but he wanted the house and I hadn't rented it for about three months, so I figured it was o.k. Plus, he paid regularly."

"Well, that's something."

"Do you know where he moved?"

Patterson shook his head. "All I know about him is in that book," he said, pointing to the tablet. "I think I misjudged him. Drugs?" he said sadly, as if asking if I was really sure his house had been used for drug production.

"Yes, drugs." I said. "But they're gone now, so you'll be o.k." I stood up. "Mr. Patterson, thank you for your time. We'll be going now. If you think of anything else, or they call you, would you contact me. Here's my card."

He looked at the card and put it in the tablet.

"All this trouble just for renting that old house."

We left and got in the truck.

"That was a nice dead end." Jake said.

"Yeah, but we know it's a good list. So what's the next place on the list?"

Jake pulled it out and gave me directions and we headed west of Winnsboro.

We spent the rest of the morning going from one location to another, from one run-down, isolated house to another. The list was getting short, and we hadn't seen anything else helpful. They had been moving the production all over rural east Texas, whether to stay one one step ahead of the law or just to ease their paranoia, I didn't know.

It was almost two thirty when we drove past a house in the country half way back to Dallas. We were tired and bored, and the light kidding humor of the morning had given way to slogging through the list. This was becoming too much like a real job.

The house was a wood frame white house with a dirt driveway that circled around a large oak tree in the front yard. Four cars and two motorcycles cluttered the front yard. I had been slowing up to pull in the driveway, like I had done all afternoon, but when I saw the cars, I just kept driving evenly so as to not attract any attention from a change in engine noise. There were two men sitting in folding lawn chairs near the front door. They watched us casually, as if they were as bored as we had been.

We drove about a half mile past the house, and pulled into a double rutted path leading off the road into a hay meadow. A gate made out of barbed wire supported by fence posts blocked the entrance to the pasture. The post on the end of the wire gate was held in place by two wire loops over the top and bottom of the post.

"That's it. Want to park here and walk back?" I asked.

Jake nodded. "Has to be. Did you recognize any of the vehicles?"

"No, but I was trying to get out of sight without arousing their attention, so I just glanced."

Jake got out and open the gate and shut it behind me after I had driven into the pasture. I stopped and let him get back in, then drove to the back of the pasture and parked where the field circled behind the trees and you couldn't see the truck from the road. The winter pasture grass was thick and dark green so I drove along the edge of the field, where the pine trees had kept the grass short so as not to leave much of a trial. If I drove directly across the field, there would have been two deep, pressed-down furrows in the grass, leaving a trail as obvious as a bleeding elephant in the snow to any and all passing cars.

We got out and leaned against the truck. I drained the last of my Dr Pepper, and crushed the can and tossed it in the bed of the truck.

"I think we ought to hike back there and set up on the house and see what's happening. Then tonight we can decide what we want to do."

"Yeah. That is the place we've been looking for. I'd be surprised if Ketting wasn't in there or around here. But I'm like you. We need to know a little more about what were getting into before we actually barge into the middle of it." He pulled the back of the seat down and pulled out his bag. "You want to just go in there light this afternoon?"

I nodded. "Yeah, we might run into somebody or be seen, and if we are loaded for bear, the word will get out, either to the land owner or the police, or maybe even to Ketting. Just carry your pistol."

He put his pistol under his shirt tail. He slipped a spare clip in his shirt pocket. I got my Berretta and we closed and locked up and headed into the woods towards the house.

CHAPTER

29

It took us about forty-five minutes to find our way back to the house through the forest. Our path was blocked by briars and fallen tree limbs, then it led across a narrow, dry creek bed. The creek bed, carved through the thick east Texas sand over millennia, was five foot deep with steep banks. I picked my way carefully down the bank, and hauled myself up the other side by grabbing hold of a wild muscadine grape vine. Jake chose another way down. Suddenly I heard a commotion and looked behind me as Jake slipped and fell sideways the final couple feet, landing on his butt.

"Damn," he muttered under his breath. He got up and dusted himself off, then pulled out his pistol and made sure it didn't get dirty. He put it back, and pulled his shirt back over it.

"Here, pull yourself up on this," I said quietly, so my voice wouldn't carry to the house. I swung the vine to him. "Bad to be getting so old you can't even hike this little jaunt."

"Screw you," he said as he pulled himself out of the creek bed with the vine. "Ain't that something. I do two combat tours, and now I almost break my leg in a cow pasture."

I slapped him on the back and said, "I think you'll live."

"Let's hook'em, buddy, it's gonna get dark pretty soon."

I turned and continued picking my path towards the house. We came to an opening in the woods, but the dewberry vines and thick new growth pine trees, barely four foot tall, formed a near-impenetrable barrier. We skirted the glade and headed up a small rise. A cool front had blown through, leaving behind little warmth in its wake, as east Texas spring weather often does. But our struggling through the forest and the briars, and the thick stillness in the thicket had me getting hot. Sweat was running down my spine, my shirt wet from the sweat.

Ahead I could see a break in the forest, and slowed down and let

Jake catch up with me. He was breathing heavily. Maybe he ought to quit smoking, but since he was helping me for free and was carrying a pistol, I decided not to mention it to him. We eased forward until we were behind a thicket of sumac bushes and winter-killed elderberry branches. I looked through a space between the dead leaves that still clung to the thin branches. Jake pulled a branch to one side and looked at the house. We had ended up just west of the house. The sunlight was blocked by the trees around us, putting us in the shade, and helping hide us.

The back yard was not a lawn, more of the forest chopped back in a hundred foot circle around the house. Neglect had permitted the forest to ease back toward the house, a wave of new growth scrub trees and shrubs leading the forest's assault on the outpost of humanity. Fortunately for us and for the forest, the humanity that was staying in the house wasn't putting up much of a fight. About the last forty feet of the yard was roughly mowed, as if they had used a tractor and brush hog instead of a lawn mower. As rough as the area was, though, it might have been the only way to keep the forest out of the living room. Of course, the way the place looked, I didn't figure that lawn care was a regular weekend chore.

We watched the house for about forty-five minutes. No other cars came. I recognized a car I had seen at Hank's. One lean man with a sleeveless shirt and tattoos on his neck and arms came out the back door and relieved himself against a shrub, then zipped up, and went back inside. The two men in the front yard finished the beers they were drinking. One of them went inside and got a couple more and returned and sat down and handed one to the other guy. They laughed and talked, their voices rising and falling. I couldn't make out what they were saying but they seemed to be having a good time killing the afternoon.

The windows were covered by what appeared to be bed sheets, dingy white and hanging loosely, not neat pleats like window curtains. There were no blinds or other window coverings, and from my vantage point, I could see glimpses into the rooms around the edge of the sheets.

About four o'clock, three men came out and started getting in a blue Toyota with a cracked windshield. The front yard guards yelled at them good-naturedly and waved to them, and they left. The guards leaned back in their lawn chairs and talked more.

After about another thirty slow minutes, a white Cadillac with three occupants drove up the road. As the car slowed down, the two men on the porch sat their drinks down and stood up. The man on the left reached his hand behind his back and I followed his movement and saw his gun. The other guy backed slowly to the door, and called over his shoulder to the house. The door opened up and Ketting came out, followed by two more men who held their pistols by their legs. The two men fanned out from the door.

The Cadillac pulled into the dirt driveway and parked by the door. The driver killed the engine. Everything froze for a second, Ketting's men waiting for the people in the car to act. Then the three men slowly got out. The driver and the back seat man were bigger and were wearing blue jeans. The front seat passenger was wearing tan slacks and an oxford shirt. He spoke to Ketting, who walked to him and they shook hands. Ketting motioned them inside. The oxford shirt man spoke to the back seat passenger who reached back in the car for a brief case, and then everyone but the two guards went inside. The guards sat back down but didn't talk. They watched the house and the road, as if expecting trouble. Every few minutes one of the men would walk to the road and look in the direction the Toyota had gone. A black pick-up passed and as soon as they heard it, both men stood up and watched it pass. I saw a couple bales of hay in the back and figured it was a farmer going to check on his cattle. The men didn't sit until the truck was out of sight.

Through a gap in the window sheet, I watched several people come into a back room. I crouched behind the brush and motioned Jake over to me. He jogged over, bent slightly to stay below the brush line.

"I'm thinking about going to that window and see what's going on."

He nodded. "We've been sitting here for over an hour. Wouldn't hurt to get a closer gander at what's happening."

I pointed towards the back of the house. "I think I can stay behind brush until I'm almost to the house."

He nodded and I moved around the brush and through the low growth, stooping over and walking quietly. Jake followed me. When I got to the last of the tall bushes, Jake motioned that he would stay there. He had drawn his pistol while I was running towards the house. I listened carefully and then jogged to the corner of the house. I edged along the house to the window through which I had seen the people. I glanced in through hole in the sheet.

Ketting and two of his men were talking with the three new arrivals.

"It's good stuff, man," Ketting was saying to the man in the oxford shirt, who was holding up a large plastic baggie of beige powder. "Keep you flying all day. Ed's really cooked up some good meth this week." He motioned towards a guy holding another large baggie, then pointed to a folding card table.

The man with the baggie put it on the table. Ketting told the man with the brief case to put it on the table beside the baggie. The guy in the oxford shirt pulled up a chair, and he and Ketting sat down. The buyer opened his briefcase and took out a box the size of a shoe box that was covered in black cloth, like a band instrument box. He unclasped the lid and opened the box. He took out a set of scales and started weighing the speed. As he measured it, he put the weighed speed into his own large baggies. He and Ketting kept talking about the quality of the drugs, and Ketting mentioned that he had a large shipment of cocaine coming in the next couple days. They discussed prices of various drugs and made small talk. After a few minutes, Ketting asked someone to get him a beer. He asked the other man if he wanted a beer and when he said yes, asked the man to go get them both a beer. A man left and returned with two cans of Budweiser. They both opened their beers and drank, then returned to weighing the speed and talking. When Ketting's baggies were empty and all the drugs had been weighed, the man in the oxford shirt put his large baggies of speed into his brief case. Then he brushed off the scales and put them back in the box, and closed the lid and put the box in the briefcase. Then he pulled a thick white envelope from the briefcase.

"Nineteen thousand dollars, right?"

Ketting nodded and watched the man count a pile of hundred dollar bills. "Love good old Ben Franklin," Ketting said, as he pulled the pile of money towards himself. He started counting it into another pile. "That's it," he said and stood up. He reached in his back left pocket and pulled out a large black billfold on a chain that was attached to his belt. The billfold looked like the ones delivery people tote to carry their money and receipts in. He unzipped the billfold and holding it under his arm, stacked and straightened the bills. Then he put them in the billfold and zipped it up. He put it back in his back pocket. Keeting and the buyer shook hands and, picking up their beers, everyone all went out of the room and towards the front of the house.

I motioned to Jake I was heading back and quickly dashed to the trees. We moved quickly through the underbrush and were looking through the limbs at the edge of the rough-hewn yard when everyone came out of the house. The three men got in the car. The oxford shirt man rolled down his window and told Ketting he enjoyed doing business with him. Ketting said it was mutual. The car pulled onto the road and headed back south towards Interstate 20, and everyone but the guards went back inside. Jake and I waited about ten more minutes. Nothing else happened. I motioned towards the forest and we left.

When we got out of hearing range, Jake said quietly, "What now?"

"I think we ought to get our fire power and go talk with whoever wants to chat back there." I paused, "This could get sticky."

"Yep, that's why I came. To keep you from getting your ass shot off."

"I'll try to return the favor."

"You do that. You think anybody's gonna talk with us?"

"We'll know more than we do now no matter what happens. Travis with the Dallas P.D. . . . "

"Yeah, I know him," Jake interrupted.

"He said that Ketting and Keith were together in drugs. Of course I knew Keith was heavily involved in drugs from what I found in his apartment. I'll be frank, though, I don't think it'll do any good to try to strong arm Ketting, though. He's tough as a boot. He won't rattle just because we ask him nicely."

"Besides, he's with his gang and if he comes off soft, they might decide they need a tougher leader, and since there isn't a retirement plan in the Aryan Brotherhood, they would be apt to cap him. Hardly incentive to talk with us."

I agreed. "I think we'll just sit outside until he leaves. I figure he stays in Dallas, that's where the business is. He might have just been down to make that deal. Then, when he leaves, we'll just be-bop in and see if we can get some feed back from the others."

When we got to the truck, Jake and I started getting ready for the return engagement. I took the pistol out of my belt and laid it on the seat. I put on my cameo gear, then the hunting vest and checked the pistol clips. I put on the holster and slipped the pistol in it.

I looked over at Jake and he had on an open camouflage army issue field jacket. Underneath the coat, I could see his ammo belt and his Glock in its holster. A military-looking knife was in the scabbard next to the gun. He was smoking a Camel, holding it in the side of his mouth, while he stuffed banana clips in his jacket pockets. He got his rifle out of its carrying box and slipped a clip in until there was a metallic click. Then he jacked the action once to load the first cartridge. He slung it under his arm. He took a long final drag of the cigarette, then dropped the smouldering butt at his feet and stepped on it. He lit another cigarette, then looked at me and asked, "Think we'll be out there long? Figured I would carry the smaller whisky bottle if we're going to be there all night."

"Your guess is as good as mine. Whenever we think it's the right time, we'll roll in."

He nodded. He got the smaller bottle and put it in the jacket's breast pocket. "Ready?"

"As I'll ever be."

I got out the shotgun and a flashlight from the glove box. I locked the truck and we headed back into the forest.

It was after five when we got back to the house. We settled in behind the same bushes and waited. At dusk, one man left in a car. He was gone about an hour and a half, and returned with two take-out pizzas and two cases of beer. Jake and I glanced at each other. It was going to be a long night for those not invited to the party. Jake got out his bottle and took a long swig and offered it to me. I shook my head slightly and watched the house.

They turned on some music and the party got loud as they drank. At about midnight, Jake told me to call when I was ready for him to relieve me when I got tired. He settled against a tree and cat-napped.

I woke him about three as the party began to quiet down. The music was still loud, but the voices were quieter. By four the place was quiet. Seemed to be only one man awake. He must have drawn the short straw and got to be the designated night guard. He kept pacing around the house, pulling back the window sheets and looking out into the darkness, a dark shadow against the interior lights. I thought about trying to sneak up and take another look, but figured I would have to use a flashlight to keep from breaking my leg, so I decided not to.

About five o'clock I took a small nap and let Jake watch. He was still sipping his whiskey and didn't seem to mind. Sleeping against a tree is an acquired art, one which I didn't have. I wrapped my jacket tightly around me and stuck my hands in my pockets to try to ward off the early morning chill. I tried to sleep but every time I would begin to doze off, my head would sag, then I would jerk it back. By six, I had all the tree sleeping I wanted. It was for the birds. I went back to watching the house. Jake was sitting as still as a stone gargoyle.

"Anything happen?"

"Same guy keeps making his rounds. Other than that, no."

When the sun came up, there was a changing of the guard and a taller man began making the rounds. He even went outside and looked around once. At eight thirty, Ketting and another guy came out and got in a car and left. He must have had important business in Dallas early to be up that early after that beer party.

We waited thirty minutes to see if he would come back. When he didn't, we moved in.

CHAPTER
30

WE GOT OUR guns ready. I slid the Beretta action back and slowly released it, sliding a shell into the chamber and put on the safety. I partially opened the ejection chamber of the shotgun and made sure there was a shell in the chamber. I glanced over and Jake was doing the same thing with his Glock and rifle. He nodded, and we headed towards the house, going slowly to quietly and carefully pick our way through the underbrush to get to the house undetected. We went around the house and looked in the windows, but didn't see the guard. We waited by the back door listening for movement. It was quiet. I opened the sagging screen door slowly so the old hinges or the door spring would not make any sound. I turned the door knob on the wooden door. It was unlocked. I glanced back at Jake. He was holding his rifle lightly pointing just to my left. He nodded and I opened the door and went in.

The kitchen was simple like most farm house kitchens of the forties and fifties. But the stench almost knocked us out of the room. The dining table was covered in cardboard take-out pizza boxes and scraps of uneaten pizza and crust. Beer cans were piled on the table and had fallen on the floor. Three chairs that matched the broken one at Patterson's house and two aluminum folding lawn chairs were scattered around the table. A black plastic trash sack leaned in the corner. It had flopped over and paper towels and cans had fallen out of the trash sack and onto the floor.

One end of the kitchen counter was covered with trash and beer cans. On the other end was a large plastic vat the size of a beer keg. A water hose ran from the kitchen faucet to the vat. A drain hose emptied into the sink. They were still cooking speed.

We went into the hall and glanced in the empty bathroom. Then we looked in the open door of the bedroom on the right. Two men were sleeping in their camp cots. One man, sleeping on his back, was snoring loudly. The other man, one of the guards from the day before, was turned over to towards the wall. Several beer cans lay on the floor. A half-empty Tequila bottle was at the head of his bed next to a blue steel revolver. The stench of beer and sweat and body odor was nauseating.

We looked in the bedroom across the hall. One man was asleep on a mattress on the floor with a dirty blanket over him. I saw a shotgun and a pistol in a holster against the wall next to him. Clothes were piled beside the bed. I looked carefully in the dim light that diffused through the sheet curtain and realized there was someone with him. I raised two fingers and Jake nodded. We went down the hall to the living room. A dirty red and blue plaid couch, stained by countless spills and unwashed men was under the window. The cushions were not straight and the floor skirt was half torn off and kicked under the couch. There were two cloth recliners, one yellow and one green corduroy, and three green and white folding aluminum lawn chairs. Two rickety end tables and a coffee table completed the decor. There were no pictures, except a magazine picture of a large breasted naked woman with her legs spread taped to the wall with duct tape.

The guard was sitting in a recliner, flipping through a men's magazine. His gun was on the end table beside him. Several more magazines were on the coffee table covered by the cans and liquor bottles from the previous night. He was tired from the party and his long night watch and was not alert. I eased forward and nudged my shotgun barrel against his neck. He jerked his head around and said "What the . . ." and saw the black void of the twelve gauge barrel aimed at his face. I put my finger to my lips to signal him to be quiet. His face froze, his eyes wide open. The magazine was frozen in his hands. He looked from me to Jake and back to me.

I motioned him to rise and he laid the magazine on the end table. He paused a second with his eyes on the pistol. I shook my head, then nudged him again with the shotgun and he got up. Jake reached over and got the pistol and put it in his jacket pocket.

We headed down the hall with him in the lead with me behind him on his right and Jake trailing and on the left side of the hall. I signaled the guard to stop when he got past the bedroom doors. Jake took the bedroom on our left with the two men, I took the other one.

We positioned ourselves at the door so we could see the guard and the people in our rooms. I glanced at Jake and he nodded.

"Everybody up. Rise and shine." I yelled.

They cursed us, then when the woman rose to see who was waking them up, she screamed and everyone jumped to their feet. One of the men in Jake's room knocked over his cot.

"Stand up," Jake snapped.

The man in my room leaped to his feet, knocking the covers off into a pile at the foot of the mattress. The naked woman started standing up then realized she was naked and lunged for the blanket.

"Freeze, honey," I said. She froze in a half crouch, then put her hands over her breasts.

I flipped on the light switch and motioned them to a clean corner of the room. I motioned to the pile of clothes beside the bed. "These your clothes," I asked them. They nodded. I kneeled on one knee and quickly patted the clothes for a weapon. I kicked them to them. His arms were covered with tattoos and he had a Harley Davidson tattoo covering his chest. She had a rose tattooed over one breast and a flower bracelet around her ankle. They got dressed quickly.

I half backed out of the room. "Come this way, slowly." I said. They walked towards me with their hands raised, their eyes on the shotgun. I backed out into the hall, watching them, and kept the guard in the corner of my eye. "O.k." I said to Jake, "I've got mine out."

I motioned them down the hall about two feet and said, "Put your hands against the wall."

"Is this a raid?" asked the guy with the woman. "Where's your search warrant. I'm going to have your badge for this. I know my rights." He seemed to have a lot more courage with his pants on.

"Surprise, punk," I said, emphasizing the name, "I don't got no stinking badge," I said in a bad Mexican accent.

"Who the hell are you then," he said, half turning towards me.

I motioned him to put his hands back on the wall. He did.

"I just wanted to talk with you."

"Screw you." He snapped.

I tapped his head lightly with the barrel of the shotgun.

"Ohh. That hurt man."

"Then shut up until I ask you a question."

Jake backed out with his two men. They had evidently slept in their clothes. He lined them up besides the other people.

"Watch them for me, Noah, while I pat them down. You know the position." They leaned forward, their hands against the wall.

I positioned myself and watched Jake as he patted down everyone.

When he started to pat down the woman, she said, "Don't touch me."

"Why not, everyone else has. Shut up." He quickly patted her down and moved to the man who had been with her. "They're clean."

"Down the hall to the kitchen," I said, motioning with the shotgun. They filed down the hall and lined up against the back wall.

Jake pulled over a chair and rested one foot in it. He lit a cigarette and took a long drag then exhaled and took another drag.

The people watched us, looking from me to Jake and back to me. Two of the men had been in Hank's with Ketting.

"Let's get some rules straight first off." I said. "I want some answers. You'll give them to me. Give me the information and nobody will get hurt. Otherwise. . ."

"What do you want? Take the drugs." Said the tattooed man I had pulled out of the bedroom.

"I don't want the drugs. I want answers. Weren't you listening?"

He nodded but he did not seem to comprehend that anyone would not want to get the drugs if they had the chance.

I pointed my shotgun at the two on the end that I had seen at Hank's. "You two, you know Keith Holland?"

One shook his head; the other glanced over at him, then shook his head. I rammed my shotgun barrel hard into his solar plexus. He collapsed against the counter, and slid to the floor, his flailing right hand catching a couple empty beer cans and drug them on top of him. He lay coiled on the floor, trying to gasp.

The others started to jump towards me when I hit him, but at the first sign of movement, Jake stiffened, his rifled aimed chest high. They froze, then stepped back against the wall.

I looked at the other man from Hank's. "I asked you a question. Next time I ask a question, I want the truth. And I'm going to get the truth. You understand?"

He stared at me, his face hard but his eyes glancing at the gasping man on the floor.

"You understand, punk?" I yelled.

"Yeah, I understand." He said flatly.

"Do you know Keith Holland?"

"Never heard of him." he said with a faint smile.

I moved the shotgun just to his right and pulled the trigger. The explosion roared through the room, the flash from the shotgun reaching past him. The buckshot tore through the drug vat, knocking it into the wall. The vat ricochetted off the wall and rolled and fell to the floor. The lid came off and the liquid spewed across the floor. The shot tore a ragged four inch circle through the wall. Outside sunshine stabbed through the hole, glistening in the liquid spreading across the floor. The empty red shotgun shell casing bounced across the floor at the feet of the druggies. The shotgun blast reverberated in the small room, half-deafening everyone.

The man grabbed his arm and fell against the wall into a crouch, and screamed, "God damn, man, you shot me." Blood was oozing from a small hole in his forearm where a stray pellet had caught him. His skin was pink streaked with black debris from the burn of the shotgun blast.

The others were getting flighty, their wide eyes darting around looking for somewhere to run and hide, like trapped deer. The smoke from the shotgun blast filled the room, and drifted in the corners of the room. The woman began crying, slowly collapsing and folding over, her face hidden in her cupped hands.

I looked at the wounded man again. "Should have answered right. You were there at Hank's when I came in. Remember?" I paused as he looked at his arm, his attention focused on his pain. His face was pinched and pale. "Remember?" I yelled.

He glanced up at me, trying to focus on me then looking back at his arm. He nodded slightly.

"Speak up, before I aim a little closer next time. Remember Hank's Place?" My voice was loud and echoed in the room, the silence when I wasn't speaking was palpable after the shot gun blast.

"Welcome back," I said to him. "You remember Hank's, too."

"Yeah."

"You remember a guy that came there a lot. Keith Holland?"

They both nodded.

"Out loud."

"Yeah," they said together.

I looked at the one I had hit. "Tell me what you know about Keith Holland."

He looked at me blankly.

"Speak up." I paused. "Now."

"I don't know much. Met him there a couple times."

"He knows Ketting, right?"

"I suppose so."

"Don't give me any trouble. I'm getting impatient," I screamed.

He cowered back. "Yeah, yeah, they knew each other."

"They were in business together, weren't they?"

"Yeah, they did a little business, sure."

"Drugs?"

"What drugs?" He said blankly.

"What drugs?" I yelled. I kicked the vat against the wall and it reverberated in the room as it rolled and crashed against the wall. "We're up to our ass in this crap you're cooking here and you say 'what drugs?' I ought to shoot your sorry ass right now and then ask someone who won't bullshit me."

He shrank slightly with each outburst.

"O.k., man. Keep cool. Yeah, yeah, they were in business together. Coke, speed, ice. Pretty much anything."

"Shut up," the tattooed man spat at him.

I hit him in the face with the shotgun, knocking him against the woman who screamed and started wailing "Oh, God. Oh, God. Oh, God."

The man screamed in pain and grabbed his mouth. Blood ran down his arm. "Damn, man. Damn." He mumbled. He stumbled against the wall, then sat weakly on the edge of the window sill.

"If I want your input, I'll ask for it, o.k." I said. He nodded, not looking up at me. The woman had shrunk against the window and was partially turned toward the window, as if in an attempt to shut me out.

I turned back to the other man. "Was Keith involved in this drug manufacturing operation?"

"I don't know, man. Really. I don't know about that."

"Was he ever where you were cooking?"

"I don't cook, man." He pointed at the tattooed man. "He's the cooker. I just stand guard."

"O.k. Was Keith ever out where the drugs were made?"

He nodded.

"Speak up."

"Yeah, he came out sometimes with Bob."

"Bob Ketting?"

"Yeah."

"You know Holland was killed, right?"

"Yeah, you said it at the bar."

"You knew it before then, didn't you?"

"I had heard, yeah."

"Who from?"

"Just talk at Hank's. You know, they were talking about Holland."

"What did they say?"

"Not much. Just that he had been shot."

"Any idea who shot him?"

He shook his head. "No one seemed to know. It was a shock to all of us. Keith was an stand-up guy. No one could figure out why anyone would cap him." He continued to slightly shake his head as if he was still pondering the eternal injustice of a stand-up guy like Keith getting shot on the street.

"Did Ketting have anything to do with Keith's murder?"

"Naw, man. They were close. Bob was really upset about Keith's murder and I heard he spent several days looking into it hisself."

"Did Ketting have any idea who could have. . . " I caught the tattooed man glance over my shoulder and down the hall, a look of relief in his eyes. I half-spun when the first shot rang down the hall, catching Jake in the right shoulder. Blood splattered into the face of the man I had been talking to. The second shot missed Jake and caught the man in the throat, knocking him against the wall, his hands clutching at his throat, his scream turning into a gurgle as he slid down the wall, the blood on the back of his neck smearing down the wall. He lunged and twisted like a headless chicken, trying to tear himself away from the pain. Everyone was screaming and the other two men leaped at me, knocking me to the side. I slid in the liquid on the floor and sprawled face down.

I rolled up on my knee and shot down the hall at Ketting and another man as they crouched, their pistols targeting me. The shotgun blast was off to the left and tore a long gash in the sheetrock, throwing sheetrock down the hall. The other guy cut loose with four more shots so close together it almost sounded like one echoing shot. His aim was high, and I heard a scream behind me.

I spun around with the shotgun aimed waist high in time to see the man with the tattoos hurtle backwards through the window, his legs getting caught in the window glass. The woman was screaming, and the guard and the man I had clipped with the first shot were yelling.

The guard jumped toward me, but Jake's Glock spat several bullets. Jake was holding the pistol with his left hand, his right arm, scarlet with blood pouring from a ragged hole in his shoulder. Jake's first bullet hit the man like a baseball bat, knocking him back against the wall and tearing a hole the size of a thumb in his chest. The second shot caught him in the neck. The third shot took off part of his cheek. He fell to the floor and quivered, his blood gushing across the floor. The woman flung herself across the room into the far corner. She cowered in the corner, covering her head with her hands, speckled with blood that had splattered on her.

The other man ran out the door and into the underbrush, darting left and right. Jake shot twice at him but missed.

We spun back as Ketting ducked into the bathroom. The other man stood crouched in the hall and started emptying his gun at us, the bullets hitting the wall and glass behind me. I pulled the trigger on the shotgun but nothing happened. Enpty. I dropped it and grabbed the Beretta and started shooting down the hall. I missed the first shot, but the second shot caught him in the thigh, knocking his leg out from under him. As he fell, his last shot caught me in the left side. I spun around, slipping in the blood. I tried to get my breath. My side felt like a hot poker had been shoved through me. I tried to tear my mind from the pain and rolled onto my right side and slid my knees under me and sat up, bracing myself with my two hands. The movement tore the breath from me.

I glanced down the hall and the man was screaming, holding his leg. I could see the blood spurting from the wound. I had hit an artery. Ketting stuck his head from the bathroom and shot two quick shots at me. One was wide, but the second clipped my left arm. I fell back against the wall and snapped off two quick shots. Jake staggered towards the bathroom his gun at the ready. Ketting must have heard the footsteps and stuck his gun out around the door jam and cut loose with three more shots. Jake started shooting at the edge of the door and traced a line of holes through the thin sheet rock across the bathroom. Ketting's gun fell to the floor and I heard him crash into the metal bathtub.

The house was still, but my blood was pounding and my ears were ringing from the echoing roar of the guns that had blasted through those small rooms been fired in the house. Gun smoke filled the rooms, wafting in the eddying breezes coming through the broken windows.

The woman was still sobbing in the corner. I glanced at Jake. He was holding his right shoulder, and reeling against the walls as he went to check on Ketting and the man in the hall. There was no sound from either one. Jake came back to me, his gun in his belt. He reeled against the kitchen counter, and sagged to the floor. He glanced over at me.

"Hey, hotshot. I thought you were supposed to keep me from getting shot." He grimaced with pain. His jacket and pants were covered with his blood. "Got a band-aid, Noah?"

I glanced around the room. A thick cloud of smoke filled the room. Blood was splattered all over the walls. Tattoo's feet still stuck through the window.

I pulled myself to my feet and went to the bathroom. I was weak on my feet, and every step sent hot knives through my bleeding side. Ketting was arced in the tub, his head in the bottom of the tub, his feet in the floor. His blood was splashed across the wall of the room. Large holes, where the bullets had hit, lined the walls. I found three old bath towels in the bathroom cabinet and brought them back to Jake.

I kneeled down in front of him.

He was pale from loss of blood, but he smiled thinly at me. "Medic," he whispered.

I tore the towels into strips, laying them across my legs. I stuffed a wad of cloth in the wound in his shoulder. He sucked in sharply from the pain. I leaned him forward and stuffed another wad of towel in the wound in the back. I wrapped a strip of towel around him and tied it to hold the two cloths in place.

"Thanks, buddy," he said quietly.

I wrapped some towels around my side and tied them tightly.

I pulled my cell phone out of my shirt pocket and dialed "911." When the operator answered, I asked for the Sheriff and two ambulances. I gave them directions to the house and put the phone back in my pocket, my bloody hand print crimson on the phone.

I leaned against the wall and listened to the woman whimper, and we waited.

CHAPTER
31

I HEARD A siren growing louder as it approached, and then another distant siren joined the chorus. The first car arrived in less than five minutes. I leaned against the wall, my hand on Jake's front bandage, trying to apply pressure. His blood puddled under us, a red lake trying to pull him under. His breathing was growing shallow.

"Hang on, Jake. We're almost out of here."

His eyes flickered and he looked up at me. "Noah?"

"Yeah, buddy?"

His eyes flickered and closed again.

I caught a glimpse of a uniformed man go past the window, sidling towards the kitchen door.

"Get a medic in here now," I yelled.

He kicked open the door. It swung back violently, then bounced off the leg of Tattoo, hanging out the window. He shoved it open again and stepped into the room in a slightly crouched stance, holding his gun in both hands, and aiming it in an arc as he surveyed the destruction of the room. He glanced at the woman, then, ignoring her, turned his attention to Jake and me.

"Slide the gun over here," he snapped.

I slid it across the floor.

He squatted down and quickly checked Jake's and my wounds. Satisfied that neither of us would escape if he moved into the house, he started towards the body in the hall. I heard someone kick in the front door. I heard the crackle of radio transmissions, and one of the officers talking. In a second the officer came back. Behind him the other officer was looking at the drug vat. Neither man touched anything.

An engine gunned outside the kitchen, and then brakes squealed. Doors creaked, and then two men in pea green uniforms rolled a stretcher into the kitchen. They slid me aside and rolled the stretcher beside Jake. They quickly glanced over his wounds and my bandages. One of the sheriff's deputies helped lift Jake on the stretcher.

"Will he be o.k.?" I asked the nearest medic.

"Yeah, sure. Don't worry. We got him now." He said, never looking at me or slowing his work on Jake. They rolled him out to the ambulance.

A deputy leaned over close to me and said, "They're taking him to the hospital. They'll get you next." He patted me on the shoulder. "Hang on."

As Jake's ambulance pulled out, its siren already full volume, another ambulance rolled into its place, and the drill began again, with me the center of attention. The same officer walked along side of my stretcher. He looked down at me and said, "I'll ride with you to the hospital. I need to ask you some questions."

I nodded.

"Any problem me riding along, Ed," he asked one of the medics.

"No, just don't get in the way."

They rolled my stretcher to the ambulance, trying to soften the unevenness, but their rush to load me took precedence. Every bounce shot fire into my side, as waves of nausea cascaded through me. I must have groaned, because the man at my head apologized.

The ambulance doors slammed behind me. As the ambulance rocked across the yard and hit the highway, it sped up. Its siren grew louder, but then seemed to fade. I felt the ambulance darkening. The medic connected me to an intravenous tube, the fluid bag swinging above me. He raised my eyelids and glanced at my pupils, then quickly checked my vital signs. He called the hospital on the radio, and gave them numbers and then opened a case and filled a syringe.

He rubbed an alcohol pad on my arm and said, "This is going to sting."

He gave me the shot. The deputy and the medic leaned over me.

I blinked twice. Each time, they seemed farther away, shrinking in the distance.

When I awoke, Alice was sitting beside my hospital bed. She was holding my right hand in hers, her other hand stroking my forearm. When I glanced at her, she was watching the slow drip of the i.v. I turned my head slightly, and my movement caught her eye. She stood up and leaned over me.

"Noah, how do you feel, Baby." Her hands caressed my cheek and face.

I nodded. "How's Jake," I whispered.

"He's fine. He's resting. He'll be o.k." Her eyes searched my face for a reaction.

I nodded again. I started to say something but lost the train of thought. I looked into her eyes and said, "I love you, Babes."

She tried to smile, but a tear rolled down her face. She wiped it away with her palm and tried to daub her eyes. Her face tightened as she tried to smile. "I love you, too."

I faded again, feeling warm and secure.

CHAPTER

32

WHEN I AWOKE, the room was dark. I was momentarily lost, and wondered where I was and how I got there. Then I moved slightly and the pain in my side reminded me. I glanced towards the door that was ajar, sending the thinnest sliver of light against the far wall. In the dim light, I could see Alice curled in a chair near the head of the bed. She had a blanket pulled up to her neck. Her head was resting precariously on a pillow that had almost slipped off the back of the chair. I listened carefully to her low breathing. I thought how lovely she was, and wondered how long she had been there. I wondered what time it was. I slowly raised my left arm, but the tug of the i.v. tubes kept me from seeing my wrist. I lay still and dozed again.

I felt a hand on my left arm and awoke to see a nurse checking my I.V. She gave me a killer smile, her short blond hair a halo. "How are you feeling?" She asked.

"Fine," I said.

"Do you need anything?"

I shook my head.

"Let me get the doctor." She said. As she went out the door, she turned and said, "Don't go away now."

She had left the door half open, and the room seemed bright.

Alice had awakened and was standing beside the bed. She looked tired and drawn, her face lined with worry. I suddenly realized that this adventure had been more stressful for her than for me.

"I'm sorry, Babe," I said. I touched her face with my hand, stroking down her neck, and resting my hand on her shoulder. I pulled her gently to me and kissed her lips. My right hand circled the nape of her neck, my fingers intertwined with her hair. She hugged my shoulders. I heard her gasp slightly and realized she was crying. A tear fell on my cheek and ran down my face. She nuzzled against my neck and wept. "I'm sorry, Babes,"

I said again, my voice hoarse. I lifted my left arm slowly and laid it across her back, my right hand continuing to stroke her hair. She sobbed again.

The lights brightened and Alice pulled away and turned towards the wall. Her face was red. Her mascara had run down her face and she grabbed several tissues with her left hand and wiped her eyes. Her right hand clutched mine.

I glanced at the approaching doctor and the deputy sheriff and a man in a suit.

I looked back at Alice, and raised her hand to my lips and kissed it. I rested our locked hands on my chest. She glanced back at me, her eyes brimming with tears. I winked at her and whispered, "I love you, Alice." She smiled wanly and wiped her eyes again and stepped over beside me to face the approaching three men. Our right hands rested on my chest, but her left hand moved beside my head and stroked my hair. We awaited the verdict.

"Mr. Starr," the doctor began, then paused. "How are you feeling?"

"Fine," I said, "Considering."

He nodded. "You will be fine," he said. You can be released by tomorrow, though you will be very sore for several weeks. And you will be a little weak. You lost quite a bit of blood. But you'll be o.k." He paused again. "Do you have any questions?"

"What about Jake, the man I came in with?"

"He's fine. You can go visit him tomorrow. It would do you good to be up and around. And do him good to have visitors." He paused. "If you don't have any other questions, I'll leave you with these gentlemen. If you get tired, or need a shot, just call the nurses desk by pushing that button by your head and they'll give you a sedative. I'll see you tomorrow." He turned and left.

I looked at the two men. The man in the suit reached into his suit pocket and took out a badge and showed it in my direction. I could not see what it was in the dim light but nodded anyway.

"Mr. Starr, I'm Detective Kyles." He gestured over his shoulder. "This is Deputy Allen. He was at the scene when they picked you up. This might not be a good time for you," he gestured towards the i.v., "But we need to talk now to decide what's our next step."

I nodded.

"Your friend told us to call Captain Travis in Dallas. Travis filled in some holes we had in trying to figure out what happened out there. When we told him one of the deceased was Robert Ketting was there, he was able to answer some of our questions." He paused. "Of course, there are four bodies and a drug lab. We know it wasn't your lab. It was Ketting's or his friends. But we still have four dead men. The papers have gone wild about this, and the Sheriff's caught in the middle. He ran on a campaign slogan of 'stopping crime' and now there's four deaths and drug lab in his county. The local paper's hounding him and the District Attorney about who will be charged with what. And you and your friend, and that drug-addled woman we found at the scene are the only ones alive who can be charged. So I need some answers."

I nodded again.

He took out a small card and read me my Miranda warnings that anything I said could be used against me, and that I had a right to an attorney, and that they would appoint an attorney if I couldn't afford one. As they went down the list, Alice's grip on my hand tightened.

When they finished, I said, "I understand. Go ahead and ask me what you need. But keep it short tonight, o.k.?"

"O.k." He said. "Tell me what happened."

I told them about Keith's murder, then explained about tracking down the drug lab from Keith's list, and how we went into the house to question them. I explained about the shootings. When I got through, the two officers were nodding.

"That fits in with what Travis said you were doing. We got a problem, though. The woman there told a very different story. She said ya'll were there trying to steal the drugs and Ketting was trying to save them from your threats to kill them."

Alice's grip tightened again, but she didn't waver.

"Have you caught the guy that ran out the back door?"

"Kinda tall, blue flannel shirt, jeans?"

I thought for a second. "Yeah, that's him. Have you talked with him?"

"I haven't yet, though, I planned to. We picked him up walking down the highway about two miles away. We knew he wasn't local, and from what we had learned out where you were at, we were keeping our eyes out for anything or anyone unusual. We stopped him and questioned him, but he didn't have any i.d. We arrested him for failure to i.d. It's a bullshit charge, but it got him in so we could talk with him later. I was going to see him this morning to see how he figured into this."

"Compare his story with hers."

He nodded. "From what Travis said about you, and, by the way, I've even checked out Travis 'cause I didn't know him either, but from what he said, you're o.k. about the drugs. It's the shootings I'm having trouble with. You broke into the house. That's a second degree felony, two to twenty years. Murder in commission of a burglary is a capital charge, with the death penalty. This county is too poor and small to indict you for that, but there could be some murder charges coming up against you and your friend, Jake Brooks. Based on what the woman said, and your admission you shot them, you could be looking at charges against you for the murders." He glanced down and then said, "If that happens, though, I'll recommend the judge set the bonds low, maybe, five thousand dollars apiece."

I nodded.

"I'm still checking, of course, but I'll tell you right now the woman's a flake. She's got a long drug rap sheet. And Myerson, the guy that ran off, has a rap sheet a mile long. I figure their stories won't match. I'll talk with Brooks some more when he is able to talk some more. The Justice of the Peace has ordered autopsies, so that may help you some. That'll still leave the burglary charge, but if the murder charges go away, I figure the burglary charge will too."

"I understand. And I appreciate the low bond. Will you get back to me as soon as you can about which way the D.A. will go on the charges?"

"Sure, no problem."

"Thanks."

"I'm sorry to bother you." He nodded his head towards Alice. "Ma'am." They left.

Alice sat on the edge of the bed. Her eyes were full of tears. She clutched my right hand with both of hers.

"Oh, Noah," she sobbed and fell on my chest, crying.

"It'll be o.k., Babes," I whispered, stroking her hair. She lay there crying for several minutes, with me caressing her with my right hand.

She finally rose slightly and looked into my face. Her hair was wet and a wisp of it stuck to her cheek. I brushed it away. "What should I do, Noah?"

"First, don't worry. It may be a little rough for a while, but it'll work out. The druggies' stories won't match, and where they do, it'll confirm what I told them. So don't worry about that. I'll need a lawyer and a bond. Call Ken. He does mainly family law, but he's done a lot of criminal work. I don't need a hot shot trial lawyer to threaten to kick everybody's ass and stir up the district attorney. But I do need a real lawyer to finesse this situation. Ken will be good. Do you have his number?"

She shook her head. I started to give it to her and she went to her purse and got out her phone. "O.k.", she said, and keyed in the number. "Next?" Her law training was taking over.

"Ken can likely make any bonds they set. Have him call Kyles at the Sheriff's Office and verify. A lots of these small counties let the lawyers just make the bonds themselves. That'll save some money." I was getting tired and my side was throbbing. "What time is it?"

"Eleven-thirty," she said, glancing at her phone.

"Alice, I feel like I've been rode hard and put up wet. If it's o.k., I'm going to get some sleep. You call Ken tonight and ask him to be here tomorrow. I'll try to get out of the hospital tomorrow, and if he's here I can bond out if necessary, and then we can head home, o.k.?"

She nodded. She brushed the hair from my forehead.

I pulled her to me and we kissed again.

"Bye, Noah. If you're asleep when I come back, I'll just be waiting for you right here," she said.

"Thanks, Babes." I kissed her again and she left, turning out the light, and closing the door.

I faded as quick as the light and fell asleep.

CHAPTER
33

I FELT SOMEONE ram an ice pick in my side. The pain caused me to attempt to sit up suddenly. My whole body screamed with pain. After a split second of confusion, I remembered where I was and why I was there. I felt like I had gone ten rounds with George Foreman. I hurt from the top of my head to the soles of my feet.

Alice threw off her hospital blanket, got out of her chair and came to the bed.

"How are you feeling, Noah?"

"Fine. What time is it?"

She looked at her watch in the dark, then turned the watch towards the half-opened door so the pale hall light could illuminate the dial. "Six twenty."

I moved slowly to the edge of the bed and slowly lowered my feet off the side and, with her help, sat up. I sat very still, my head spinning. I felt light-headed.

"When can I check out?"

"Let me go find out." She left. I braced myself with my arms and remained sitting up while she was gone. After a few minutes, my head stopped spinning, and I felt a little better. Alice came back after about ten minutes. "The nurse said that we can start the check-out procedure at seven when the office opens, and we can leave after the doctor's rounds, if he releases you. She said he usually comes by around seven thirty or eight."

I gingerly laid back down. Alice stood by the bed holding my hand for a few minutes, then she went over and sat down in the chair. And we waited. And waited. Nothing is slower than waiting in a hospital. 'Slower'n molasses in the winter time,' my grandfather used to say.

CHAPTER

34

WE PULLED INTO our driveway by noon. I don't think was I ever so happy to get to Dallas in my life. As we had driven home, Alice held my hand, releasing it only to shift gears. I was feeling pretty bad by the time we hit Dallas' 635 Loop, so Alice had suggested we pick something up for lunch. We pulled into a drive-through hamburger joint and got some burgers and onion rings and took them home with us.

I unfolded from the MiniCooper and tried to stand straight, but the ache in my side and almost two hours bouncing in the little sports car had worn me out. I leaned against the car and stretched, the gunshot wound causing me to catch my breath. Alice was getting the sack of food out of the car and when she heard me gasp, she turned to me.

"You need a hand?"

I smiled thinly, "No, I'm fine, I can make it."

I pulled myself erect and walked stiffly to the house. She went ahead and unlocked the door, and watched me approach, evaluating my condition.

Alice took my arm as I went in the door, then turned and locked it behind us. We went to the kitchen and she got out two glasses, filled them with ice and poured the tea. I laid out the hamburgers and put out napkins. I tore the sack open and spread out the onion rings. I opened the ketchup for Alice and put it beside her burger. We ate quietly, Alice thinking her own thoughts and occasionally looking at me quizzically, I was just enjoying her presence and being home. After we finished eating, Alice suggested we go to the den. She refilled our tea glasses while I threw the trash away. We carried our tea to the den and sat down. Alice turned on the stereo and we listened to it for a while, each of us immersed in our own thoughts.

Finally, I glanced over at Alice. She was looking at me, as if from a distance, her eyes almost vacant in her thought.

"What's the matter, Alice," I asked.

She looked a bit surprised, having been interrupted in her musings. "Nothing, I guess, Noah." Her voice was low.

I moved from my chair to the couch beside her, putting my right arm across the back of the couch, my hand resting on the nape of her neck. "Babes, what's the matter."

She was looking blankly into space, still thinking. I put my left forefinger under her chin and turned her towards me.

"Just tell the truth. I can deal with it, whatever it is. What's bothering you. Let's talk."

Her lower lip trembled slightly, and her eyes partially closed, causing the tears to well up. She laid her head on my shoulder and I wrapped her in my arms. She clasped her arms around me, and nuzzled her face against my neck, her breath warm.

I waited, stroking her hair.

She slowly drew in a breath and pulled back slightly and looked me in the eyes.

"Do you have to do this?" she finally said.

"What 'this' are you talking about?"

"This macho private eye thing?" She paused, her mouth open as if she was trying to phrase her thoughts carefully. "The guns." She paused, choosing her words. "I guess I never realized how dangerous it was. I know you've told me stories about what you've done, but until now that's all they were, stories. It wasn't reality. Maybe I've been ignoring what you do, but generally you just go to the office and make telephone calls."

I nodded, listening to her as I massaged her neck with my right hand.

"And you could have been arrested. Tried for murder. Even capital murder." I felt her shudder slightly as she paused. "You could have gone to prison." She paused again. "You could have been killed. When you left, I tried not to worry, but when I saw the guns . . . I've never seen you take all those guns with you. And Jake. You were hunting. Hunting people. And they tried to kill you, Noah." She turned toward me and touched my face with her hand. "When the police called . . . I've never had the police call me before. And when they called and said you were in the hospital with two gun shot wounds, Noah, I fell apart." She paused, then looked into my eyes. Her gaze was weak, flitting, her voice without conviction, as if she had had the breath knocked out of her. "I can't take this kind of life. As much as I love you, Noah, I can't go through this again."

She seemed so far away, the cold gulf between us growing, like the Arctic Ocean between two drifting icebergs that were moving apart and out to sea.

"I'm sorry I worried you. This isn't what my life's generally like. This was different." I kissed her hand and then held her face between my hands and slowly kissed her. I pulled back a few inches and looked in her eyes again. "I don't know what to say. I'll try to keep you from worrying. I'm here to make your life happy, not cause you grief. I am sorry. This just got out of hand. We never intended it to end up like it did." I paused. "And with Jake hurt."

"And you killed those people, Noah. You killed people, human beings."

I nodded.

"I've never known anyone who actually killed someone. Every since we saw your friend's body, something's changed. You've been driven by it. You have been different. Is this your real life, or is it just Keith. Please tell me, Noah."

"It's just Keith. And Carolyn. I can't seem to get any answers. Just dead ends. I'm not sleeping well. Other cases, I can keep perspective, keep my distance. This mess, Keith, Carolyn, Pete and Helen, her parents, and Mrs. Holland, too. I've known Keith and Pete and Mrs. Holland almost all my life. Mrs. Holland practically raised me and Keith was like a brother to me when we were kids." I looked away and then half-turned and rested my chin on my knuckles and tried to think how to express my feelings of, what was the word? I looked across the room, and continued. "I've always been able to do anything I set my mind to. If I decided to do it, by grit and determination, I've done it. With this case, I can't seem to do that. I tried everything and ended up killing four people and getting my friend shot."

"And you shot."

"And getting me shot. I, I don't know, I'm feeling inadequate. I know how Pete feels. There is an answer out there, if I can just find the right thread to pull. And it's driving me crazy trying to find it."

"You're the best thing I've ever seen, Noah. You're good at what you do. You will figure it out."

"But this whole thing has gotten out of control. It seems like everything is snowballing. And now you are added into the mixture. I knew when I saw you at the hospital this was hurting you as bad as me. I accept a little rough-and-tumble in my line of work. I've done it for years, whether as a cop, or as a private investigator. But I've tried to keep you out of any of the unpleasantness. And you know what's so strange about this? It's not really business. The Keith thing is free. So even if I was an insurance salesman, I would have been involved. So it's not my work, it's a loose thread from my youth that's reached across time and miles to pull me back."

I looked at her. She was looking at me intently, her head cocked sideways resting on her palm, her elbow resting on her crossed knees.

"Does any of this make any sense?" I asked.

She nodded.

We sat silently again.

"Noah, I'm sorry, too." Alice said quietly.

"What for, Babes?"

"I've been thinking about me. How all this has affected me. From the time we saw Keith until the hospital call, right up until now." Alice paused. "I've spent my time thinking about me, and how Keith's death upset me and caused you to leave me several times the last week. I was lonely and it's bothered me. And it's brought violence into my life, violence like most people only hear about on the news." She looked at me with sad eyes. "I haven't thought about how it's affected you. You always are so strong and sure. It never occurred to me that you were really troubled by this. I knew you stayed up most of that night we saw Keith. But I've been so busy with me I've forgotten you. We're a team, Noah. You should have told me."

"I haven't really thought about it until I was in the hospital flat on my back and watching you cry. That just underscored my inability to handle this. I just kept working harder and harder, and when that failed, working even harder. And it didn't change. It never occurred to me that I would end up in a gun fight and almost get Jake killed."

"How are you going to get out of this, Noah?"

I shook my head. "I'm going to think about it. I can't keep on with it like this. I have to get off this merry-go-round. Tomorrow I'll go over everything one more time, call Bill to see what they've figured out, call Linny Lowry to see if he's found out anything in Ohio. And if it doesn't add up to anything, just wash my hands of it and go back to real life." I looked at my open hands. "But, Alice, I thought I could handle it. I really did."

I stood up slowly and held out my hand to Alice. She took it and I drew her to her feet. I wrapped my arms around her and gently brought her to me.

"Feeling better, Babes?"

She nodded.

I kissed her gently, then kissed her neck.

"Let's go to bed. I need to be with you as never before. I need to hold you and kiss you and . . ."

She kissed me and led me to the bedroom.

We lay together for hours in the darkened room, kissing and caressing. The gulf between us had evaporated and we were together again. Later we made love. And then we kissed and caressed more, until we finally drifted off to sleep, nestled together.

CHAPTER
35

I AWOKE THE next morning with Alice's arm around my neck, her face against my cheek. Her breath was low and even. I kissed her and she opened her eyes and, seeing me, smiled.

"Good morning, Beautiful," I said. "I love you, you know it."

"Forever and always, as I do you, Noah."

I leaned over her and kissed her. She wrapped her arms around my neck and kissed me back deeply and slowly. We lay still, holding one another.

"You doing o.k. now, Babes?" I asked.

She nodded. "You?"

I nodded. "You're always my answer. And if you're not the answer, I'm just not asking the right question."

She smiled again. Then she touched my side. "How are you feeling?"

"Sore, but overall, fine. One night with you offsets a week's abuse. You're my cure for what ails me."

"You want some breakfast?"

"Sure, if it's light."

"Toast and jelly?"

"Perfect."

"O.k., I'll go and you shower and shave, and come in when you're ready." She turned to get out of bed, but I caught her and rolled her back to me.

I kissed her and said, "Please, don't ever leave me, Alice."

"I'd be a fool to. You're the best thing that ever happened to me." She leaned up on an elbow and kissed me. "I love you." She rolled over and stood up, her beauty flashing before my eyes as she put on her robe and she left the room.

I showered and put on a robe and went to breakfast.

Alice had laid out the good china and the silver.

"What's the occasion, Babes?" I asked.

"Last night. And today. And forever, Noah. Our conversation yesterday made me realize that I've let too much slip by. Too much. Let's not let it happen again. O.K.?"

I patted her hand. "O.k. Beautiful."

We ate breakfast slowly, then dressed and returned to our work, she to school, and I to my office. I rode with her to S.M.U. and dropped her off and borrowed her car for the day.

On the way to the office, I thought about how nothing seemed to fit. Keith was heavily into drugs and crime, but his death didn't strike me like it was drug related. Carolyn was a cipher. Nothing about her added up to a missing person. She was into drugs, but only peripherally. She knew Keith to some extent, but he was dead, and no one had seen her with him since long before his death, and nobody noticed anything odd that would suggest why he was killed. And why had Carolyn left home? I was going to call Pete again. Maybe he had heard something new.

I pulled into the Carrington building parking lot. I parked on the back side of the lot and went to the office. I was beginning to think the nine-to-fivers that worked for the oil company maybe had the right idea: a regular paycheck, regular hours, and the love of their life didn't have to worry about them being shot at work. Alice's comments yesterday still rang in my mind. I hadn't decided what to do, but I knew I would have to do something to resolve the uncertainty in Alice's mind.

I unlocked the door and shoved the door open, the mail that had piled through the mail slot onto the floor wedging against the door. I opened it enough to squeeze through and picked it up and shut the door. I piled the mail on the desk. I hated being out of the office for very long because the answering machine would be filled, and I would spend the next week returning the calls of those who had left messages until the answering machine was full, and then explaining to the rest of my clients why the machine didn't take their message and why I was gone.

I sat down and got a pen and a yellow tablet and pushed the 'play message' button and started writing down the messages. I had twenty-six messages when recorder ran out of space. I had three calls from Linney Lowry with important information. Pete O'Brian and Mrs. Holland had also called. Detective Kyles had also left a message. The rest were regular clients.

I called Linney first. He left his office number, but the secretary said he was away from his desk. She put me on hold for five minutes, coming back on occasionally to advise me that she thought she knew where he was. He finally got on the line.

"Noah, what happened to you? It's unlike you not to get back quick."

"I've been out of town investigating a case. Did you find anything about the Dentons?"

"Oh, yeah, did I." He said emphatically. "You wanted me to check out the Chad Denton kid. He checked out fine. No problems, no criminal record that I could find. I even checked at his old school with some school personnel I knew. He was well liked and popular."

"So what's the big news? That's the same thing I heard here."

"What have you heard about the father, Walter Denton?"

"Nothing much. Just that he moved to Columbia to run a factory. Why?"

"He's why they had to leave Ohio."

A light flashed on in my mind. "Oh. What happened?"

"He was investigated for, how should I say this delicately, having affairs with young girls."

"How young?"

"Sixteen and seventeen. Still under the age of consent in Ohio, though."

"What happened to the cases?"

"They were dismissed just before he went to Texas. He was ordered to get counseling. I'm not sure exactly how he went from possible statutory rape to a counseling session, but he had a local hot-shot defense attorney who is pretty good at pulling off miracles. Anyway, the cases went away, and so did he. 'Gone to Texas', as they used to say." There was a pause. "Noah? You still there?"

"Oh, yeah. I was just thinking."

"I bet you are. I'm just a lowly public servant, but even I can see this one. You're thinking dear old Wally got involved with the girl, Carolyn?"

"Yeah, something like that. How did he meet those girls in Dayton?"

"At least two were his son's friends."

"Hmm, and the others?"

"Not sure, but another girl's home address is near their home. Maybe he met her on his own, maybe met her through his son. Just don't know about that one."

"Any record of violence by either Chad or Walter?"

"Not Chad. But Walter, no violence, but it seems he uses heavy duty coercion when necessary. I've read the police reports on Walter's cases and one of the girls said he harassed and intimidated her to get her to have sex with him, then he paid her off to keep her quiet."

"How does Chad figure into his father's activities?" I asked.

"No way that I can figure. He was investigated, of course, because at least two of the women were his friends. But he and the girls all said that Chad was not involved. Seems that he would date them, and that's how his father would meet them. Then dear old dad would work on them until he nailed them. From the police reports, it seems that his wife and Chad both might have known what he had been doing, but didn't know how to stop it. They just tried to keep it quiet and hoped it wouldn't happen again. Talk about your dysfunctional families."

"You ought to meet Mrs. Denton." I said, "Of course, this sure puts a different light on her. I'd drink, too, if I was in her situation."

"You think Walter put the make on Carolyn?"

"Don't you? It's the only lead I have right now and it sure fits. Explains a lot. I think I will talk to Chad again. And this time I'll meet with old man Denton. Can you send those police reports?"

"Sure. I can send it as an email attachment, or mail it to you."

"How long is it?

"Pretty long."

"Email it. Got the address?" I gave it to him.

"I'll have it to you within the hour."

"Thanks, Linney. I owe you one."

"Glad to help out. Maybe you can catch his ass on something and make it stick down there. We seemed to let him skip up here. Of course, the way you described the girl's father, he will skin Denton alive if he so much as gave her a kiss."

"Yeah, Pete's pretty protective of his family. If Walter made a pass at the girl, he'd better get out of town before Pete finds out. Again, thanks, Linney. Give Diane my love."

"Same to Alice. We'll call when we're coming down next."

"And dinner's on me, Linney."

We hung up.

I called Detective Kyle. He told me that the latest word from the District Attorney's office was that they would not be filing any charges against Jake and me. I thanked him for the good news and hung up.

Then I called Mrs. Holland and Pete. Both had heard about the shootings and were concerned about me and were wondering if the drug lab was involved in my search for their children. I lied and said no.

I called the hospital to check on Jake. I got his room number and called. It took him six rings to get it. I was just about to hang up.

"What took you so long? Chasing a nurse around the room or something?"

"No, hell, they have me bandaged up like a mummy. Just took a while to get to the phone."

"Have they said when they'll release you?"

"Not really, but I'm ready to go now."

"I bet."

"I've been walking the halls and flirting with nurses, so I think I'm feeling pretty much back to normal."

"I'm going to try to be back in town tomorrow. I'll stop by. If they'll turn you loose tomorrow, I'll give you a ride home."

"Hell, boy, figure that's the least you can do." He laughed. "I'll see you tomorrow."

We hung up.

I returned the rest of the calls and even opened a file I was involved in trying to find some missing oil field equipment. But my mind kept wandering to Columbia, and to the O'Brians and to the Hollands.

By eleven, I was tired and restless. I called Alice at the law journal office and asked her if she wanted to join me for lunch. She told me where to pick her up. I hung up and left. She was standing under an oak tree on the edge of the campus when I drove up. She waved when she saw me and dashed toward the car. I pulled slightly out of the flow of traffic so the cars could go around and she jumped in and leaned over and gave me a quick kiss.

We went to a nearby Mexican restaurant. I told her what Linney had said.

"But what happened to Carolyn? Did she just run off? Was she pregnant? What?"

I shrugged. "Your guess is good as mine. I just don't know. But at least I feel like I'm on to something." I ate a bite of my chicken enchilada. "What's your schedule tomorrow?"

"Flexible. Why?"

"I wanted to go to Columbia. I talked with Jake and he's feeling pretty good. I wanted to visit him and, if they will release him, you can bring him home. Plus I need to get my truck. I appreciate the use of your car, but I feel like I'm on a skateboard after driving my truck sitting up high. And I need to see if I can wrap up Carolyn's disappearance. I'm going to hit the Dentons one by one. They are the key. I figure Chad is the weak reed in this quagmire. I want to corner him away from his family and see what he knows. He said he returned Carolyn home that night. I just don't see it. I don't know what happened, but Pete was right. The Dentons know where Carolyn went. Pete may be a wild, irrational father, but he may be right."

"What if the boy doesn't know what happened to Carolyn?"

"He said he took her home. He lied. He may not be involved with her disappearance, but I've got him right there. He'll tell me what he knows, whatever that is. Then I'll go to mom and dad Denton and squeeze them. Maybe get a lead on which way Carolyn went. Then I'll take whatever I have to the police and let them see if they can indict the son-of-a-bitch for something, anything."

She nodded. "Yeah, I'll go with you. I'll be glad when this case is over.

I guess it's affected you so much because you are so personally involved. I've never seen you so upset. When do you want to leave?"

"I figured we can leave before seven and beat the traffic."

She nodded. "What are you going to do this afternoon?"

"I figure I'll go home and review the stuff Lenney is sending me. Plus, I'm pretty worn out."

She patted my hand. "You've had a bad week, Baby. Why don't I drive you to the house. That way you won't have to come pick me up this afternoon."

Alice dropped me off and I went in the house.

I poured a glass of tea and turned on the laptop and pulled up and printed Linney's email, and then carried the printout and tea into the den and turned on the stereo. I sat in the recliner and began to read the email. It was mainly police reports. They expanded on what Linney had said. Walter Denton had a pattern of making advances towards young women who his son knew. In addition to the three cases involving Denton possibly having sex with young women, investigators had interviewed numerous other girls that his son and his son's friends had brought around his house. Many of the girls reported Walter Denton making suggestive comments and propositions for affairs. The police reports indicated that Irene Denton, Walter's wife, refused to talk with the investigators. His son, Chad, had talked with the police but had denied any knowledge of his father's activities.

After I read all the reports twice, I put them aside and thought about tomorrow's trip to Columbia. I knew how Alice felt: I would be happy to have this case over. The frustrations of trying to solve problems I was too emotionally close to, together with my concern about its impact on Alice, as well as guilt for getting Jake shot, all added together into a witches' caldron of unresolved emotions and doubts.

I called Jake again. He was feeling better, and would be released the next day and would appreciate a ride home. He said Detective Kyles had come by earlier and interviewed him about the shooting. Kyles had told him that he didn't think any charges would be brought against us. I said we would be there mid-morning and hung up.

I sat in the recliner and thought about Keith and Carolyn and how divergent paths sometimes cross. I thought, then dozed, and dreamed of Alice and me, of our lives together, and apart.

When I awoke, I had a crick in my neck and an uneasy feeling about how Alice's and my own divergent paths had crossed. I wondered whether our future paths would be one, or would they diverge again. Alice's comments yesterday about this case was about more than just Keith's murder. It was about what I do for a living. And since what I do for a living is so much of me, I wondered if the comments weren't also directed about me. I thought of an old John Pryne song that said "She asked me to change the station, said the song just drove her insane; But it wasn't the music they're playing, it's me she was trying to blame."

I thought about Alice and me and us. And I thought how much I loved Alice and knew that we would survive.

It was almost five so I got up and made dinner, and was setting the table when she came home. We had dinner, and a quiet evening at home, and we didn't discuss Columbia or Keith or Carolyn.

CHAPTER
36

We were headed east on Interstate 20 by seven thirty. Northeast L.B.J. Freeway was packed with office workers heading downtown, but as we continued to head away from the city, the traffic quickly thinned out. The Interstate was almost empty except for a couple eighteen wheelers.

We reached the hospital by nine thirty. Jake was sitting up in bed watching t.v. when we came in. He looked tired, pale and drawn. He didn't have his regular good humor, but he was eager to get back to Dallas for the rest of his recuperation. Over the neckline of his loose hospital gown I could see the thick white bandages and tape on his chest and shoulder. He had already checked out and was just waiting for us to go get him some clothes and to give him a ride. The clothes he had come in wearing had been as bloody as mine. I told him that Alice and I would go to the police impound lot where Kyles had said they towed my truck, and bring him his clothes bag.

Alice and I left and drove to the police station. We went into the station and filled out the forms, paid the towing fee and storage fees, and went through the sacks of items the police had taken from my truck and inventoried for storage. The officer at the property desk told me that I could not get our guns until he received a written decision from the D.A.'s office that they were not going to file any charges against us.

Alice and I lugged the sacks to my truck in three loads. The truck had been thoroughly searched. Everything from jumper cables to cigarette butts and gum wrappers had been raked from under the seats and left on the floor when the officers determined that it was neither incriminating nor of any value. When we had everything in the truck, I found the sack that contained Jake's overnight bag and put it on the front truck seat. Most of the rest was tossed behind the seat or on the front floor. I gave Alice a peck on the cheek and cranked the truck and followed her back to the hospital.

I carried the overnight bag up to Jake's room.

Alice and I waited in the hall while he dressed. It took him quite a while. Between the bandages and the pain, he was slow as Christmas. We heard him groan several times. Finally, Jake called us into the room. His shirt was hanging open. He sheepishly asked Alice to button his shirt because his arm was too sore and stiff to bend to the buttons. She buttoned his shirt, then he turned around and tucked in the tail of the shirt into his jeans and zipped up.

While he finished dressing, we all made plans for the day. I told Jake what Linnie had told me about the Dentons. I said I was going to the Dentons and see if I could get some answers about Carolyn's disappearance from them. Jake and Alice agreed that I should go as soon as possible, but Jake declined to join me. As he said, he felt like he had been "rode hard and put up wet," and he just wanted to get home in bed with a bottle of Jack Black and a Laura Blond, as he called her. He figured between the whiskey and his current blond girl friend he would either recover or it would take the mortician a week to get the smile off his face.

We buzzed the nursing station and they brought a wheel chair and rolled Jake to Alice's car. We took all of Jake's stuff out of my truck and put it into Alice's car, and they left for Dallas.

I went looking for Chad Denton. I wanted to find him away from his home so I could talk with him without his mother or father interrupting. I hit all the places I saw teenagers hanging out and asked if they had seen Chad. He had been out during the morning, but hadn't been seen since then. After lunch, I made another round of the hang outs, and asked again for Chad. At the pizza joint, one young man said that Chad had told him that he was going to the golf course that afternoon. I thanked him and headed out to the Columbia Country Club.

I parked under an old oak tree at the edge of the parking lot near the driving range, its gnarly branches reaching almost to the ground. I got out and locked the truck and stooped under the branches and stepped onto the green. I wandered across the course looking for Chad.

I didn't see him on the driving range, so I circled the club house looking across the manicured grass fields and artificial sand dunes for him. I finally found him on the practice putting course behind a small grove of trees. I liked the location because it was secluded and no one else was around. He was wearing khaki shorts and white golf shoes, with a red Texas Rangers baseball cap. A golf bag lay on the grass. He was deep in concentration as he lined up his putts. I walked up behind him and waited until he made his shot before I spoke.

"Chad Denton," I said.

He jumped, and spun around.

"I didn't mean to startle you," I said.

"No problem, I just didn't hear you come up."

"You were lining up a shot, and I didn't want to disturb you."

He nodded amicably, then the smile faded when he realized this wasn't a social visit. "What can I do for you today, Mr. Starr?"

"I wanted to talk with you about Carolyn."

He stiffened, his grip tightening on the putter. "What else can I tell you." He said guardedly. He pulled his cap down over his eyes, the brim shading his eyes.

"Tell me again about what happened on ya'll's date."

"I told you, we drove around town a little, then I took her home."

"O.k. But you didn't take her directly home, did you?"

"What do you mean?"

"You took her parking, didn't you?"

"What do you mean, parking?"

"You know, you took her to the woods for kissing, romance, 'watching the moon rise', hooking up, whatever you want to call it."

He crossed his arms, the putter dangling from his hand. "I told you what happened."

I shook my head. "No, Chad, let's get back to reality. I'm tired. I've run all over Dallas and east Texas. I've been shot. I've shot and killed men on this wild goose chase. Get real. I'm not in the mood to put up with your bull. Now tell me," I said, standing taller and looking menacing, "Where did you take Carolyn?"

"I didn't. . ."

"Chad," I said loudly, "Cut the crap."

"I, I, o.k., so we went parking, it's no big deal."

"No, it's not. But this'll be over a lot quicker if you'll just tell the truth. Where?"

"Where what?"

"Where did you go parking?"

"Up by the lake."

"On the east side overlooking the lake?"

"Yeah, that's it," he said, then looked at me suspiciously. "How did you know?"

"We used to go to the same places when I was your age."

He nodded, as if surprised that young people from my youth actually dated or went parking.

"How close was it to your house?"

"Not far. Maybe a couple miles or so."

"How long did ya'll stay?"

"About an hour, maybe less."

"What happened?"

"Nothing. Really. Nothing, we just talked and kissed a little."

"Chad, this is going awfully slow. Tell me the truth. Did you make a pass at Carolyn. Did you try to have sex with her?"

He looked confused, his eyes darted from me to the ground and back again, glancing around looking for an out. "Hey, look. This has been hard on me. I'm new in town and then this. And everyone thinks I had something to do with it. I don't need this hassling, man."

He turn to get his golf bag and leave. I grabbed his arm and turned him back towards me. I felt the muscles in his arm tense and saw him grip the golf club tighter.

"Chad, dammit, I'm not enjoying this discussion any more than you are, but we're going to stay here until I know what happened. I've been through too much to just pat you on the back and walk away. Now tell me. What happened."

He glanced around and didn't see anyone. He wilted and leaned his club against his leg.

"What do you want to know, Mr. Starr." His voice was flat, without inflection, the fight gone.

"Did you make a pass at her?"

"Yes, I did."

"Did you have sex?"

"No."

"Why not?"

"Hell, I don't know. She had been. . ." He cut himself off in mid-sentence.

"She had been what, Chad?"

He glanced around, like a trapped animal.

"Nothing."

"Don't nothing me, Chad. She had been what?"

"I don't know. Just things I had heard around school."

"What things?"

"I had heard she had been going to Dallas, had a friend up there, that she was hot stuff in Dallas. Then we go parking and she's Miss Touch-Me-Not. I mean, we had been going out together for a month. Then I hear about her in Dallas."

"Did you ask her about it?"

"Yeah, she said he was just a friend and she enjoyed the big city life."

"What was his name?"

"She wouldn't say. But somebody at school said he used to be from here and was older than we were. Like out of school for years." He stretched out the word "years" to span the decades I felt in my battered body.

"So you made a pass and she didn't agree. What happened then?"

"We argued and then I backed up and drove back to the highway."

I nodded encouragingly. "What were you driving?"

"Dad's Mercedes."

I raised an eyebrow. He caught it.

"I have a Toyota Camry. Ever try to, uh," he caught himself. "Ever try to have sex in one?"

I shook my head.

"And you won't. You can't. Too small. So I took Dad's car. Big seats and I thought it would impress her. Did too."

"I bet it did. When did you knock a hole in the oil pan?"

He had been looking at the head of his golf club as he spoke, unwilling to talk and look me in the eye, but his head jerked up, his face anguished.

"What do you mean?"

"I saw the oil pan on the moss green Mercedes. That's the one you took, isn't it? Do ya'll have another Mercedes?"

"No, that was it. Why do you think I tore it up?"

"You have to be off the beaten path to tear up an oil pan. I don't figure your mother or father would take that car across the pasture too often. So it was you, wasn't it?"

He nodded. "Yes, sir." He said quietly.

"What happened?"

"I don't know. I was pissed off. She kept saying 'no,' 'no,' 'no,' and I knew she was going to Dallas with that guy, and I bet she was, you know, I bet she was doing it with him. You understand why I'd be mad, don't you."

I nodded, trying to encourage him to speak.

"I mean, we went to the Senior Banquet together. I thought we were really close, then I find out about this other guy. I mean, hell, he's grown. What's he doing dating high school girls?"

I shrugged slightly and let him run.

"So I was mad, sure. I backed out and floored the Mercedes. That big car can run. But as we came out of the woods, I guess I was a little off the path. I hit a tree stump. I went back the next day. It looked like someone had cut a tree with an ax. You know, kind of pointed up."

I nodded again.

"Anyway, I hit it going pretty fast. We were bouncing around because I was coming out of the woods wide open, and she was up against her door and she was pissed off at me. And then we hit that stump." He stopped, remembering it in his mind. "I heard a sound like someone hit Dad's Mercedes with a sledge hammer. I hit the brake, but the car kind of ricochetted sideways and kept going, so I just hit the accelerator again. I didn't want to stop until I hit the paved road. You get off in the boondocks and if you stop, you can get stuck and have to get towed. That was the last thing I wanted. So I pulled up on the road and stopped the car and got a flashlight and got out. I looked all over and didn't see anything. Not a dent. I was so relieved. I mean, I knew my old man would have killed me if I dented his car." He looked down. "I hadn't told him I was taking his car. And he is awfully touchy about it." He paused, searching for words. "But I knew he would think it was for a good cause."

"What do you mean, 'for a good cause?'"

"Getting Carolyn. You know, doing her. If I came home and told him that I had nailed her, he wouldn't have minded me using his car, you know."

I nodded agreeably.

"Do you discuss your sex life with your father?"

"What are you getting at?"

"You said that if you told him you had sex with Carolyn, it would be o.k. with him for you to have borrowed his car."

"Yeah, so?"

"So did ya'll discuss ya'll's sex lives with each other?"

"Well, I mean, we talked, you know. We're both grown men. We get around."

I thought about his mother with a glass in her hand. I wished I had a strong drink about then.

"Both of you?"

"Well, you know, I've had sex, o.k. And Dad, he really gets around. He's real good with the girls."

"Girls?"

"You know what I mean," he said quickly. "Women. Skirts. You know."

I nodded. "So get back to the car. What happened then?"

"I got out and looked around like I said, and just when I was relieved that everything was o.k., Carolyn called to me. I looked in and she said, 'What's that red light for?.' Shit. It was the oil light. I looked under the car and there was a big puddle of oil. That's when I figured out that I had screwed up Dad's car. First Carolyn, then this. What a night."

"So what did you do?"

"I turned off the engine so I wouldn't burn it up, you know." He paused. "Then I called home on my cell phone. Mom answered and I asked for Dad. She said he was upset about me taking the car, but I said I had to get Carolyn home. You ever meet her old man?" He looked at me and I nodded. "The man's a lunatic. He was always so protective of her and I knew if I didn't get her home pretty quick he would kick my ass all over town. So I didn't have any choice. I mean, here I was, out in the woods, just tore up Dad's car.

He was pissed at me. Carolyn was pissed at me. But Dad got on the phone and he yelled at me for taking the car. Then I told him what happened and he went ballistic. But he finally calmed down enough to say he would come and get me in my car. I told him where we were and we waited. Boy was it a long wait. Carolyn wouldn't talk to me. And waiting for my old man. I knew I was going to catch hell when he got there."

"So what happened?"

"He showed up in about twenty-five minutes in my car. He had to call once on the way, trying to find the place, but when he got there, he was raging mad. He got a flashlight and looked at the busted oil pan, then he began screaming at me. And Carolyn tore into me, yammering about needing to get home so I asked Dad about taking her home and he said he'd run her home and would send a tow truck in the morning. Told me to stay with the car to make sure nothing happened to it. Then they left."

"What did Carolyn think about the plan?"

"Didn't bother her. She was so mad at me, I think she would have walked home."

"Did he take here home?"

"Sure, why not?" He said defensively.

"Because she didn't get home."

"How do you know?"

"Look, you've told everybody you took her home. Now you tell me that your father took her home."

"So?"

"So how do you know she got home?"

"Well, let me tell you. I waited a while, then I just left the car and started walking home. When I got home, Dad was still up and was walking in the yard. He was really wired then. I've never seen him so upset. He kept saying he decided I needed to think about what I had done to his car and that's why he had left me. He said we'd go get it when we got up in the morning."

"Did you go get it the next morning?"

"Yeah, Dad called a tow truck in the morning and they pulled it in and parked it in the driveway."

"Yeah."

"How was your father that morning?"

"You mean about his car?"

I nodded.

"Didn't seem too upset about it. You know, Mr. O'Brian called in the middle of the night and yelled at me about Carolyn. Dad told me to tell him that I had brought her back. Said that would be better than telling about taking her parking, the mood he was in. So that's what I told him."

"Did your father tell you he took her home?"

"Yeah, sure, said he had taken her to the door, and they had talked and Carolyn kept saying she was tired of Columbia and wanted to leave and go to Dallas. Said she had friends up there she could stay with. So when she left, Dad and I just figured she had called her friends and run away to Dallas. That's what she had told Dad she was going to do."

"Had she ever mentioned running off to Dallas with you?"

"No, but then I didn't even know she had a boyfriend in Dallas until that week. I mean, he's the reason I took her parking and tried so hard to, you know, do her." His gaze dropped by to his shoes. He looked back at me. "I mean, I guess didn't know her like I thought I did. I looked like a fool. I mean, I thought she and I had a good thing going. We went to everything at school together, and then a friend of mine told me his girl friend said Carolyn was bragging about running all over Dallas with this older dude. I didn't even know about it. Hell, she went shopping in Dallas a lot, but I just figured she was a girl and, hey, that's what they do, you know, shop a lot. And I knew of a couple times a couple of her friends went with her. Then I learned they would shop, then go to the clubs with this guy and his friends."

"Who were the girls she went with?" He told me their names. And you told the police the same story about taking her home?"

"Yeah, I mean, after she ran away from home, I couldn't change my story then. And Dad backed me up so we just stood by the story."

"Anything else you remember about the night that I should know about?"

He shook his head, his shoulders sagging, his eyes downcast.

"You know, if I find out anything different, I'm going to come and we're going to have to discuss it, and I'm not going to be as nice as I've been today."

"No, this is really what happened. Really, man."

"O.k., Chad, thanks." I clapped him on the back and turned and walked back to my car. As I went over the rise, I glanced back at him and he was still standing where I had left him, his head still down, thinking.

CHAPTER
37

I DROVE FROM the golf course to the Dentons' house. I didn't know if I would find Walter there during the day, but figured that, if I did, I might be able to get further than if I confronted him at the office. I drove slowly along River Road, catching myself glancing through the trees at the lake and wondering if this hideaway or that clearing was where Chad and Carolyn went parking. I slowed and turned into the driveway. The construction workers had finished cleaning up the debris from the job site, and the lawn had been sodded. Pop-up sprinklers arced water across the new grass, the sun prisming the spraying water into rainbows as I drove to the house. I noticed that the flower bed in the center of the circle drive way was filled with rose bushes and flowering plants, and neatly covered with fresh pine bark chips for mulch. The entire place had the look of being prepared for a photo spread for a gardening magazine.

The moss green Mercedes was still parked in the drive next to the red brick walkway to the porch. I pulled beside it and looked over it carefully. Then I knelt down in the white gravel and looked under the car. The oil pan had been replaced; the new one gleamed with fresh paint. I reached up to the front driver's side fender, and was pulling myself to my feet when a man bellowed at me from the house. I spun around and saw a stocky man standing holding the open door.

"What the hell are you doing?" he demanded. He was wearing dress slacks and a white shirt, his red and blue rep tie loosened at the neck. He held a tall glass in his left hand.

I started walking towards the house, but he didn't move, but stood glaring at me. As I reached the first step of the porch, he stepped out and pulled the door closed behind him.

"Who the hell are you and what are you doing here?" he yelled, his voice loud and demanding. He was agitated, his left hand slightly trembled, the ice in his drink tinkling. "Well, who the hell are you? Tell me or I'll call the cops and they'll haul your ass out of here."

I walked upon the porch and stuck out my right hand. "I'm Noah Starr. I'm ..."

He didn't move to shake my hand, but interrupted me. "I've heard of you." He took a long drink, then paused as it went down. It must have been a strong drink because he shuddered slightly as he swallowed. His voice had a hoarseness when he spoke again, so he cleared his throat and said, "You're the one that came out here and harassed my wife." He said it like his wife was a possession, like a dog or t.v. "And Chad said you've been asking about him all over town." As he spoke, his voice grew more menacing and louder.

I rested my hands on my hips and nodded, waiting for him to either wind down or for his anger to come to a head. Having talked with Chad and having re-read the police reports from Dayton, I was in the mood to kick his ass, but had decided to try to talk with him first and see what I could find out.

"What the hell are you nodding about?" He glared at me. He was about six foot tall and had the broad shoulders and build that suggested he had been an athlete when he was younger, and he kept himself in pretty good shape. His hair was wavy. His well tanned complexion was flushed from his anger and the alcohol.

"I'm just agreeing with you."

"Why are you bothering my boy?"

"He was supposedly the last one to see Carolyn alive."

He took another quick drink. "What do you mean 'supposedly the last one to see Carolyn alive?'" He stabbed at me with his left hand, causing the ice in the glass to clank.

"That's what he told the police, right?"

"That's what happened and that's what he told the police. So, what's your business in this?"

"Carolyn's parents have hired me to find her."

There was a long pause as he stared at me, then slowly finished his drink, crossed his arms, the ice cubes rattling in the empty glass of ice cubes.

"So, why are you here? Go find her. The police think she's in Dallas last I heard."

"Thoughtful of you to keep track of her that way."

"What's that supposed to mean?" He uncrossed his arms and the damp glass slipped from his hand and fell to the porch beside the wall, breaking into large shards and scattering glass and ice cubes across the porch beside him. He didn't even look down.

"Just that you are keeping track of this girl's disappearance closely."

"Hey, let me tell you something. That girl's father's been harassing us.

The police have been here time and again. My boy's an outcast at school because that bitch decided to take a hike after their date, like he had something to do with her leaving. I've heard about her and her trips to Dallas. She wasn't some pure virgin out here, you know. Now you take your ass back to Dallas and don't you ever come back here or I'll stomp your ass. You got that?" He hammered the last three words into my chest with his index finger.

I looked at him evenly, but I could feel the tension rising in the back of my neck. I smiled slightly and said in a low, calm voice, "You touch me one more time, you son of a bitch, and I will kick your butt all over this porch. And I'm wearing the boots to do it with." I paused, then said, "And Carolyn didn't go to Dallas."

"What the hell do you mean, she didn't go to Dallas?"

"I've checked around Dallas and she hasn't been seen. She isn't there. She's still here."

"What the hell do you mean, still here?" The pitch in his voice grew higher. "No one's seen her in Columbia since she disappeared."

"I've talked to Chad."

He didn't reply, but his eyes squinted a little, and his neck grew redder.

"Just now, at the golf course."

"So, who gives a damn who you've been talking to. Besides, what right do you have bothering my boy. He's been hectored enough by that O'Brian guy and the police. Can't you people just leave him alone?"

"I won't talk to him again. I know what happened."

He leaned slightly towards me and said, "What do you mean?"

I pointed to the Mercedes. "You got the oil pan fixed, I see."

"Yeah, so what. What do you mean, you know what happened."

"Denton, Chad told me about going parking with Carolyn, ripping the oil pan, and about you coming and getting Carolyn." His head was slightly shaking from side to side as I spoke. Then I said, "And he said you took her home."

"What? No, he took her home. He told the police he took her home. That's what he's told everybody."

"Yeah, that's what he told everybody. But it's not what happened, is it?" I reached into my back pocket and took out some of the printouts of the police records Linney sent me. I unfolded them and held them in my right hand and waved them in his face. "Know what these are?"

"No, and keep that out of my face." He brushed at them with his hand, like swatting gnats.

"These are police reports from Ohio. Ever hear of a young woman named Crystal Johnson? How about Natalie Anderson? Denise McFadden?"

He was shaking his head.

"No? Think again, Denton. You knew these girls. They were Chad's girlfriends. And you made what we used to call 'passes' at them. Had sex with at least one of them. Tried to have sex with the other ones and most likely a lot more girls like them. Remember them now?"

"Where did you get that stuff." He grabbed it from my hands and started glancing at the pages. "These are lies. It's all a bunch of crap."

I nodded agreeably. "That's good. And I'm sure the Columbia police will love to hear it. But why don't you save the bull until you meet someone who cares. Now, where is Carolyn?"

"I don't know. We haven't seen her since Chad took her home."

"Look, Denton, if I have to repeat everything a dozen times, we'll never make any progress here. Listen carefully, now. Read my lips. I'll even talk real slow for you, Denton. Chad didn't take Carolyn home. You told him you took Carolyn home. But you didn't take her home."

"Where did I take her then, you know so much."

I gazed slowly around the newly sodded yard and the flower gardens and the lake and the nearby forest. "That I don't know. There's lots of places she could be. But you didn't take her home. She's right here somewhere."

"Where, what, what do you mean I didn't take her home and she's here?" He swung his arms wide and said, "I don't see her. Do you? Where is she if I didn't take her home?"

"I'm glad we're off the 'Chad took her home' story."

"O.k., so maybe I took her home. Chad had tore up the Mercedes. Wasn't even supposed to have been in it. Why should he take her home? Let him walk car. That would teach him a lesson about tearing up my car and not asking permission."

"Yeah, but we're not talking about Chad learning from his past mistakes. You're the one who keeps repeating his mistakes."

"What do you mean?"

I waved the police reports. "This." I stuck them in his face. "These police reports about you chasing and trying to have sex with your son's young girl friends. First in Ohio, now here with Carolyn?"

"I didn't have sex with Carolyn."

"But you tried, didn't you? Didn't you, you sorry son of a bitch?" I shoved him back against the front door and he stumbled. He tried to catch himself and his elbow went through the glass beside the door. The glass flew across the hallway floor.

He staggered and caught his balance and looked at his elbow. Scattered red dots exploded onto the white shirt where the glass slivers had cut him. He clutched his arm. "Damn you, look what you did."

I grabbed his tie just below the knot and slammed him against the door again then held him close to my face with the tie. "Denton, that's the least of your problems right now."

The door opened suddenly behind him, and his wife, holding a drink in her hand and looking half drunk screamed at him, "Look at my window. What's going on?" Then she saw me holding his necktie and she yelled, "You, you again. Walter, what's going on?"

He half turned and looked over his shoulder at her. At that moment she saw the bloody red arm of his shirt.

"Oh my God, you're killing him." She threw her glass at me, and I dodged it, but the alcohol caught Denton on his shoulder and sprayed over onto me. She tried to swing at me but Denton pushed her back away from us.

I shoved him back again and he fell back into the hall. She screamed and ran into a room. "I'm calling the police," she yelled to her husband.

Denton staggered against the hallway table, trying to get his feet under him. The vase on the table fell on the floor and broke.

"O.k. Denton, one more time. You say you took Carolyn home, right?"

He glanced at the doorway his wife had gone through and then back at me. His face was beet red. "Yeah, so what."

I grabbed his tie tightly and hit him in the solar plexus as hard as I could. As he fell, I slung him to one side by the tie.

He fell against the table that collapsed under him and he lay on the floor gasping for breath. I could hear his wife screaming on the telephone to the police that I was killing her husband. I grabbed the tie again and pulled him to his feet and slammed him against the wall again.

"You didn't take her home, did you?" His eyes were wide with terror. He didn't say anything so I slammed his head against the wall again. "It's going to take the police several minutes to get here, and by then you're going to want them to arrest you to keep me away. And to keep Pete O'Brian away from your sorry ass. You didn't take her home did you?"

He shook his head slightly.

"You made a pass at her, didn't you?" I was yelling at him at the top of my lungs. He didn't say anything so I slammed his head against the wall again. "You tried to have sex with her, didn't you?"

"No, no I didn't." His voice was cracking with panic and fear, his hands clutching at the wall behind him for stability.

"You sorry son of a bitch, you tried to screw her and she refused and you killed her, didn't you? Didn't you?"

"No, I didn't, I . . ."

I slammed his head again the wall again. The sheetrock broke and crumbled behind him.

"You tried to force yourself on her, she fought you off, and then you killed her, didn't you?"

"It was an accident. She was going to then she said no and we wrestled and, and, I don't know, I didn't mean to hurt her. It was an acci. . . "

I hit him as hard as I could, putting all my weight in the punch, driving my fist into his face. Blood splattered onto me as I broke his nose. He fell through the wall into the next room, his feet caught in the broken sheet rock of the hallway. He didn't move.

I leaned through the hole in the wall. He slowly shook his head and his eyes fluttered and he focused on me. Blood poured from his nose and busted upper lip onto the carpet and his shirt. He half sat up and tried to rub the blood from his face.

I pointed my finger at him. "I'm on my way to tell Pete O'Brian you killed his daughter. When the police get here, you had better tell them what happened and go to jail. Because you and I both know that if Pete gets the chance, he's gonna kill your sorry ass. And I just might help him. Because you just don't deserve to live."

I turned towards the open door and caught a movement to the side. Mrs. Denton was standing halfway in the hall, her eyes wide with fear.

"Did you hear that?"

She nodded.

"You can tell the police what he said. He'll be better off in jail than trying to deal with Pete. But you know what? If I were you, I think I might just shoot the sorry bastard myself." I turned and walked to the car. I was a half mile down the road when two sheriff's cars passed me, their overhead lights flashing and sirens wailing.

CHAPTER
38

I knew I had to tell Pete and Helen before the police called them. I pulled out my cell phone and called their house. It rang three times before Helen picked it up. I asked if Pete was there. She said that she expected he would be home from work in about fifteen minutes. I told her that I was on my way, and that I had news about Carolyn. She choked a gasp.

"It is good news?" She asked quietly.

"I'll tell you when I see you." I heard her start to cry. "I'll be there shortly." I hung up.

I looked at myself in the car's rear view mirror, glancing at my beat up face and then at the road and back again. I turned the mirror downward so I could see better. I had spots of blood on my face and on my shirt. My shoulder was red from blood oozing from my gun shot. I figured I had torn the sutures. It was throbbing like hell. I glanced down at my hands. My right hand was turning purple from hitting Denton. There was a big scrape along the back of my left hand that I didn't recall getting. Two buttons had been torn off my shirt and the corner of my pocket was hanging down. I figured Denton had grabbed my shirt towards the end and I hadn't noticed. I readjusted the mirror.

My head was hurting and my throat was sore from the yelling and the fight. I was getting too old to brawl like that any more. I realized the radio was playing so I turned it off. I drove by the O'Brians' house but Pete's red SUV wasn't there yet so I made the block. I didn't want to have to report that Carolyn was dead more than once. When I passed again, his car still wasn't there, so I drove down town and then back. By then his car was in the driveway, so I pulled up behind it.

By the time I parked and got out, both Pete and Helen were on the porch, their arms tightly around each other's waist. I walked slowly to the house, and they withdrew into the house, Pete holding the door open for me. Helen led me to the living room again and we all sat down. We were quiet for a minute as they waited for me to speak and I tried to find the right words.

"Pete, Helen, I found out what happened to Carolyn." I finally said.

They clutched each other's hand. Helen's left hand held a crushed tissue. Her eyes were red and swollen from crying.

"Where is my baby?" She asked quietly.

"She's dead, Helen."

Helen collapsed into Pete's lap, crying in loud gasps, saying, "Carolyn, Carolyn, oh my baby."

Pete's right hand covered his eyes. His head bowed, then shoulders slumped. He cried quietly, his body limp. He laid his right hand on Helen's hair and caressed it. He put his left hand on her waist and held her like he was trying to quiet a little girl awakened by nightmares. Helen's sobbing grew quieter, and when we could talk over her sobs, he wiped the tears that had streaked his face and looked at me.

"What happened to Carolyn?" His voice was broken and he had to clear his throat twice to get the words out.

"Walter Denton, Chad's father, killed her."

He looked at me suddenly. "Walter Denton? How? Why?"

"Chad had car trouble and his father offered to take Carolyn home. Denton . . . ," I paused and tried to think of what to say, but couldn't. "The police were on their way to his house when I left a few minutes ago. When I leave here, I will go and give them a statement. But he admitted it to me. He had made passes at Chad's girl friends in Ohio. That's why they came to Columbia."

Pete was silent. "I never suspected Walter Denton. At first Chad, but never his father."

I took a deep breath. "You thought it was Keith Holland didn't you?"

He looked stunned. "How did you know?" He said in a quiet voice. Helen stopped crying and sat up and looked at Pete, then at me, and back at Pete.

"You heard about Carolyn going to Dallas and meeting someone, didn't you?"

He nodded.

"You checked around and found out that she had been seen with Keith Holland. And that he was into drugs, right? And that Carolyn was known to use drugs, right."

He nodded again.

"And it all added up, didn't it? Keith had taken Carolyn to Dallas. And had disappeared."

"I checked him out some, Noah. I even heard that some of the girls he met got into prostitution and drugs. Noah, it had to be him. I just knew it."

"But you knew wrong, Pete. It wasn't Keith, it was Walter Denton." I paused. "Witnesses said that the car Keith's killer used was black or dark. You have a red car, Pete. You know why they don't paint fire trucks red any more, Pete?"

He shook his head.

"Because at night in bad light, red looks dark. Black."

His shoulders slumped.

Helen looked at him, the confusion in her face circling her eyes with wrinkles. "What's he talking about, Pete?"

He reached over and patted her hand. "It'll be o.k., Helen." He looked back at me. "How did you figure it out, Noah?"

"I just kept coming across people who mentioned or recognized Carolyn while I was investigating Keith's murder," I said. "And there were rumors here in Columbia about her running around Dallas with a fast crowd. When I figured out what happened to Carolyn, the only loose end was who killed Keith. You had threatened to kill whoever hurt Carolyn. You thought you had the reason to kill Keith. You just figured wrong."

Pete took a deep breath and rubbed his eyes with his hands. He clasped his hands in his lap, his arms tight against his body. Helen leaned over and wrapped her arms around him, her face close to his.

"What's he talking about, Pete? What's this about Keith?"

"I'm sorry, Helen. I've messed every thing up now. First Carolyn, now this." Tears had begun to run down his face. "I'm sorry Helen. I thought I was taking care of our baby." He started crying. Helen began crying too, her mascara now long streaks on her face. She put her face against his cheek, their tears mixing and running together.

I looked away, unable to bear seeing their sorrow and feeling like a voyeur at the most personal time of their lives. I got up and went to the dining room and looked out the window at a robin building a nest in a tree beside the house.

After a few minutes, Pete came into the room, his hands deep in his pockets. He looked out the window for a while. I waited for him to speak.

"What now, Noah? I don't know how to handle this. Do I turn myself in or do the police come and get me?"

"If you want, I'll contact a friend on the police force, and schedule a time for you to come to Dallas to turn yourself in. I'll call a lawyer friend of mine and he'll meet and go with us."

"Thank you, Noah. You've always been there for me, buddy." He paused. "I don't know why I did it. I just knew he had done something with my baby. And it just ate me up. I didn't mean to kill him. I just went to threaten him and get him to tell me where Carolyn was, but I spent the whole day and I just couldn't get him by himself. And then when I saw him strutting the street that night, I just . . . I just couldn't take it any more. I mean, yeah, I shot him. Dead in the streets like the dog he was. I mean, I've known Keith since we were in school together. And for him to be doing . . . that . . . with my little girl. You shouldn't do that with your friends' kids." He was shaking his head and looked over at me.

"No, he shouldn't have done it."

"But I should have just let the police handle it. And then to have shot the wrong man. That's the worst part. All the heartache, and then I destroy everything that's left with killing him." He stopped, then looked out the window.

"Call me in a couple days, Pete. We'll face the next step together, o.k.?"

"Thanks. I appreciate it."

"I'll be going now, Pete. Tell Helen bye for me, o.k.?"

He walked me to the door and I left.

CHAPTER
39

I DROVE OUT to the Hollands. I told Mrs. Holland that Pete O'Brian had shot Keith because he thought that Carolyn was in Dallas with him. I assured her that Keith was in no manner involved with Carolyn's disappearance. I didn't tell her about the drugs, or his connection with the shoot-out, or what I had found out about Keith's life. Some things a mother doesn't need to know. I wondered how I would explain the money I had found in Keith's apartment, but didn't mention it. That could wait till she had healed some. She thanked me for finding the murderer. But there wasn't much else to say. I said goodbye and promised to come visit again later.

I walked out to the cemetery. The flowers on the bouquets and sprays were now dried and brown. The rain had packed the dirt hard on his grave. At the head of the grave the first shoots of daffodils that Mrs. Holland had planted were sprouting and swelling with the promise of spring flowers. There was only a small metal marker on his grave while the marble tombstone was being made. So little to mark an entire life, I thought.

I thought about Keith, and of me, and how we started together, and parted, and how our paths met again. Both of us back on the farm we used to play on as kids.

"How're you gonna keep them down on the farm?" the old song asked.

"Well, Keith, you're home for good now." I thought of Robert Louis Stevenson's line: "Home is the sailor home from the sea, and the hunter home from the hill." I said a short prayer for Keith, and for me.

I walked back to my truck. The brisk, cool wind was blowing across the open fields, and Keith's grave, and the dead flowers, and the new daffodils of spring.

I drove fast to Dallas, my mind filled with thoughts of Alice and her love and our home. And I was happy.

www.ingramcontent.com/pod-product-compliance
Lightning Source LLC
Chambersburg PA
CBHW020521120726
47904CB00003B/915